Praise for *Ceda*

'There's a fragility at the core of her characters and an intimacy that adds depth to their quirks and peccadillos; there is such heart in her storytelling. Readers who loved *Goodwood* will find even more to love here.'

—*Books + Publishing*

'A charming epic of intimacy . . . a moving affirmation of the sustaining grace of community that animates and enlivens this impressive work. Large and luminous.'

—*Australian Book Review*

'Ingenious . . . *Cedar Valley* is a sweet and sad ode to loss in all its guises.'

—*Weekend Australian*

'Throsby has talked of *Cedar Valley* as existing in the same fictional world as its predecessor, something akin to Kent Haruf's Holt, Colorado novels or Thomas Hardy's Wessex tales. By the end of the beautiful and humble *Cedar Valley*, you may yearn for another dot on the map of Throsby's imagination.'

—*The Sydney Morning Herald*

'Throsby's talent for affectionate, satirical portraiture is sharper the second time around with moments of real heart that make [*Cedar Valley*] difficult to leave.'

—*The Adelaide Review*

'Holly Throsby writes with a dry wit and a keen eye.'

'[*Cedar Valley*] delivers in spades . . . Throsby's rich characterisation left this reader feeling as though she'd made lifelong friends by the final page.'

Praise for *Goodwood*

'The kind of big-hearted, emotionally bruising story that reminds you why you love fiction . . . *Goodwood* is many things: a satisfying and conscientiously constructed mystery, an affectionate but clear-eyed portrait of a time and a place, and a darkly lovely coming of age story. But most of all, it's a complete revelation, the conjuring up of a sad, beautiful, indelible little world of its own.'

'Goddamn brilliant. This funny-sad mystery about growing up, missing persons and dark truths about your neighbourhood will gently, gorgeously demolish you.'

'Lyrical without being abstruse, colloquial without being contrived. Her characters, while familiar, are nuanced and authentic, and her depiction of small-town life is bang-on in both its endearing and suffocating ways.'

'*Goodwood* is gripping, moving, often funny and written with a sure ear for Australian country-town vernacular. Very good.'

—Mark Colvin

'A little bit *Twin Peaks* and a little bit *Picnic at Hanging Rock*, *Goodwood* is a terrific, thoroughly Australian novel . . .'

—*The Australian Women's Weekly*

'. . . the world Throsby builds around her teenage narrator in this book is so vivid it can occasionally feel more like fact than fiction . . . *Goodwood* is wonderfully lush and well-realised . . . The intrigue slowly builds to the point where the urge to learn the truth about the disappearances becomes overwhelming. The ending does not disappoint.'

—*The Australian*

'A lyrical, rolling ballad of a small country town hit with a one/two punch of grief and a one/two punch of burgeoning sexuality for the story's narrator, seventeen-year-old Jean Brown. The characters are rich and myriad, from family and friends, neighbours, shopkeepers and barflies. All are beautifully realised . . . Refrain and reprise are used brilliantly in a composition that's rich in rhythm with a melodic tone conceived from a keen imagination, an observant eye and a fine ear for idiom and the colloquial.'

—*Sydney Arts Guide*

'The small town of Goodwood is rocked when two locals disappear in this chilling, evocative and buzzed-about debut.'

—*Who Weekly*

'So much truth, so much aching and pain by humour . . . What a wonderful book. I can see the Australian novelist continuum from Patrick White and Thea Astley in her explicit representation of the character of Australians in regional towns. Others have compared Throsby with Tim Winton. I hope she is writing another book.'

—Lindy Morrison

Holly Throsby is a musician and novelist. She has released five solo albums, a collection of original children's songs and two albums as part of the band Seeker Lover Keeper. She has been nominated for five ARIAs.

Holly's novels, *Goodwood* (2016) and *Cedar Valley* (2018), were both critically acclaimed bestsellers. For her fiction, Holly has been shortlisted for the Barbara Jefferis Award, an Indie Book Award, two Australian Book Industry Awards, two Sisters in Crime Davitt Awards and a Ned Kelly Award.

Clarke is her third novel.

Also by Holly Throsby

Goodwood

Cedar Valley

Clarke

HOLLY THROSBY

ALLEN&UNWIN
SYDNEY·MELBOURNE·AUCKLAND·LONDON

First published in 2022

Allen & Unwin
Cammeraygal Country
83 Alexander Street
Crows Nest NSW 2065
Australia
Phone: (61 2) 8425 0100
Email: info@allenandunwin.com
Web: www.allenandunwin.com

Allen & Unwin acknowledges the Traditional Owners of the Country on which we
live and work. We pay our respects to all Aboriginal and Torres Strait Islander
Elders, past and present.

 A catalogue record for this
book is available from the
National Library of Australia

ISBN 978 1 76087 874 0

Set in 14/19 pt Perpetua by Bookhouse, Sydney
Printed in Australia by McPherson's Printing Group

10 9 8 7 6 5 4 3 2 1

The paper in this book is FSC® certified.
FSC® promotes environmentally responsible,
socially beneficial and economically viable
management of the world's forests.

For Zoë, Alvy and June

1

Little Joe went up the hallway in his singlet and shorts and crept into the poky room where the curtain was closed and Leonie was sleeping. With her back to him in the dim light, Leonie's form was a hill on the bed, covered in a sackish nightie, the new one she'd got on sale at the Plaza. Leonie went up and down with her snoring—the sound of it like a soft motor—and she stirred then as if noticing Joe from a dream.

'Joe?' she said, still facing the dresser, not properly woken.

'It's me, Leelee,' said Joe.

'I'm up, sweetie.' And Leonie rolled onto her back, making a different landscape now on the creased sheet. The quilt had been sleep-kicked to the floor in the wee hours, such was the heat of the summer.

Joe went wide-eyed across the carpet to the edge of the bed. He said, 'Lee, there are lots of ambulances next door.'

•

In the kitchen, it was hot and Leonie made breakfast. Joe ate his Rice Bubbles from a plastic bowl and Leonie ate her fried eggs and toast with margarine. The two of them watched through the kitchen window as men in blue uniforms mingled outside next door.

'Is Barney died?'

'I don't think so, sweetie. Those are actually not ambulances. They're police cars.'

'Oh,' said Joe.

Then he asked more questions about the police cars and Leonie answered most of them with, 'I'm not sure, sweetie,' and after Joe had finished asking questions there were spilled wet Rice Bubbles and droplets of milk on the red formica table.

Leonie brought a sponge over and cleaned up. She kissed Joe on the forehead and tried to act very blasé about the police vans and police cars, and she was glad when Joe didn't ask more questions. He sat up on his knees on the chair, staring out the window, and soon Leonie went over to the living room and switched on the television. She could feel a little perspiration coming out on her body, under her bosom.

'Why don't you come in here and watch some telly, Joe. It's probably getting boring out there now anyway.'

And when Joe was settled in front of the television, Leonie went back across to the kitchen. She picked up the telephone and dialled.

'Hello, Dorothy speaking.'

'Shit a brick,' said Leonie.

'I can't believe it,' said Dorrie.

Leonie leaned over to the window and held up her hand. Dorrie waved back from the front window of the red-brick house across the street. Leonie could see Dorrie was in her new nightie too, it was a nice pattern of blue flowers.

'She's in there after all.'

'Well, that's what they must be thinking.'

'I knew it, Dorrie,' said Leonie, rippling with a sad sort of excitement. 'We both did. We've always known she was in there.'

2

Next door, Barney Clarke was half-woken by the sound of knocking. He sat up in his bed and listened. *Knock knock.* There it was again. A seed of hope sprouted in Barney's chest. He went quickly down the hallway in his bed shorts.

Deb? he thought implausibly.

Ben?

Oh, but the bright day and a policeman on his doorstep. Barney squinted, barely awake. This was not what he'd expected. Who would? The policeman looked a bit like every man who worked at the bowling club, but tall and with a navy hat on. Two other policemen were on the front lawn, and on the street there were three police cars and two police vans.

The policeman on the doorstep introduced himself. Barney forgot the man's name as soon as he heard it. He looked down at the official-looking document in his hands. Had the policeman given this to him? Barney could not remember taking it. *Occupier's Notice.* Barney read it over, without reading it at all.

'So basically we'll be executing a search warrant, mostly at the rear of your property.'

Cockatoos screeched in the street trees and Barney was informed of his rights.

'We're acting in relation to a missing person.'

The policeman was so tall—kind of up-there—and Barney looked past him now to the street, where a contraption that resembled a lawnmower was being removed from a van.

'Any evidence we take from the property will be stored as exhibits.'

'I'm just renting,' said Barney. 'I just rent the house.'

'That doesn't matter, Mr Clarke. You're the occupier.'

The sound of Comfrey trotting softly down the hallway behind him. Barney stepped out onto the porch and closed the screen door.

'You stay inside,' said Barney to Comfrey, and the cat did frustrated circles on the floorboards.

The policeman looked down at Comfrey, and then up at Barney. He said, 'I used to have a tortoiseshell myself but now I have two blue Burmese.'

'Okay,' said Barney.

'Burmese are very muscular cats,' said the policeman.

•

An hour later, Barney—the 'occupier'—stood on the patio at the back of his house, where there was a small table and two chairs. It was impersonal plastic furniture. Barney's old house had been charming and homey. This, his present house, was generic and mostly empty. He watched as the unexpected group of police people stood conferring in front of the shed next to the pool.

Virginia Lawson. At first, in his drowsy confusion, the name meant nothing to him. But then it did. *Ginny Lawson.* A twinge of recognition as the police people brought in various pieces of equipment.

'This is *that* house?' asked Barney.

'This is that house, yes,' said the policeman.

'Imagine my surprise and disappointment that the real estate agent failed to mention it.'

The policeman smiled. 'Bit of bad luck, I guess.'

The policeman's name was Levins. Detective Sergeant Levins. Barney had recovered the ability to read a name tag.

'Worse luck for Mrs Lawson, I imagine,' said Barney, as he was police-escorted to his own shed, which was Colorbond and green. The pool next to it was kidney-shaped, a pale blue organ. Morning light shone on the water while Barney answered questions about the shed, which would be such a dull subject on any other day.

No, he did not purchase it. No, he did not assemble it. Yes, it was here previously.

Barney was on the lawn now, next to the pool fence, and he saw a eucalyptus leaf fall from the overhanging tree. Then he moved to one side as a policeman dragged the lawnmower-like contraption over to the concrete. And he moved to the other side as a policeman carried past parts of a portable blue marquee.

Several leaves floated in the pool, and Barney had the distinct feeling of being in the way—in his own home. Which, of course, was such a familiar feeling to him—it reminded him of Deb, and the way it had been with Deb, towards the end.

Deb! Wait till Deb hears about this! I need to tell Deb!

And then of course the silent chiding of himself: that he somehow thought it was still possible to talk with Deb. He was deluded and irrational and moist under his shirt.

Barney stared at the lawnmower. It had big wheels with rubber tyres and seemed, closer up, less lawnmower and more like something they'd send to investigate the surface of the moon.

'What is that, some kind of radar?' asked Barney.

'Ground-penetrating radar,' said Levins.

'How sophisticated,' said Barney.

3

Joe sat on the edge of the couch and Leonie put a little shoe on him, and then another. She fixed the velcro straps down and Joe unstuck one and smiled at the crackly sound it made. Leonie let him stick and unstick the velcro over and over while she switched off the television and looked around for the bag Joe took to preschool.

'Do owls know that their name is owl?' asked Joe. 'Like that they're called owls?'

'Yes.'

'No,' said Leonie. 'They wouldn't know that.'

She went over to the window above the table and watched a policeman open one of the van doors and disappear inside it. In the red-brick house across the street, Dorrie was moving about in her kitchen. Leonie could see the movement of her in the window and it always consoled her to see that Dorrie was there.

'Are owls in real life?' asked Joe.

'Yes, sweetheart, they are,' said Leonie.

Leonie, only two years ago, would not have dreamed that someone would ever cohabitate with her in her modest, ordinary house. Yet here was Joe. Before Joe, it was a little lonely for Leonie, but she only really noticed this in retrospect. She hadn't been fully aware of how quiet it had been and how long the evenings were. Now there was Joe and not enough hours in the day. Now there was Joe and a lovely kind of chaos. Joe slept in the second bedroom, which Leonie used to use for Maurie's visits. Two years ago, Leonie had made the single bed with new striped sheets and tried to make the room more suited to a child, arranging Joe's things in the way they'd been in his old bedroom.

All the while as she did these things—tucking the sheets in under the mattress, hanging up his pin board with the photographs on it, plugging in his night-light, which was the shape of a bear and glowed orange when she switched it on—all of this time Leonie had hummed and held her grief in with every muscle she had. Leonie had never met a sad feeling she hadn't tried to ignore. She hummed until it turned into a strange whine.

•

Barney was in the kitchen now, spooning cat food into a bowl on the floor. He pushed the switch on the kettle and took out two slices of bread. He noticed that his toaster was still so clean—a bright little toaster. Barney had bought all his appliances at the Plaza in one go and had received a discount of ten per cent for purchasing more than three products that said Breville. There were posters all around the store for this promotion, this offer of a discount, and Barney made calculations at the counter, stunned to be buying appliances, momentarily pleased with his modest saving.

Now a toast smell filled the kitchen and Barney looked up to see the police people carrying out items from his shed and setting them on the lawn in the sun. The red toolbox that had belonged to his father, an old Remington typewriter, a crate of empty Grolsch bottles. Barney spread butter on the toast and then honey.

Deb used to talk about Ginny Lawson—it was all coming back to him. She used to read the newspaper every morning at the kitchen table with her cup of coffee and her breakfast of soaked oats. She used to watch a television show called *Unsolved Mysteries*. It had always amused him how much she loved that show. Barney briefly smiled, standing there in the middle of the kitchen. Comfrey was licking the last of the cat food, pushing the bowl against the wall. And then a policeman appeared at the sliding door and Barney set his toast down and went over. He squinted at the name tag: O'LEARY.

'Does the shovel belong to you, Mr Clarke?'

'Actually, no, that was here. Mine's got the orange handle.'

'Would you mind coming out and confirming which items belong to you?'

Barney stepped outside into the stinking morning and closed the sliding door behind him.

•

There was no way of driving from Leonie's house to the Plaza without crossing the train tracks. The tracks divided the town of Clarke. Leonie's house was on one side, and the Plaza was on the other. So Leonie crossed over at Horsham Street, where there was what she considered to be adequate signage and traffic signal interfacing. A boom gate went down when a train was coming, and up again once it had safely passed.

'When I was a little baby I was so excited of tunnels,' said Joe from his car seat.

'Were you, sweetie? I didn't know that.' Leonie was preoccupied, thinking about all those police cars. So many police cars! The train went past and Leonie looked down at her pale, freckled hands on the steering wheel.

'Leelee, why don't we see any tunnels?'

'Because there aren't any tunnels in Clarke. The tunnels were in the city.'

'Oh,' said Joe.

Leonie glanced up at him in the rear-view mirror. He had his toy rabbit on his lap and was turning it around in his hands. The boom gate went up and they crossed the tracks and, several blocks later, pulled into the underground car park. Then Leonie led Joe up the ramp and onto the street again, past the McDonald's and through the gate of the preschool—a brick bunker of a building with a cartoon kangaroo on the sign. It had a shade-clothed sandpit and an astroturfed lawn.

Joe hung his bag on a silver hook and Leonie had her brief morning interaction with Kaye. Joe hovered, holding Leonie's leg, staring at the children playing on the colourful rug. Leonie wrote the time and signed her name on the sign-in form. It was 8.47 and she was Leonie Wallace.

'I could take you to the underpass near the showground one day soon. It's like a baby tunnel,' she said, and Joe nodded. Then she let herself out and waved goodbye to Joe from outside the front window, as always, and Joe waved back with Rabbit in his hand and sorrow in his eyes, and the sorrow killed Leonie every time, even as she smiled through it.

Leonie went back up the footpath and in through the main entrance of the Plaza. *Clarke Plaza: Experience the Lifestyle.* She rushed past the disposal store, the newsagent, the Wendy's. She felt an urge to laugh or to cry. She hadn't been able to talk to Dorrie properly in front of Joe. Dorrie had stayed in her house and Leonie had packed Joe into the car. She'd talk to Dorrie this afternoon. She'd set Joe up with a puzzle so they could talk.

Leonie pushed open the glass door and went along to where her desk was, right next to Wanda's.

'You'll never guess what happened this morning,' she said, breathless.

'What?' said Wanda, who had a Garfield mug in her hand and cat hair on her shirt. A map of the world hung behind her on the wall, with red pins stuck all over it and red lines joining the pins together.

'Well,' said Leonie, 'half the police in Clarke showed up next door looking for Ginny's body.'

4

The shed in Barney's yard was dismantled in an hour, and sections of shed were stacked against the back fence, under the eucalypt. The blue marquee was erected on the grass and a folding table was placed underneath it. Four white plastic chairs were arranged near the table. It looked like the Clarke police were setting up for a bleak party.

'This has quite the air of semi-permanence to it,' said Barney, indicating the plastic furniture.

'That's because there's a bullshit amount of concrete,' said Detective Sergeant Levins. 'If you'll excuse the expression.'

'Do I have to stay here the whole time?'

'I'd love it if you did.'

'How long will it take?'

'How long's a piece of string?'

'So I'm not legally required to stay.'

'Well, I'm not going to arrest you.'

Barney wondered what it would be like to be so tall. He realised that Detective Sergeant Levins reminded him of his father. Barney's father had been a stoic, courteous man who never read a book that wasn't about war. Barney's mother had been a quiet, pious woman who seemed devoid of passionate feeling. Barney looked now at the filthy square of concrete where the shed had been.

'You obviously think you're going to find Mrs Lawson's body—in my yard.'

'I'm an optimistic man,' said Detective Sergeant Levins.

•

'Hello, Harvey World Travel Clarke Plaza, Leonie speaking.'

Oh, it was Clarice.

'Clarice, hi, you were on my list to call and you beat me to it.'

Leonie sounded so sunny. She surprised herself sometimes with how well she could turn it on.

'Ian wants to do it,' said Clarice, and so Clarice and Leonie spoke a while about going ahead and booking that stopover in Singapore because Sydney to Heathrow really takes it out of you and Singapore has a lot to offer. Leonie had a great price on an airport hotel and suggested the Long Bar at the Raffles Hotel for a drink in the evening.

'Would you believe that there're peanut shells all over the floor? I'm serious, Clarice, it's like a carpet of them.

You just walk right on top of the shells and they go crunch under your feet.'

Clarice loved the sound of that. 'How unusual,' she said. Clarice and Ian lived in Clarke Hill, the only suburb of Clarke considered to be in any way fancy and it was hardly that. It was just that the people who lived there had bigger houses and hadn't seemed to notice the recession.

'Have a Singapore sling for me, Clarice,' said Leonie, who had never had a Singapore sling nor been to the Long Bar at the Raffles Hotel and felt the peanut shells go crunch under her feet. She hung up and made a note to update Clarice's itinerary. She had a sudden urge to eat peanuts.

Leonie turned back to Wanda, who had several car hire catalogues all open in a pile. She said, 'So anyway, my new neighbour, Barney, he seems very pleasant. He's much nicer than that last lot. But you know, I don't think he had any idea that he's renting *the* house.'

'Ugh,' went Wanda, leaning back in her swivel chair. 'When did Barney move in? I don't remember when he moved in.'

'I don't either. Maybe six months ago?'

'Well, I bet the real estate agent didn't put it in the ad.'

'Quaint two-bedroom murder scene and burial site.'

Wanda chortled. She said, 'But imagine living there!'

'I know.'

'Imagine that being your yard.'

'I know.'

'Honestly,' said Wanda. 'And it's been even harder for you being next door this whole time, Lee. Ginny was your friend.'

'I know,' said Leonie. Wanda was so validating. And Leonie had the odd sense of being adjacent to her feelings. She couldn't join with them. Her feelings for Ginny were kind of *over-there*. Or they were *back-then*. Or maybe, if she were honest, they were *too-much*.

'And with everything else you've been through,' said Wanda carefully.

'Yes,' said Leonie, who felt very hot all of a sudden. 'Is the air conditioning on in here? Is it hot?'

Wanda smiled kindly and said, 'You know what, it could be hot.'

'I think so.'

'Ladies.' This was the disembodied voice of Varden, from his office. 'More shoosh.'

'We're shooshing,' said Leonie loudly.

'You should go tell Vard about Ginny,' said Wanda.

'I'll wait till he emerges. I think right now I might just nip out and get some peanuts.'

●

Leonie's mother was so dismissive of peanut butter, that dreadful American spread. The idea of mashed peanuts on toast was absurd to her. Full of calories, full of cholesterol was what she thought of it. In England they had Marmite and they had jam, so Eunice Wallace liked Marmite and she liked jam. These were the condiments of her ancestors.

When Leonie was nine, Eunice took her and Maurie to the old grocery store that used to be on Colonial Road.

'It's so American!' said Eunice. 'So fattening.'

So Eunice did not buy any peanut butter for Leonie and her sister Maurie, even though they were desperate to eat it.

On the way home that day Maurie had a fit in the car. If Leonie was nine, then Maurie would have been eleven. It started with the jerking of her hand, like an animal was in there, trying to escape.

'Mum,' said Leonie from the back seat. *'Mum.'*

Maurie's leg was flipping up and down erratically, and she emitted a stifled noise. Her odd breaths, her absent expression, her body announcing its soundless mysteries.

'Maureen?' said Eunice sharply, and she pulled over into a spot where you shouldn't stop. There was a sign that said *No Stopping* and Leonie felt very distressed that they had stopped there. She felt that the police might come and take Eunice away.

Maurie didn't seem to notice anything; she only stared out the window.

'Maurie!' Eunice screamed. She unbuckled herself and opened her car door, while other cars flew past. She hadn't got close enough in to the kerb. A car went past so fast and let out a long and shocking honk, and Eunice yelped as she went around the back of their Holden and appeared again at the passenger door with a stricken look. She wrenched open that door so hard it looked set to come off its hinges.

Maurie's body fitted silently. But Maurie herself was not there at all; she was somewhere else entirely.

Lucky Maurie, thought Leonie.

She watched from the back seat as her mother crouched in the dirty gutter and gripped Maurie by the shoulders, trying to shake the awful animal free.

You should have bought us peanut butter, thought nine-year-old Leonie.

And now, here was present-day Leonie, in the nut aisle of the Clarke Plaza Woolworths. She chose a five hundred gram bag of salted peanuts and proceeded to the check-out.

Leonie was a grown woman and only mildly superstitious. Yet, for going on two years now, she had not been able to bring herself to buy peanut butter.

5

The McDonald's building, adjacent to the Plaza, was red and yellow and faded with sun. Barney pulled into the car park and wound around to his spot under the spindly tree. He kept the engine running and the air conditioning on and was glad for the small amount of shade. This was the place where—largely hidden by the drive-through signage—he could get the best view of the counter inside. And look, there he was. There was Ben.

Barney watched Ben at the counter. He was working the register, serving a woman, then serving a man. Barney knew the way Ben moved so well, the foal-like youth of his limbs.

This would just be a quick visit. It was Monday, so the girl was there too. She'd been doing this extra Monday morning shift for the past three weeks. She was a nice-looking girl, although waifish and pale. Ben was facing her now and they were talking. Even at a distance they looked flirtatious.

Barney smiled, his right hand still holding the wheel.

Then he looked down quickly, hiding his face as Helen Last drove into the car park and pulled up on the other side, near the glass doors. This was the fifth time he'd seen Helen Last here in ten days. She got out and strode into the McDonald's. Barney watched as Ben appeared to talk with Helen, no doubt exchanging familiar pleasantries. Ben was smiling.

What a privilege for Helen Last! She had no idea. But Helen Last was a good person. Barney missed Helen and her husband Phil, and everyone else at the Gather Region Bushwalkers Club. But the club was his past life. This here, in the hot car park, was his present life. And without Deb, how could he blend that past with this present? He couldn't, it was impossible. Those times with the club were their times. It was their club. Those walks were *their* walks.

Helen Last was departing the McDonald's now, sipping some sort of enormous drink. She wouldn't see him here, under this desolate tree. Ben, as far as Barney knew, had never seen him here. And if Ben had, well, it would not be the first time that Barney had embarrassed his son.

The important thing was that Barney could see Ben— which had become something of a compulsion. Just to see him going about his life. Ben, behind the counter, was laughing now with the girl. Look at them in their brilliant youth, in their McDonald's uniforms.

'Hello, Ben,' said Barney aloud in the car, looking across the asphalt and in through the glass doors. 'Hello, son.'

•

The Local Heritage Room was downstairs at the Clarke Library. It was an airless, low-ceilinged room that stored copies of the *Gather Region Advocate*, dating back to 1909, on microfilm. Barney stood with arms akimbo, a selection of small boxes on the table near him. The librarian, Rosalie, picked up the boxes labelled *1985* and carried them into the dimly-lit annexe on the western wall, where there were two chairs and a microfilm reader.

'I can't believe it was that long ago,' said Rosalie. 'I would have said '88, '89.'

Barney followed Rosalie and watched as she sat down and put the first roll of microfilm onto a spindle on the projecting machine, demonstrating to Barney how to work it. She fed the film under the reels and pressed a red button to make it go through.

'Then you just push the tray under the microscope,' Rosalie said, pushing the tray. 'And look, here it is, it comes up on the screen.'

A page of the newspaper from 1985.

Barney stared at a picture of his house; but from six years ago, when there were rosebushes under the study window and a mini-tramp on the front lawn.

'I live in that house,' he said, pointing at the screen.

'Goodness,' said Rosalie, with a kind of horror. She paused to look sideways at Barney. And then she went on, using a grey button to demonstrate how to scroll through the article. NO TRACE OF MISSING WOMAN, said the headline, and next to the photo of the house was a photo of Ginny Lawson and her husband on their wedding day.

'I remember this picture,' said Rosalie the librarian. 'She looks so happy, don't you think? It was such a terrible thing.'

Rosalie the librarian was a very beautiful woman. This was not lost on Barney. And she had this way of speaking so *slowly*. She spoke like Deb did after the fifty-minute body scans she used to do in the sunroom.

Barney stared at the screen. Ginny was so young and her hair was styled like she watched a lot of television. She did look happy. And her husband looked enormous, like he could lift a car over his head. Rosalie made the machine zoom in and Barney read the name: *Lou Lawson*.

'Six years ago. I feel a hundred,' said Rosalie, and she laughed. 'Well. There you go. Do you have everything you need?'

'Yes. I'm just having a quick look today, I have to get back soon. Thank you, Rosalie.'

Rosalie offered a weak smile. 'It's *Rosamie*,' she said, in a new voice that sounded less musical and more tired.

'Oh,' said Barney. 'I'm sorry. Rosamie.'

Rosamie stood up from the chair and Barney saw that she was wearing a name tag. And then off she went, back upstairs, leaving Barney in the sad annexe with the boxes of microfilm she had found for him: every *Gather Region Advocate* edition from 1985 featuring the name Ginny Lawson.

Rosa-*mie*. Barney was so embarrassed.

He looked at the screen. He would focus on Ginny Lawson. Ginny Lawson was thirty-one when she disappeared. She left behind a three-year-old son, as well as her husband. Barney read the short article and then he read it again. Ginny had left the house on foot, heading for the bus stop. According to her husband, Lou Lawson, Ginny said she was going shopping at the Plaza. According to Lou Lawson, he had no idea why she didn't come home. According to Lou Lawson, off Ginny went and—*poof*—she vanished, and he never saw her again.

•

On the drive home there was light traffic on Colonial Road and Barney half-listened to the radio. The ABC was running a call-in with a veterinarian. *Cats over the age of eight years are considered 'senior'. Many cat owners don't realise the practical things they can do for their ageing cats.*

Barney drove past the auto-electrician and through the lights at Clarke Hill. He glanced sideways at the turn-off to the inland mountain.

Of course Clarke Hill reminded him of Deb. The inland mountain reminded him of Deb. The afternoon reminded him of Deb. Everything reminded him of Deb. There must be a word in another language for being constantly reminded.

When Deb was still Deb, they went one sunny day in winter to their favourite spot just off the Birrung Track—a natural rock platform with views over the treetops. The sandstone was almost warm and only a little moist. They had sat on their canvas mat and eaten egg sandwiches. Deb had brought a thermos of tea.

On the way back to the car they crossed the plank bridge and went down the steep slope of the gully. Barney remembered that day because he had seen two memorable things. The first was a superb lyrebird. They saw it just near the creek. Barney had heard it first; he often heard them rustling, but he and Deb had always had such terrible luck when it came to actually seeing one. It had become a running joke at the club. Helen and Phil Last seemed to see a lyrebird on every other walk, and Barney and Deb walked more than anyone.

The frogs went quiet as they approached the creek. Then a rustling and a gasp from Deb as the shy bird walked slowly across the trail. They stopped very still. The bird scratched at the earth. Barney saw the long curved feathers of its special tail, the net-like lyre parts, stretching out behind it. And then it was gone, rummaging off invisibly through the undergrowth.

'How about that,' Barney whispered.

'Finally,' said Deb.

'We can tell Helen the lyrebird curse has been officially lifted,' said Barney, and they had this way of talking very softly when they walked, as if not to disturb their surrounds.

The bird had put them in a good mood and Deb was whispering away. As they neared the car park she stopped and said, 'Bush wee.'

'Okay.'

So Barney waited on the path while Deb trampled in a bit to pee. And that was when he saw a dead baby kangaroo on the other side of the track, a few metres into the bush. A raven was standing on the little furry body, tearing off chunks, looking up between each bite.

The bush was so quiet that Barney could hear Deb peeing. He stared at the stiff joey. Poor thing. Ants swarmed in the spaces where eyes had been, now just fluffy sockets.

Deb trampled back to the path and Barney turned and nodded that they should keep going on to the car.

He hadn't shown the baby kangaroo to Deb and she didn't see it. Why had he felt this odd need to protect her? As if Deb was some delicate flower? Deb was tougher than Barney was. And yet, he had kept it to himself as they talked on the way home, louder now they were in the car, about the luck they had had that day—the lovely rarity of seeing a lyrebird.

Barney smiled sadly now, alone in his car on the highway. There was so much of this highway in Clarke. The showground, the underpass, a church, more highway. On the radio, the veterinarian was suggesting perching options for elderly cockatiels. Barney tried to concentrate. He learned that a padded perch can be offered to cockatiels that suffer from arthritis, stiff toes or dubious balance. *Owners may wish to connect perches with bird-safe rope or miniature ladders.*

Barney turned off at the lights, down the wide road, towards his new house. A grown man rode past on a child-size BMX.

Rosa-*mie*, he thought, shaking his head.

6

'There was a whole troupe of them. There was four police cars and a couple of vans, and they put that blue-and-white police tape all across the front of the house,' said Leonie. 'Peanut?'

Wanda took some peanuts from the plastic bag.

'So they just showed up first thing in the morning and went in?' said Varden, who was sitting on the edge of Leonie's desk. 'Just like on television.'

'It was just like on television. I popped out the back to have a look before I left, and I could see them all around the shed, looking at that bloody concrete.'

'The stuff the husband poured,' said Varden. 'The *grieving* husband.' He made air quotes and gave an eye roll.

'The stuff he poured and the stuff the next lot poured,' said Leonie.

'It's slab on slab,' said Wanda.

'Well, that might take them a while,' said Varden.

'I imagine it will.' Leonie emptied a hill of peanuts onto her palm and ate a few and went on: 'Because the guy who bought the house off Lou Lawson wanted this great big shed—before he moved out of town and just rented the house out, anyway. But, long story short, he needed to pour a new slab for his great big shed, which went right over the concrete that Lou put in.'

'The suspicious concrete,' said Varden.

'Yes, because that's what you do when your wife and the mother of your child has just disappeared,' said Leonie. 'You landscape.'

Varden laughed. Receding, bearded Varden—he looked ten years younger when he laughed. Leonie's phone rang. She picked it up and began one of her chirpy workplace conversations—this one about Fairstar (the Funship!). Leonie was always so wonderful with her customers, she knew she was. Everyone loved Leonie! She chuckled away now, even though she could barely understand the woman on the other end of the line.

'No, I'm sorry, we don't have a Dutch speaker here,' said Leonie. 'Right now we have an Armenian, a second-generation Chinese Australian, and a woman who speaks very poor Italian. That's me. *Buongiorno.*'

Varden got up and held out his hand and Leonie filled it with peanuts. He put the whole lot of them in his mouth at once—he just threw them all in there—and wandered back to his office.

'Why don't you pop your daughter on now,' said Leonie, the phone wedged between her chin and her shoulder. 'Hello? Hi. Yes, we're in the Plaza. Yes, next to the RTA.' And so it went on.

A few minutes later, when Leonie hung up, Wanda was on a call. So Leonie leaned back in her chair and sighed and stared at her collection of snow globes, which sat in a row on her desk. Her clients were so kind—and everyone loved Leonie! She picked up the smallish one that said *Paris* (a gift from the Hamiltons) and tipped it upside down. She set it back on her desk and watched the snow fall on the Eiffel Tower. Then she looked up at the big Qantas clock on the wall and calculated it was two hours and forty-nine minutes before she could head home and look over the back fence with Dorrie.

•

Barney actually tried to work. In his study, at the front of the house, he managed to finish off the last corrections for the Eccles manuscript (*Ethics in Engineering*). He stared at a small pile of books on his desk. He read the first paragraph of the Duncan article. He couldn't focus. What was he doing?

How could he work when a dead body might be unearthed from his yard at any moment? The answer was: he couldn't. Minutes later he was watching from the patio as one of the police people ran the radar over the concrete.

A string line had been erected around the perimeter of the old shed site. And chalk lines had been drawn on the slab, dividing it into columns and rows like a big concrete spreadsheet. The man with the radar proceeded along column three while Levins stood nearby with a third man, the one who seemed lower down the chain of command—O'Leary? They spoke in quiet voices and Barney could not hear the content of their conversation.

Rosa-*mie*, he thought. He had seen her around town, not just at the library. The office for the South Coast Philippines Association was in the building next to Deb's old work and Barney had seen Rosamie coming out of there several times over the years. He'd also seen her coming out of Con's Convenience and Deli, which was in the same dreary row of shops. Rosamie always had a tremendous amount of groceries, just bags and bags.

It was agony now to think of those times when Barney would park the old Subaru outside Deb's work and wait there for her to finish. Those shops had been so familiar—the deli, the video store, Clarke Chainsaws and Mowers, the tired building with all the offices in it. He'd liked picking Deb up in the afternoon, even if he hadn't realised it at the time.

At the time it was mundane, routine. Now it was painful, sublime. It broke his heart to think of Deb coming out of the building. The radiance of her, the way she walked, smiling at the sight of him. That special quality he thought would never be extinguished. Oh, Deb!

And now, fragments of conversation reached Barney where he was, near the sliding doors.

Features, as opposed to depth . . . subsurface . . . other potential obstructions.

Something about megahertz?

'Who's doing a run to the pie cart?' asked O'Leary—this Barney heard clearly, and it sounded like O'Leary had a head cold.

Barney opened the sliding doors and let himself inside. Comfrey was lying on the floor in a rectangle of sun. From the fridge, Barney retrieved a packet of sliced ham and a packet of sliced cheese. From the counter, he took a packet of sliced bread. Deb would have been *fascinated* by this. Absolutely fascinated. That Ginny Lawson's body might be found right here with a radar. Unsolved mystery solved! Deb would have lain awake at night thinking about it, talking Barney's ear off with her wilful enthusiasm. How Deb would berate him for his 'obsessions', as she would call them, never seeming to notice how obsessive she was herself! Deb was so wonderfully passionate; she was the opposite of Barney's mother.

Barney neatly assembled cheese and ham on a slice of bread. He set another slice on top and pressed down, his palm making an imprint on the soft white surface.

'You and your obsessions,' was what Deb would say, sometimes with genuine annoyance. He smiled to himself at that. Even when she was cranky she was warm.

Except, of course, after everything happened and the rages started.

7

When Leonie got home, a policeman was standing at the bottom of Barney's driveway, in front of the police tape. Police cars still lined the street. Doug and Sandra from number seventeen had dragged out camp chairs and were watching from their lawn.

Leonie pulled in and parked in her carport. She looked at her own lawn and the grass was long, long—Clive would surely come across and mow it soon. It astonished her how much the grass could grow in the summertime.

'The police are still here,' said Joe.

'Yes, they must still be working.'

'Why?'

Leonie turned around in her seat and said, 'It's grown-up stuff, Joe,' and Joe didn't say anything but let out a protesting groan.

Oh, Ginny. Leonie tried not to think about her beautiful friend.

It was blessedly cooler inside the house. Leonie had shut the windows before leaving that morning, and she went straight to switch the floor fan on in the living room and the ceiling fan on in the kitchen. The dank air began to move around and Leonie wondered if she should buy some air freshener like they had at work. Something that smelled of lemons or lily-white flowers.

She fetched the zoo puzzle and put it on the coffee table, and she poured Joe a glass of milk and cut half an apple into thin slices and put the slices on a plastic plate. Then she opened the puzzle box and spread the pieces out on the coffee table, and she saw that there were so many crumbs on the carpet. There was a potato gun on the carpet too, and a torch, and a Hot Wheels car, and one of Joe's hats.

Joe sat on the floor and drank some milk and looked at the puzzle. He placed two pieces together and started to sing. 'Row, row, gently boat, gently down the stream.'

Leonie smiled and said, 'That's a good song. Did you learn that at preschool?' and Joe said he did.

Leonie went over to the window. Dorrie was coming across already, she would have seen Leonie's car. Dorrie, in a denim dress and a red neckerchief and a pair of leather clogs. Leonie filled the kettle and switched it on to boil, even on this boiling day.

'It's jolly hot,' said Dorrie as she let herself in and kicked her clogs off near the door. 'Hi, Lee. Hi, Joe!'

'Hi, Dorrie,' said Joe's small voice from the living room.

'Doing your puzzle?' said Dorrie loudly, and Joe nodded.

Dorrie hovered near Leonie's kitchen table, which was always covered in piles. A pile of books to go back to the library. A pile of Joe's drawings. A pile of shopping lists and letters and bills.

'Joe, Dorrie and I are just going out to the yard—we'll be back in one minute.'

Joe chewed his apple and didn't look up.

The two women went outside and peered tentatively at the fence that went along the boundary of next door. A male voice floated over, along with the sense of activity and movement.

Dorrie went up on tiptoes. 'Is that a gazebo?'

'I think so,' said Leonie, as she walked out into the tall grass.

'Clive needs to come and do your lawn.'

Leonie walked slowly over and stopped short of the fence, not wanting to be seen looking. She squinted from where she was near the Hills Hoist, her arms folded, and then she came back quickly to where Dorrie stood near the back door.

'They've dismantled the shed. And there's a blue gazebo thing next to the pool.'

'Why don't you just go and talk to them?' said Dorrie. 'It's a whole new bunch. Marrel isn't there. I've been looking out for him all day.'

Leonie looked at Dorrie sharply and said, 'I'm not talking to them, Dorrie. I'm done talking to them.'

•

Inside, Leonie made two cups of tea and set them down on the table and switched on the radio. An Elvis Presley song came out. Leonie turned the radio around to face the living room, where Joe was sitting, and then she sat down opposite Dorrie at the table.

'Earl was out on his porch pretty much all day, just *watching*,' said Dorrie in an almost-whisper.

'I don't like the way he watches.'

'Neither do I. It's like he took a course on being creepy.'

Leonie sipped milky tea. 'How long was Barney gone for?'

'Not long. Maybe an hour and a half? And the newspaper people came, but that policeman who's been standing out the front all day is like a guard, so he told them to go away. They still took pictures of the house, though.'

'Does anyone need more pictures of that house?'

'Someone might like to see what they've done with the front garden.' Dorrie grinned.

'But where did Barney go? I mean, if every policeman in town arrives looking for a dead body in your yard, wouldn't you stay?'

'I would,' said Dorrie. 'But maybe he had to go do something. I'm told people have things to do.'

'And I guess you don't know him well enough to have gone over and asked twenty questions.'

'I thought I'd practise restraint.'

Leonie hooted and said, 'Now you're going to make me look bad,' and Dorrie laughed too, and then they stopped laughing and Leonie sighed. She said, 'He seems lonely, don't you think?'

'Barney? I don't know. He seems preoccupied.'

'Yes, he does.' And Leonie looked past Dorrie at the little group of photographs displayed up on the mantel above the fireplace. She could see old Eunice. And, in the nice brass frame, Maurie. Sometimes when Leonie thought of her sister she thought of Ginny, and vice versa.

'She would have been thirty-eight this year.'

'Ginny? Would she?'

'She would,' said Leonie. 'And Tobias was three, so he's, what, nine now?'

'Gosh, he would be too,' said Dorrie, shaking her head. Elvis was singing 'Love Me Tender' and Dorrie stared into the middle distance. 'Imagine that. Little Tobias is nine years old. I bet he's still a sweet boy.'

'I bet he is,' said Leonie. 'And I bet Lou Lawson is still a complete arsehole.'

8

B arney remembered exactly when the first rage happened—
it was on Deb's fifty-second birthday.

In the kitchen, Barney was making sandwiches for the
walk they had planned. Or the walk Deb had reluctantly
agreed to go on. Barney was spooning curried egg onto
slices of bread and listening to the radio. The ABC, same as
always, and it was not turned up much louder than usual, just
a little louder because the dishwasher was on. The woman
on the radio was interviewing a Scottish comedian and she
got the giggles and it was so funny the way she was laughing,
and so Barney laughed too. He let out a deep laugh.

Deb had come into the kitchen like a flash, white hot in
that moment.

'Stop it,' she'd said, in an unfamiliar tone.

'Stop what?' Barney asked, still smiling.

'Stop laughing,' said Deb. 'Turn it off.'

Barney was so shocked he didn't do anything at all.

So Deb picked up the radio and ripped it out of the wall. It was an old radio that had belonged to Barney's father and Deb knew this, of course. They had both loved that dear little Sanyo. But Deb yanked the radio right out of the socket and lifted her arm up high before she threw it down on the floorboards, so it hit with such force as to properly smash it; it all came apart. And then Deb made a swipe at the container with the egg in it. There wasn't as much precision in the flinging of the egg, it was like an afterthought, and yet egg went everywhere. There was egg on the broken radio and on Barney's bare feet and the side of the kitchen cupboard.

'It's too loud!' screamed this woman who was Deb but was not Deb, and Barney felt himself stop breathing. He just blinked at her hopelessly until she made a disgusted noise and left him there in the kitchen, where there was so much egg and radio to be cleaned up and put into the bin. Then Deb had taken to bed and slept all afternoon, and they did not go on her birthday bushwalk after all.

•

Barney stood now in his characterless bedroom, looking upwards, where a pull-down ladder extended at an angle from an opening in the ceiling.

The police people who had disappeared up there wore blue paper overalls and hairnets and coverings over their shoes, and Barney could hear them now, shuffling around.

The one called O'Leary asked, 'Nothing at all stored up there?'

'I've never been up there,' said Barney.

Murmurings emanated from above. There was a flash of light, and then another.

'They'll be taking pictures,' said O'Leary, who, along with Levins, seemed to be supervising the forensics people in everything they did.

Barney said, 'I'll leave you to it,' and wanted nothing more than to depart entirely. He wanted to get into his car and drive straight back to his old house, park in his old driveway and walk casually through his old front door.

But no, he couldn't. He went instead to the kitchen. Through the sliding door, he could see Levins outside, next to the slab, pointing to the chalk lines on the concrete. Then Levins walked several paces backwards onto the grass and put on a pair of ear muffs.

Why?

Because of the godawful screaming of a concrete saw, so loud that Barney could feel it right to his bones.

•

'What's that?' asked Joe.

'That's loud is what that is,' said Leonie. 'I'm going to close the doors.'

Leonie went over and closed the front door, and she closed the kitchen window, and she closed the back door. She turned up the radio. Oh, Robert Palmer. Leonie loved this song.

'I want to go see,' said Joe.

'I don't think we're allowed to go see.'

'Why?'

'Just because. They have rules about police stuff.'

'I want to go to Milo's.'

'Milo's still away. They get back on Saturday.'

And did Joe cry. He really wailed. And so Leonie went over to the living room and put her arms around him and said, 'I know you really want to go look, and you really want to see Milo, but you can't do either of those things, so why don't we find something else to do.'

Leonie and Joe played Snap for what seemed like a year, but was actually twenty minutes.

An hour later, Joe was colouring in and Leonie was still wincing at the ghastly noise. She washed up the dinner dishes and the house was full of six o'clock light. When Dorrie called, Leonie had to strain to hear her through the receiver.

'I just got back from aerobics and I tell you, you can hear that thing as soon as you turn off the highway. Clive says it's one of those doovers they use to cut concrete.'

'It sounds like they're killing someone else over there,' said Leonie. 'I don't like it.'

'I know.'

'It's giving me the horrors, Dorrie.'

'Well, they can't keep it up all night. They'll have to stop soon.'

Leonie sighed. She fiddled with the phone cord and stared at the floor. 'Remind me that this is what we wanted.'

Dorrie said, 'This is what we wanted.'

•

Leonie poured Mr Matey into the bath and watched the bubbles form as the water rushed out of the tap. She helped Joe in, and she sat on a low stool while he played with his plastic boats. The tiles in Leonie's bathroom were pale pink and she had a framed print of sunflowers above the toilet. It was a famous painting by Vincent Van Gogh and she'd bought the print at the poster shop in the Plaza. She was very fond of it. She thought it gave a warm feeling to the room.

Awful, awful noise. Everything about it. And yet Joe barely seemed to notice.

'Are police nocturnal?'

Leonie laughed. 'Not in the way that owls are.'

'And possums.'

'Yes.'

'Leelee?'

'Yes, Joe?'

'When I'm older, like when I'm bigger, will I still be Joe?'

'Yes, you will. You'll always be Joe.'

Joe nodded seriously and held a plastic boat against the bottom of the bath, and then he let it go and it rose up fast, surfaced, and capsized sideways.

'Good,' said Joe, and he put his mouth down to the bathwater and blew bubbles, making a sound like a motor in the water.

'Don't drink the bathwater,' said Leonie.

Joe ignored her and kept making bubbles. And here we go: yet another instance of Leonie sounding exactly like her mother! Like Eunice. She had said to herself so many times: *Don't be Eunice.*

When Leonie was little, she and Maurie would bathe together in their dinky bathtub. Eunice was such a fusspot, she'd always be worried that Leonie would mess everything up somehow. She thought Leonie would injure herself getting out, or that she'd irritate Maurie. And Leonie felt she'd displace too much water by getting in the bath in the first place.

'Don't drink the bathwater,' Eunice would say, because Leonie loved drinking the warm bathwater. 'Maureen never drinks the bathwater, do you, Maureen? It's full of germs.'

The fact that Eunice favoured Maurie was so obvious that Leonie hadn't ever thought to mind. It was just the way it was:

Maurie was delicate and clever, and Leonie was messy and enormous. Often, as a child, Leonie felt grotesque. Often, as an adult, Leonie felt like a child. And any resentment she briefly felt for Maurie back then had all receded. In fact, Leonie's love for Maurie was such an intense and tender pain that she mainly tried not to let herself feel it.

•

The sawing noise mercifully stopped sometime before 7 pm, while Leonie was helping Joe into his singlet and pyjama shorts. She made him a small bowl of honey yoghurt and he ate it at the kitchen table, while Leonie had some cream cheese on a Salada.

Then she read him three picture books and, after, he asked if she would lie with him while he went to sleep, as Leonie often did, even though it was so squishy.

He was such a cuddly thing, Joe was. Leonie lay on her back and Joe put a knee up against Leonie's belly and his leg was so small compared to her body. Then he flung an arm up over her, onto her chest, and burrowed his face into her neck.

'I can feel your heart beeping.'

'Well, I have a great big heart,' said Leonie, and she shut her eyes.

Joe went off to sleep like that, a tiny weight against her, and Leonie felt the hot air of his breaths go against her neck over and over again. Maurie is in those breaths, thought Leonie. Particles of Maurie. The warmth of Joe's breath was so small and lovely that Leonie lay awake for a long while—squished there on his single bed in the soft glow of the bear light—just to have the gentle feeling of it.

9

Barney slept poorly, what with the floodlights on in the yard all night and the police officer stationed there like a sentry. Dreams came and went. Most involved Barney in some mundane scenario (walking down endless Escherian stairs at the library) before quickly mutating into surrealist semi-nightmares. Rosamie was in one of his dreams, raging at him in the Local Heritage Room, tufts of her glorious hair falling from her head in clumps. Troublingly, this was followed by an indescribable erotic frisson.

Barney woke, moist with confusion. The bedroom was pallid and grey. He went over to the window that faced the backyard and opened the curtains slightly. There, on a white plastic chair, was the officer who drew the short straw, reading a magazine by torchlight. There was the illuminated slab, half removed. There was the kidney-shaped pool, as still as a bone. Barney watched the water a while before returning to bed. He lay in the dark and tried to visualise the creek systems that wound their way down the inland mountain.

•

At first light, there were rainbow lorikeets. A short time after, cockatoos. Barney listened to the birds. He rolled over in his bed and looked at the empty space beside him. His sheets were new and smelled of the same phosphate-free detergent that Deb used to buy. Without thinking, he had bought the same brands of everything, and now the smell of his bed was somewhat familiar. Not unpleasant—but so singular, so unmingled. How he missed the morning ylang-ylang smell of Deb. The warm form of Deb. Now there was this gaping area of bed on which Barney lay an extra pillow, longways, so he could rest his arm over it in the night-time.

The sound of car doors opening, car doors closing.

Knock knock knock.

Such forceful, manly knocking. Barney rose and walked down the hall, slowly this time. No rush, he knew who it was.

'There'll be noise,' said Detective Sergeant Levins.

Barney nodded. As the police people disappeared down the side path, he descended the front steps. It was already humid. Bees on the clover. Barney retrieved the newspaper from the warm lawn. On the front page of the *Gather Region*

Advocate was a photograph of his house. Not an old photo, but one that must have been taken yesterday. There was his blue house with the dull row of lavender plants he'd inherited from the previous tenant. There was the trim lawn and the fantastic *Banksia integrifolia*—the main reason he had chosen to rent the house in the first place. Barney's car was not in the driveway, though. They must have come with their cameras when he was out. This whole experience was very unusual.

POLICE SEARCH SOUTH CLARKE HOME FOR MISSING WOMAN. Barney read the article, there on the lawn, and was intrigued by new information not reported in the articles he'd read yesterday from 1985. Lou Lawson now lived in Queensland with his second wife, Janice. Lou and Janice Lawson had two daughters. Tobias—the son of Ginny and Lou Lawson—lived with them too. Fascinating. Barney could have done with ten more articles, each with slightly more and different detail.

The concrete saw started up again. If ever a noise should be illegal. Barney folded the newspaper and set it down on the front step. He unravelled the hose and regarded the row of leggy lavender. Just five lavender plants and, at one end, an agapanthus. Barney turned the tap on and held the hose, watering them as a kind of reflex from his past life. All he could think was: Deb would have found this *so* unimaginative.

Deb would have planted obscure medicinal herbs and made a tincture.

'What are you doing?'

Barney turned around and saw Joe, the little boy from next door, standing in the carport beyond the low brick wall.

'I'm watering the garden. What are you doing?'

'I don't know,' yelled Joe, and he swung himself around the pole, one eye on Barney, one eye on the policeman in Barney's driveway.

'I don't know what I'm doing sometimes either,' said Barney.

'You need to water plants or they'll get died.'

Barney smiled. 'That's true.'

Joe hung off the pole with one thin arm. He was wearing a white singlet and pyjama shorts, and was staring at the policeman now in that particular way that children stare.

'What's he doing?'

'I suppose he's doing his job.'

'Joe?' said a woman's voice. And then the mother—Leonie—came out of the house next door. 'Golly, there you are. I couldn't find you.'

She was much paler than her son. Curly hair, the colour of sandstone. And she was old—or was she young? She was young, but she seemed old? Joe swung himself around the pole and Leonie looked over and said, 'Hi, Barney.'

'Hello, Leonie.'

This was all a triumph of name-remembering. And it was not because Leonie was wearing a name tag—although she was. She wore a name tag pinned to a polo shirt with an embroidered logo: *Harvey World Travel, The Travel Professionals.* Barney turned off the hose, and Leonie looked across at the policeman and the police cars, and then back at her neighbour. She yelled, 'This is all a bit dramatic, isn't it?'

'Dramatic and loud.'

'Yes,' said Leonie, and she looked like a woman who wanted to say a whole lot more on a subject, but who suffered that attendant maternal instinct of wanting to protect her child from the content of the conversation.

Joe let go of the pole and swung himself off onto the concrete. He made a noise of fake pain upon landing, followed by laughter. Barney grinned. Joe was showing off, thought Barney. Joe was putting on a little show.

'Let's go get you dressed,' said Leonie, who was, upon closer inspection, definitely young. She couldn't be much more than forty. She took Joe's hand, but Joe yanked it away, and Leonie said tiredly, 'Come on, Joe.'

'You better go with your mum,' said Barney, as he looped the hose around the metal hanger.

'She's not my mum,' said Joe.

Leonie took hold of Joe's hand again, more deftly this time, and led him up the front steps and into their house.

'That's true, isn't it, honey,' she said to Joe as they went. 'I'm not your mum, I'm your Leelee. Now I'm just going to help you to walk back inside so we can get you dressed.'

Barney thought that she said this so kindly, over the wailing saw, and he heard Joe say, 'Barney was watering his plants so they don't get died,' as they disappeared into the house.

10

'H e settles in very well,' said Kaye, the woman who ran the preschool with the kangaroo sign. Earthy Kaye, who had the look of a farm woman and smelled of instant coffee. 'After you go, it'll only be a minute and then he's off playing with the other children.'

Kaye pronounced 'off' as if it had an 'r' in it. *Orf he goes! Orf goes Joe!*

'Well, that's good,' said Leonie. 'I just thought I'd ask, you know. It's hard to get anything out of him.'

'He loves dancing. He loves painting. He's a gorgeous, gentle boy. You really don't need to worry. He's doing very well, considering.'

'Oh,' said Leonie. 'Yes.'

Leonie looked over at Joe, who was next to the bookshelf by the window. He was standing with a small black-haired girl, holding a wooden train.

'You're doing a wonderful job, Leonie. He's very lucky to have you.'

Leonie's eyes filled fast with stinging tears, which was most unexpected. She smiled and blinked furiously.

'Leonie,' said warm, earthy Kaye.

'I'm *fine*,' said Leonie, and she let out a peculiar laugh. Then she looked at her wristwatch and said, 'I'd better be getting to work.'

Kaye did a closed-mouth smile. And Leonie composed herself and went over to where Joe was and kissed him on the top of his head and said, 'See you this afternoon, sweetheart.'

'Can we go see the baby tunnel?'

Leonie crouched down and looked at Joe and said, 'The underpass? Sure we can.'

•

At Harvey World Travel, Leonie sat at her desk, and Wanda sat at Wanda's desk, and Varden sat on one of the chairs opposite Leonie, where her customers usually sat.

The newspaper was open on Varden's lap. Leonie could see the photo of the house next door—of Ginny's house—from where she was sitting. How many times had there been a picture of that house in the newspaper? So many.

'So we still don't know why they've suddenly come digging *now*,' said Varden.

'Exactly,' said Leonie.

Wanda nodded and got up and went over to where Varden was. She bent down, looking over his shoulder. 'The garden looks nice,' she said, and took a sip of tea.

'The real estate agent had some mob come in and clean it all up,' said Leonie. 'The last lot had really let it go.'

'The *grieving* husband lives in Queensland with the new young wife,' said Varden. 'How sunny.'

'As if Ginny wasn't young enough,' said Wanda.

'And that's the thing,' said Leonie. 'Because Lou took Tobias and moved up to Queensland so fast. He was all packed up within a few months. So god knows why he needed that extra concrete bit next to the pool. For what? A chaise lounge? He didn't get a chaise lounge.'

'And then he ended up selling the house anyway,' said Varden.

'After he'd moved all of Ginny's assets into his name.'

Varden shook his head and stared at the article—Wanda hovering behind him—and after a while he said, in a dramatic voice, '*Ground-penetrating radar.*'

'Followed by an ear-penetrating concrete saw,' said Leonie.

'Ah,' said Wanda.

Varden got up and went back to his office, taking the newspaper with him. Wanda went back to her desk. And then Mr Liu came in, in a nice suit jacket, and Wanda raised an arm to welcome him.

'*Ni hao,*' said Wanda.

'*Ni hao ma.*'

'Very well, thank you, Mr Liu. Have a seat.'

And the two of them began to discuss flights.

Leonie folded her arms and stared out the front window into the Plaza.

Kerry from the RTA walked past. Then a man on a mobility scooter, a woman with three small children. Leonie could see the backs of the people at the fish shop opposite. Glass cabinets full of fillets, chalkboard of daily specials. The reassuring glare of fluorescent lights.

Leonie closed her eyes and conjured the inscrutable face of Ginny Lawson. That tentative look Ginny would give whenever Leonie pressed her about Lou. Even the lightest press. *Don't press her*, Leonie would tell herself, back in 1984, in '85. *Don't push.*

•

In 1985, Leonie had waited for the police to come to her.

'Why?' she had said to Dorrie. 'Why haven't they come and asked us any questions?'

Leonie lived right next door to the Lawsons and Ginny Lawson had been missing for seventeen days, and yet no one from Clarke Police had shown up on her doorstep ask her a single thing.

'Maybe they don't want to know,' said Dorrie, the prophet of South Clarke.

'Don't be so cynical,' said Leonie. 'They'll come.'

But they did not come. And by day twenty-four, Leonie couldn't wait any longer. She put on a neat red dress and drove to the Clarke Police Station, naive as a child.

'What type of information would you like to tell us?' the policeman had asked Leonie.

'Information about Ginny Lawson,' she said, in her silly dress, before she was led into a small room to give her statement.

The police officer made notes in a little book. And she realised as soon as they sat down that this policeman was the old mayor's son, because his name tag said SIMMONS and he bore a strong resemblance.

'Are you Neville Simmons's son?' Leonie asked warmly.

'I am,' said this younger Simmons, in a way that made clear how tired he was of being asked that question. Or was it that he longed for a different answer?

'Neville Simmons was a wonderful man.'

The look on younger Simmons's face was one of quiet patience. Or was it quiet fury?

Golly, thought Leonie, and so she rattled it all off about Ginny so quickly—much faster than she'd rehearsed it in those long days prior. She told the younger Simmons how she had grave concerns about the fate of her neighbour. She told him how she had heard the big horrible fights, and how Ginny would come to Leonie's for cups of tea. She told him how obvious it was that Lou Lawson was controlling, volatile, needy.

'I heard him say some terrible things to her. From my yard, and from my bedroom.'

'What kind of things?'

'Would you like me to repeat them verbatim?'

'I would.'

'Once I heard him say: "You're a nasty fucking whore. Look at this. Look at this, you nasty fucking whore."'

'Look at what?'

'I have no idea.'

'Right,' said Simmons, and he wrote a note in his book in an oddly childlike scrawl.

But then another policeman knocked and entered—this squat, blond man with not much neck. And the new man called Simmons out of the room.

Leonie waited. She realised her hands were trembling. After a short time, the other man came back in and sat down where Simmons had been.

'I'm Senior Constable Marrel. Sergeant Simmons has an urgent matter to attend to, so I'll be taking the rest of your statement, Miss . . . *Wallace*, is it?'

'Yes.'

And so Leonie had to go over it all again, with this new compact blond person. He was so stocky. He was like a wheelie bin. Leonie watched as he wrote everything down in *his* little notebook—and would it have killed him to show some feeling?

'So you'd say Ginny wasn't getting enough sleep? She was exhausted?'

'Yes, because Tobias wasn't sleeping. But the point I'm making is that Lou's suggestion was to give Tobias sedatives. He wanted to sedate a three-year-old boy. I mean, on top of everything, there's another reason why Ginny would never have left Tobias with Lou. She was so protective of her son. She loved him more than anything in the world. It's a ridiculous suggestion that she just ran off and started a new life somewhere else.'

Marrel said, 'And if she was so exhausted, as you say, how would you describe her mental state?'

'What do you mean, her mental state?'

'I mean, how would you characterise it?'

Leonie was puzzled for a moment before she was absolutely furious. She detested this man. She made her tone as robust as she could. 'Ginny Lawson did *not* commit suicide.'

'We just have to explore all avenues,' said Senior Constable Marrel casually.

'Was the avenue of interviewing her friends and neighbours a bit too obvious?'

The policeman kind of smiled. He gave Leonie the distinct impression that, as soon as she walked out of that room, he would disregard everything she'd just told him.

And so, resignation. Leonie delivered the rest of her information flatly, until the whole interaction came to its merciful end.

'Is that everything?'

'I think so,' said Leonie.

'Thank you for coming in, Mrs Wallace.'

'I'm not *Mrs*.'

'Of course you're not,' said Senior Constable Marrel.

Leonie wanted to cry.

But not here; not in the presence of this man.

Ms Leonie Wallace walked out of Clarke Police Station that day in 1985 and across the car park. She got into her crappy old car, hit the steering wheel hard with the palm of her hand, and burst into tears.

11

Barney stood in his study, wondering what he'd gone in there for. He stared blankly at the pile of manuscripts on his desk. Did he come in here for a manuscript? No, it wasn't a work thing. God, he was so distracted. He looked around the austere room. Bare walls, bare shelves. Just a pile of manuscripts here, some books there, and on the other side of the room a stack of unopened boxes.

This was nothing like the study at Barney's old house. Barney's old study had been like an eccentric personal museum.

Paper! That's right. Barney wanted lined paper. He opened a drawer and retrieved a pad and pen. He wandered back down the hall to the kitchen. When he arrived at the sliding door, the sawing stopped. A policeman set the concrete saw on the grass in a way that indicated completion of task. There was an additional blue marquee now, which had been erected in the place where the shed had been. This marquee had walls on all sides.

Barney sat down at the kitchen table, where he had a good view if anything dramatic happened.

Dear Ben,

Barney wrote these two words before looking up again at his newly fascinating yard. He saw a police person wandering past in special overalls and gloves and paper booties and a hairnet. This police person—forensics person, whoever he was—carried a shovel across the lawn and disappeared into the marquee. It was almost lunchtime and stinking hot and Barney had seen a number of trowels and those big round sieves that were used to sift soil.

I am so sorry.

Barney thought of Ben. He really conjured Ben, the essence of Ben. He was overcome with an exquisite sadness.

'Ben,' said Barney to the kitchen.

'Ben Clarke,' said Barney to Comfrey, who sat on the tiles staring out at the activity in the yard.

Ben Clarke, who had once been as small as Joe, the little boy next door. Ben had been a fresh pink baby, pulsing with life from Barney and Deb, attached to Deb's breast. Milky, soft Ben.

Every day I think about how sorry I am. I should have
picked your mother up from work that day. I will regret this for
the rest of my life. And I know you think that I should have—

Barney felt a pain in his temple. It was like someone had taken a trowel to the side of his head. He closed his eyes until it passed. Then he drew a thick mark across the page and screwed up the sheet of paper into a tight ball.

•

Barney had first met Dr Prakash at Clarke Base Hospital. Dr Prakash had a small office that had come to nauseate Barney. The smell in there was Pine O Cleen mixed with misery. Dr Prakash had a photo of three smiling children on his desk—three little Dr Prakashes—and for some reason, when Barney looked at the image of these children, he imagined their violent, tragic deaths.

Dr Prakash had said, 'Try not to take it personally.'

Sure, thought Barney. Try not to take it personally. Sure.

Dr Prakash was a mild person with thick black hair. His voice was soft and concise.

'Encourage her to recognise your smile. For example, if something's funny,' said Dr Prakash. 'Or let her see you crying or looking sad, if something's sad. And then help her to take note of the appropriate responses in that way.'

What if nothing's funny anymore? What if everything's sad? How will she take note of 'funny'?

'Model calm behaviour,' said Dr Prakash. 'Don't challenge her. Don't confront her. Try to negotiate with her and appease her. You must be consistent.'

Barney nodded. I must be consistent. He wrote some key words down in his notebook. *Consistent. Calm.*

'You can cue her to recognise thoughtlessness or hostility. People can relearn appropriate behaviours.'

Barney had left the hospital in a miserable kind of shock. He bought a book called *The Man Who Mistook His Wife for a Hat* and read it while Deb slept. A year later he went to the video store and found, in the new release section, a film called *Awakenings* starring Robert De Niro. At that point, Barney was staying in a gloomy room at the Clarke Village Motel. *18 Colonial Suites.* Doilies sat under upturned cups on saucers. Barney watched a worn VHS of *Awakenings* and wept. He had a strong feeling that night that whatever this was that he was doing, it wasn't really living.

He wanted urgently to tell Deb: *Deb, honey, this is not a life.*

But in that sickening office at Clarke Base, it was mostly just Barney and Dr Prakash.

'Are you able to work?' asked Dr Prakash.

'Barely,' said Barney. 'There's so much to do now. Just—everything. I try to work at night when she's asleep.'

It seemed in retrospect that Barney was, at that moment, concerned with his labours. Later he experienced regret regarding this concern. As everything got worse, Barney often regarded the things that had previously concerned him as petty, and he longed for such petty concerns.

'I know you've been given some pamphlets. Perhaps you'd consider attending the support group,' said Dr Prakash.

Barney had thought: Doctor, you are overestimating your audience.

•

At 11 am, Detective Sergeant Levins broached the back patio and knocked on the sliding door.

'We're going to be applying to extend the search warrant. The concrete has slowed us down more than I would have liked.'

Barney stepped out and closed the door behind him.

'How'd they go under the house?'

'We didn't find anything of interest under the house or in the roof space.'

Barney could smell baked goods and tomato sauce. The police people were gathered in their refreshment area, eating pies from paper bags. O'Leary was drinking Fanta.

'Are you able to tell me why you're looking now? Do you have new evidence?'

'In regards to the search warrant, you can make an application at the courthouse to view the documents. You can view that information.'

'Can I now?'

Levins smiled. 'You can, Mr Clarke. You're the occupier.'

Barney said, 'Lucky me.'

12

'**D**orrie's husband, Clive, he thinks Ginny's under the lemon tree. Have I told you this? About Clive's lemon tree theory?'

Wanda and Leonie were having lunch in the Clarke Plaza food court in their matching polo shirts. Wanda's lunch was homemade noodles. Leonie's was a serve of lasagne, warm from the bain-marie at the Oasis Café.

'Why does he think that?'

'Because there were all these woodchips all of a sudden, under the lemon tree. Clive was doing my lawn, right after Ginny went missing, and he thinks that was the first time he'd noticed this new woodchip area under the lemon tree.' Leonie had pepped right up after a drowsy morning. She'd done a group booking (Honolulu, Maui) for three retiree couples, one of whom kept calling her 'pet'.

'So Clive thinks the woodchips were covering up some type of "disturbance", shall we say?' said Wanda.

'Yes, a disturbance,' said Leonie. 'But I don't know. It's so hard to remember. I do remember the grass was all pulled up before the concrete went in. And I just think that *can't* have been before Ginny went missing. It wouldn't have made any sense, because Ginny used that patch of lawn under the big gum tree all the time. Her and Tobias were always there on a blanket, lying on the grass.'

Wanda smiled sadly.

Leonie said, 'And I always felt the lemon tree was too close to the fence. You know? Too close to my house. Like I would have heard something.'

'But the storm,' said Wanda.

'I know, the well-timed storm.'

'The convenient storm.'

'Do you think he checked the weather report before he killed her?'

Wanda took this as rhetorical and ate the last mouthful of noodles.

Leonie could hear Wilson Phillips through the tinny speakers of the food court. Leonie loved this song. She scooped up some lasagne with her plastic fork and thought about the area under the lemon tree. 'I'm not someone to notice woodchips,' she said. 'Do you notice woodchips?'

'I don't think I do,' said Wanda.

'I guess Clive has fruit trees, so . . . '

Wanda put the lid on her empty container and put it back in her bag. The Oasis Café sign glowed above her like an aura. Wanda said, 'I don't care if it's concrete or woodchips or what have you. If a man is digging around in his yard after his wife goes missing—*disturbing* the dirt and who knows what else—I still can't believe that shrimpy policeman made out like you were hysterical for thinking it was suspicious.'

●

The sun was hot and high when Leonie pulled her Magna into the vacant lot next to the showground. Vacant, except for a bus-like thing that had been converted into a campervan. Two young people, not much older than teenagers, sat smoking cigarettes on the dusty gravel.

The heat was like an affront to Leonie in her work slacks and her work shirt. She didn't like the smell of cigarettes and she was very tired. She didn't want to walk Joe to the underpass in the sun.

'Maybe we should do this tomorrow.'

'But you said.'

Leonie took a breath. 'I did.'

She got out of the car and unbuckled Joe from his car seat and they walked in the scorching sun, a short distance that felt like a long one. When they reached the underpass, holding hands, Leonie said, 'Well, here it is. Here's the next best thing to a tunnel.'

The underpass was only the width of a few lanes. The cars on the high road above could loop down and join the highway in either direction, or continue straight on to the western suburbs of Clarke.

Joe looked up at the high road, his head tilted all the way back, and Leonie led him beneath the underpass, on the footpath between the pylons and the roadside. Leonie could see graffiti on the pylons—a big old penis and the words *ARABS OUT.*

Leonie hated this underpass. For a moment she hated the whole town. Were there even any Arab people in Clarke? She shuffled around to block the words from Joe, even though he couldn't read. He stood close by her, gripping her hand tight now with the thrill of being there, where it was so loud with cars. The ones going past were amplified by the road above and the ones above made a thumping sound, so noisy it felt almost violent.

'This is the best tunnel in my whole wide world!' said Joe.

But there were empty beer bottles strewn on the hill near the tops of the pylons, and the ground up there was just gritty dirt with rubbish scattered around.

Why had she brought Joe here? Why had this seemed like a sweet thing to do?

Joe looked up at her, beaming, and Leonie said, 'I'm glad one of us likes it.' And even though Joe wanted to stay under there much longer, Leonie said they had to go home.

They walked back along the loose gravel. Leonie buckled Joe in his car seat and went around to the driver's side and heaved herself in.

'*Foof.*'

Joe looked out the window longingly, back towards the underpass, as Leonie pulled onto the highway. And when Leonie asked him some chirpy questions, he was quiet and he stayed quiet all the way home.

•

A kilometre away, Barney parked his car outside the courthouse. He got out and walked along the paved area towards the anomalous building, which he had driven past hundreds of times and never entered. A low sandstone-trimmed arch, slit windows, short towers and—now that he was so close—was that a medieval motif? Barney had been very preoccupied with architecture for a short spell in about 1980. In that regard, Clarke had very little to offer. But he could have come here to this Federation Free Style courthouse and walked under this rock-faced stone arch and entered these double doors. Barney could have done a lot of things that Barney had not done. He gave this fleeting consideration now, as he approached the desk.

'Hello, how can I help you?' asked the clerk, who was a dour woman with little round glasses.

'I was told I could access information about a search warrant?' Barney almost smiled when he added: 'I'm the *occupier.*'

'Calboonya Avenue?'

'I guess there aren't many search warrants issued in Clarke.'

'You'd be surprised,' said the woman in the little round glasses, and she disappeared though an old wooden door. Everything smelled of a cedary polish. The clerk returned, holding a manila folder. And Barney was surprised no end to find that Levins was right: the occupier was permitted to read this document at their leisure while the clerk typed loudly and, every so often, issued a frustrated sigh.

Barney read the document closely. He read the name *Janice Clifford*. Janice Clifford who, in 1987, became Janice Lawson.

Barney read the words *abrasions, bruising*. He winced. The clerk sighed. *Changes to her voice (hoarseness), difficulty swallowing and fluid in the lungs.*

Barney put the document down for a moment. He felt light-headed. Queasy even, from past memories of reading such a report. At the blandness of the language and the unbearableness of the content. What had Deb's report said? *A thirty-centimetre intrusion.*

Barney's face had gone cold. Since when was he so squeamish? On a particularly memorable walk in the Royal

National Park, Barney had once breezily tended to a gash on Helen Last's leg that was so deep it ended up requiring seven stiches. Helen had bled everywhere! Barney hadn't flinched! He sat down now at a long wooden bench, under a portrait of a judge.

'Are you okay?' The clerk was peering at Barney over her glasses.

'I'm fine,' Barney heard himself say. His voice, and everything around him, seemed dreamily far away. He sat on the bench and waited for the blood to return to his head. He felt so foolish. This was not like him, he was not himself. Come on, Barn, hold it together. With the back of his hand, he wiped sweat from his brow. He closed his eyes and inhaled with a sense of purpose. Deep breath in, deep breath out. Now. What does this thing say? Barney raised the document and continued reading. Janice *Clifford*, was what it said. This was a start, at least: that Janice Clifford was no longer going by Janice Lawson. Good for you, Janice. And, judging by what Barney read—by what Lou Lawson had done—it would be a surprise if Janice Clifford ever used her married name again.

13

'Leelee, I want to watch over the fence,' said Joe. 'I want to see the police.'

'I know, sweetie, but I've told you already: you can't do that.'

The sound of shovels next door. The voices of several policemen near the back fence. A man laughing. Leonie went over and turned up the radio.

Joe got up on his knees on the carpet, a wad of animal cards in his hand. 'I want to go look!'

'I said no, Joe,' said Leonie firmly. She could hear anger in her voice—she was so weary. So weary that when Joe wailed, it pierced her. But Joe just wailed anyway, and then he wailed some more. Leonie set her cards down and put an arm around him. He hesitated at first, but then he hugged her back and wailed.

'Golly, you really want to go look. And I'm saying you can't look.'

Joe howled. 'Y-y-y-yeah!'

Leonie said sympathetically, 'Yes, I can see that's really hard for you.' She half-listened to The Beach Boys while Joe cried. When a new song came out of the radio, Joe let go of Leonie and stopped crying. He stared at the carpet, where there was a peg and a plastic Smurf. Leonie watched on. Joe was in a mute trance. He seemed transfixed by the Smurf. Or perhaps it was the peg.

Leonie said, 'Why don't we play another game of Animal Snap?'

With his finger, Joe traced a circle on the carpet around the Smurf. 'Okay.'

•

In the kitchen, Leonie emptied cupcake mix into a bowl and cracked an egg on top and added the correct amount of Meadow Lea. She lowered the beater and turned it on and watched it collapse in on itself and become batter.

Joe was colouring in. He was colouring a tree blue. Leonie looked at the beige contents of the bowl. Then she went over to the phone on the wall and dialled Dorrie, the receiver under her chin.

'Hello, Dorothy speaking.'

'It's me.'

'I was just about to call you.'

'I'm making cupcakes.'

'Well,' said Dorrie. 'Personal history would suggest you must feel bad about something.'

'I don't know,' said Leonie. 'Everything?'

Leonie went over to the sink to rinse the beater, the phone cord pulling tight across the kitchen, and she gave a wave to Dorrie.

Dorrie waved back. 'At least the noise stopped.'

'*That* noise stopped. But now they've started digging. I can hear these awful digging noises.'

'Which is what we wanted.'

'I know, I know.'

Dorrie was standing there, in the window across the street, but then she sat down in her chair and most of her disappeared.

'I was just thinking,' said Leonie, 'about how Lou and Ginny furnished their whole house with a package deal from that Furniture 4U place on the highway.'

'Yes, it was all very matching.'

'Wasn't it so matching.'

'But I only went in that one time with you. When we dropped over the Easter egg.'

'That's right,' said Leonie. 'Tobias's giant egg.'

'Why are you speaking so quietly?' said Joe's cranky voice from the living room, and Leonie looked over at him, lying on his belly, his head propped up on his hands.

'I'm just talking to Dorrie,' she said loudly. And then: 'Sorry, Dorrie.'

Joe coloured angrily, and Leonie stood there in the kitchen with her telephone and her cupcake batter. She felt as if it was just yesterday that Ginny was out back next door, pushing Tobias on the swing, or leaning over the fence for a chat while Leonie hung out the washing. Ginny was such a circumspect person.

'What if they find her, Dorrie?'

Dorrie said, 'I know.'

Leonie's eyes filled up with tears. 'What if they actually find her?'

•

In Joe's room, at bedtime, Leonie and Joe went through the Special Box of Maurie, like they often did. Joe looked closely at all of the things (photographs of Maurie, postcards from Maurie, knick-knacks of Maurie's), while Leonie tried not to look at any of the things.

'Here she is at class,' said Joe.

'Not much older than you,' said Leonie, barely glancing at the picture.

A Clarke Primary class photo. Little Maurie was smiling among her peers and Leonie could still remember how Eunice would do braids on photo day and frame the photos. Maurie always looked gorgeous and Leonie always looked average. Then Maurie's school photo would sit slightly in front of Leonie's on Eunice's hall table, not side by side.

Joe was holding a different picture now. He said, 'Here's me in the tummy.'

'You would have had a pretty comfy time in there, I think. Nine months of being squished up and warm.'

Leonie looked past the photo, at the blanket. She wouldn't look at the photo. She didn't need to anyhow, she knew the image so well. Maurie: out-to-here pregnant, soft in the face, a glazed look of contentment. In that photo, which Leonie was looking *past* rather than *at*, Maurie looked happier than Leonie could remember.

The ceiling fan was spinning. Some papers fluttered in the Special Box. Leonie was leaning up against the wall, and Joe brought the photo very close to his face. He studied it like an artefact in a museum.

'Why is she so happy?' asked Joe.

'Because you were in there,' said Leonie.

•

Another night of floodlights bleeding through the curtains, but this time the police worked through till 1 am.

Barney lay awake, staring at the closed manhole in the ceiling. Barney lay awake, listening to Comfrey's creaky breathing. Barney got up and switched the fan to a higher setting, and then he lay back down and composed a letter to Ben in his head.

Dear Ben, I am sorry.

This was how he should begin.

I should have picked up your mother from work that day. I wish that I had. I can understand that you blame me for what happened. I also know that you think I should have stayed on living at our family home. This is a very difficult thing to explain—

Barney closed his eyes and thought he might cry. Right now, he could go and get his keys and drive to the old house. It would still be there; of course it would be. Would he get dressed or just go in his bed clothes? He got up in the dark and went down the hall to the kitchen, which was lit up by the floodlights outside. In the shadow of the kitchen doorway, he gazed at the dim pool, the illuminated marquee, all of it a strange tableau.

What was Barney thinking? Driving to the old house was the worst idea in the world. It would ruin him, shatter him.

Detective Sergeant Levins wandered out of the marquee and over to the plastic table where, under the floodlights, he appeared to prepare an instant coffee in a polystyrene cup. Was he smiling? It appeared that he was.

Barney was about to switch the light on and make himself a cup of tea, but a forensic officer was approaching Levins, holding a dirty thing. Barney squinted. It was some kind of unearthed object. The forensics man spoke to Levins, and Levins pointed at the thing, which was soft and orange. It was a bag. Or a soft type of jacket? Levins was holding his cup, pointing now at the sleeve of the thing. A cardigan?

Another officer came out, holding a brown paper bag. Then the man in the forensics coveralls placed the dirty orange soft thing in the bag very carefully, like it was made of finely blown glass.

14

'Might be a good day for it,' said Clive, bright and early. He tilted his bald head towards next door and grinned, and Leonie shook her head.

Oh, *Clive.*

She said, 'Don't you have a carcass to attend to?'

'I'm letting the boys open up. I'm going in at ten.'

'Well, I'd be as grateful as always.'

Clive rolled the mower up the side path along the fence line. Leonie watched him as he went, his head turned in order to get a great big look at Barney's yard—at *Ginny's* yard.

A policeman approached the back fence presently, and Leonie watched as Clive started chatting and reached a hand over the fence for the policeman to shake. The policeman did not shake Clive's hand. Clive was wearing shorts and those boot-cover things that stop the cut grass getting in your shoes and socks. The policeman frowned. Clive smiled. Clive amiably set about starting the mower.

Leonie went back inside. She put a bowl of milky Rice Bubbles in the sink. She let Joe sit cross-legged on the back pavers while Clive mowed. She got dressed in her work clothes—polo shirt with logo, black trousers, name tag, footlets, flats. She put her hair up in the bathroom and peeled carrots in the kitchen. Then she lay Joe's little shirt and little shorts on the couch in the living room and thought, He needs new little shirts and new little shorts.

After a while the mower stopped and Joe rushed back in and said, 'Clive's going to do the front. Can I watch?'

'You can watch for five minutes,' said Leonie, and she opened the front screen door and Joe ran out. Down the steps, down the concrete slope of the carport, he waited on the brick wall for Clive to bring the mower back down the side path. The enthusiasm of being four! It just killed Leonie. The police guard was standing next to Barney's car. He eyed Joe. And then down the side path came hot and sweaty Clive.

He said, 'There's not much to actually see anyway.'

'No,' said Leonie, in the doorway. 'They've got their modesty tent.'

'Doesn't look like they've gone anywhere near the lemon tree.'

'Well, why don't you go tell them your theory?' said Leonie. 'Again.'

Clive rolled his eyes. 'Clarke's finest,' he said, and he looked out at Leonie's front lawn. 'I've been neglecting you, Lee. I'm full of embarrassment.' He wheeled the mower down the drive and onto Leonie's front lawn, where the grass was up past his ankles.

'My natural state,' said Leonie. 'I'll get you a cupcake.'

•

Leonie started at 10 am on Wednesdays and the extra hour allowed her to stop at Mick's Famous Pies on the way. The pie cart was right near Clarke station, and Leonie pulled into the car park and eased into a spot. She unbuckled Joe from his seat and they walked, holding hands, along the bitumen.

'Three spinach and cheese,' said Leonie.

'You like the pasties now, do you, little mate?' said Mick, the pie man.

Joe looked up at Mick, beaming.

'Good boy,' said Mick, and he put two pasties in a paper bag for Leonie to take to work, and one in a paper bag for Joe to take to preschool.

Leonie and Mick exchanged niceties while Joe held his pasty bag. A large Australian flag hung in the pie cart window, and there was a smaller flag underneath it: blue stripe on white stripe on red stripe, with a yellow-bordered red star in the centre. Leonie and Joe walked back to the car and got in.

'Mick has a ack-sent,' said Joe.

'He does,' said Leonie. 'And you know, sweetie, everyone has an accent. It just depends on who's listening.'

'Oh,' said Joe.

She pulled out and headed towards the Plaza. They went past the equine podiatry and turned left at Sunset Gardens. Leonie always felt terrible when she passed Sunset Gardens. Eunice had hung on there for longer than anyone expected. Two dreadful years, before she died from a colossal stroke. Leonie had packed up Eunice's talcy room and delivered most of her belongings to the big Salvation Army store opposite Clarke Park.

Eunice was still hanging on there when Ginny Lawson went missing. Leonie thought of it now, looking in the rear-view mirror at that awful place. Sunset Gardens had a minivan that took residents to the bowling club to play bingo once a fortnight. How Eunice had hated those excursions! Eunice considered her co-residents to be, en masse, feckless halfwits.

'That mousy thing from next door?' was what Eunice had said when Leonie told her about Ginny.

'I think she's beautiful,' said Leonie. 'And she's a very nice person.'

'The one with the dachshund?'

'She used to have a dachshund.'

'And the handsome husband.'

'Is he?' said Leonie.

She would have been making Eunice an English breakfast tea. Or making Eunice toast with Marmite. Or making Eunice's bed, because the staff at Sunset Gardens were feckless halfwits too, and they didn't do things specifically to Eunice's liking.

Leonie went and sat with Eunice three times a week. She went after work on Tuesdays and Thursdays, and every Sunday was an extended and intolerable visit for morning tea. Every Sunday Leonie hated herself and brought scones. Every Sunday, Eunice would say, 'Only a *little* bit,' before eating half a scone, and then eating the other half ten minutes later.

'She would be a fool to run off on that man,' Eunice had said.

'I don't think she ran off at all,' said Leonie.

'What do you think then?'

Eunice's room had dark grey carpet and pink walls and a window that looked sadly out over the highway.

'I think he did something to her,' said Leonie.

It was tea. Eunice had been drinking tea. Because Leonie remembered how Eunice almost spilled it when she tossed her head back, rolling her eyes.

'For goodness sake, Leonie. You're not Angela Lansbury. Don't be such a fantasist.'

Leonie, sitting in a soft floral armchair, had offered no argument. She just exuded a seething annoyance that Eunice tried to ignore.

Now she went down the ramp into the darkness under the Plaza. It always took a moment for her eyes to adjust. Joe was sitting quietly in his seat, holding the warm paper bag. The car smelled of pasties and Joe grinned when she turned to look at him in the dim light. He held up his bag so proudly.

'Aren't we lucky ducks,' said Leonie.

•

At the postbox across the road from the library, Barney stood for a moment and checked, for the fourth time, that he'd written his own son's name and address correctly on the envelope. He had. *Ben Clarke*, and the address of the house that Barney had lived in for twenty-seven years. He'd included his return address too, in faint hope of reply, and affixed a forty-three-cent stamp that commemorated the fiftieth anniversary of the Siege of Tobruk. The tiny photo showed two soldiers with bayonets crouching behind barbed-wire fencing. He could still taste the stamp on his tongue.

Across the street, in the library, he said, 'Hello there, Rosamie.'

She looked up from the index cards. 'Hello.'

'I'd like to look at more of the microfilm.'

Rosamie smiled at him—a compassionate kind of smile— and did his heart beat a little faster? How disconcerting; it did. She seemed to do everything in slow motion, this woman. She looked up in slow motion, she smiled in slow motion.

And for Barney to have even the slightest of amorous stirrings for Rosamie at this time was unacceptable. It was too soon. It would always be too soon. Deb was cemented so firmly in his heart.

In the annexe off the Local Heritage Room, Barney sat at the desk in front of the machine and scrolled through articles from 1985 to 1988, reading anything he could find about Ginny Lawson: the minor updates that surfaced because of some new scrap of information or other, of which there were few.

Barney read the *Gather Region Advocate* every morning with a cup of strong tea, but it was true that he had never paid much attention to the disappearance of Ginny Lawson. He only really remembered it because Deb had found it so fascinating. Actually, now that he thought about it, Bill and Rita Murrow had been fascinated by it too. Barney had a distant memory of one of their dinners at the bowling club. Barney and Deb, Bill and Rita, everyone talking about the missing woman from South Clarke.

Why had Barney not cared? One could probably write an essay on the reasons. But, as he considered it now, he decided it was obviously because he had been distracted by work and his various 'obsessions'. In 1985 alone, Barney had been obsessed with: cryptic crosswords; astronomy; birds; the history of Australian mining disasters; the history of Aboriginal trackers in New South Wales. Deb had referred to Barney's 'passionate relationship with home-brewing systems'. Or his 'affair with the geography of Australian lakes, rivers and tributaries'. Or his 'preternatural interest in transformative grammar'. Deb had been such a wry, smart woman.

Barney looked at the screen and learned that Lou Lawson's parents, Gerry and Yvonne, supported their son and asked for privacy at this difficult time. He read that Ginny Lawson wore what police described as 'characteristic jewellery', which was a personalised gold bracelet that she never took off.

But did she wear an orange cardigan? Would it be too much to ask for a photo of Ginny Lawson in a soft orange cardigan?

A box marked 1988, another roll of film. Barney zoomed in, as Rosamie had shown him, this time on yet another old photo of his house. The garden was a mess. And Barney was struck by the fact that the house itself looked so common— like every other house in South Clarke. Similar heritage, similar size. The houses of South Clarke were clad with brick or weatherboard or fibro. They had roofs of corrugated iron or terracotta tiles.

Barney found an article from the same year that quoted Lou Lawson's older brother, who lived on Bribie Island.

'Lou's had nothing to do with Ginny leaving. He's lost his wife and we're all very happy for him that he's moved on. Him and our family should be left in peace.'

He and our family, thought Barney.

And where are you in all this, Janice Lawson née Clifford? Barney could find no photos of Janice. But he found a statement from Lou Lawson himself. Lou had thanked the public for their support.

'I trust the police have done everything they can to find Ginny.'

Lou said his priority was caring for his children. And this:

'I realise now that Ginny was suffering from depression. I believe it was postnatal depression. I can only speculate if that had something to do with her leaving.'

15

At the Plaza, Leonie wandered around Fosseys in her morning break. She drifted through Women's Sleepwear and saw the nighties that she and Dorrie had bought the weekend before last. Dorrie's one, with the blue flowers, was almost out of sizes, but there were plenty of the one Leonie had chosen, with the pink and orange flowers. Looking at it now, Leonie felt she'd made a wrong and garish choice. The blue one was much more sophisticated. Dorrie had a real eye.

Leonie went along through to Children's Wear and stopped in front of boys pyjamas. Joe needed new clothes. Leonie chose a pair of pyjamas with planets on them, and then a little further along she found three plain t-shirts and three plain pairs of shorts. She popped them in her basket and, in a matter of steps, was amid rows of small, brightly coloured swimming costumes.

'Leonie?'

Leonie startled and turned around, and there was Verna Swan. Hands on a shopping trolley, taut smile, a strong waft of tobacco.

'Verna,' said Leonie. 'Hello.'

'Oh, *Lee*. It's good to see you.' Verna paused and the air between them felt as heavy as a wave. 'How are you holding up?'

'I'm just *fine*,' said Leonie. 'How are you, Verna? How's Ken?'

'We're alive, Lee,' said Verna. 'At our age that's a real bonus.' Verna's voice was rough and brought to mind oesophageal cancer. Her mouth had wrinkles coming off it every which way, and it had the effect of making a smile look like a real chore. Leonie could see that Verna pitied her. It was clear as day the way she was looking at her, like Leonie was some poor thing who'd gone through a terrible tragedy and now Verna just felt so sorry for her.

'How old's Joe now?'

'He's four.'

'Four? God, how did that happen?'

'Just day by day.'

'Well, he's very lucky to have you, Lee,' said Verna. Then she looked at the shiny beige floor. 'I miss your mother,' she said. 'I think of her a lot. I bet you do too. And, you know . . . Maureen.'

It took so long for Verna to get Maurie's name out, like it was some painful splinter lodged inside her. And it was such a shock to hear her sister's name spoken by someone else. Maureen. Maureen Wallace. How could it be that her name could be spoken yet she was no longer here? Leonie blinked and her eyes filled right to the brim with tears. These involuntary displays of grief were just intolerable. Here in front of Verna, of all people—her mother's old friend.

Verna said, 'I'm sorry. Oh, Lee.'

'I'm fine. Not to worry,' said Leonie, red and grinning through it. Verna pushed her trolley to one side—Leonie saw it glide across the glossy floor and bump softly against a row of swimmers. Then Verna came forward, this bird fossil of a woman, and put her arms around Leonie and held her with such surprising strength that it forced—from Leonie—a honking sob. Just the one. And no sooner had the awful sound come out than Leonie had sucked it all back in, and she endured the quiet embrace, her chin on Verna's bony shoulder.

Out of the corner of her eye, Leonie saw a nightie in Verna's trolley. The one with the blue flowers.

•

Before Eunice went to Sunset Gardens, Verna Swan would go over and watch television with her. There were two shows that they watched together: *Columbo* and *Murder, She Wrote*. Leonie, against her better judgement, would join them on occasion. She'd pull her car into the old driveway and see the lamps on in the living room through the front window.

It was *Murder, She Wrote* night. Leonie and Verna were on the settee and Eunice was in her reclining armchair with a plate on her lap. Leonie had made a quiche. Only a sliver for Eunice! But then she had two more slivers after. Angela Lansbury was trying to work out who poisoned the strawberry preserves and Eunice was yelling at the television.

'It's the chef!' yelled Eunice.

'It is,' said Leonie, grinning. 'The French chef.'

'I don't think he actually meant to kill that Betty woman,' said Eunice.

Leonie said, 'I think it's difficult to aim well with poisoned jam at a public diner,' and Eunice laughed like a drain, she was in such a good mood.

'Oh, Lee,' she said, wiping away tears. 'You're so funny. You're smart and you're funny.'

Leonie glowed with satisfaction. Affirmation from her mother! Which only really happened in company, but still. Leonie ate some quiche happily.

And Verna, perfumed to the nines, took a sip of sherry from one of Eunice's special crystal glasses. Verna smelled like sherry mixed with Red Door mixed with ashtray.

'Why would the doctor part his hair like that?' said Eunice, pointing at the television. 'It looks terrible.'

'Maybe the hair and make-up department thought it went well with his bow tie.'

'I think they could do better with Angela Lansbury's hair too, if I'm honest,' said Eunice.

'I can't believe you'd voice an opinion on someone's appearance,' said Leonie.

Verna laughed in her crackling, raspy way, which sounded like she was dying.

Eunice smiled and said, 'Be nice to your mother.'

'I am nice to my mother,' said Leonie.

'Speaking of—' said Eunice. 'Maureen called this afternoon. She's coming to visit next month.'

Eunice always had that same look about her when she spoke about Maurie. Pride so strong she'd almost blush. Maurie, the gilded one. Maurie, who had travelled overseas and had achieved the illustrious aim of living in Sydney.

'Yes,' said Leonie flatly. 'I know.'

Eunice turned to Verna and said, 'Maurie's *so* excited to see me. She misses me terribly.'

•

'I wonder if the police will still be there when you get home,' said Wanda.

'I assume so,' said Leonie. She poured skim milk in her tea, and in Wanda's tea, and she put the milk back in the bar fridge in the kitchenette. 'Cupcake?'

'Ooh,' said Wanda, and the two women walked back out to their desks carrying their mugs, Leonie with a plate of two cupcakes. Varden had stepped out to get a haircut and beard trim at the cheap hole-in-the-wall place opposite Woolworths.

Wanda said, 'That woman from last week came in when you were out on your break. Karina? The one who's organising the Bali hens trip?'

'Did you book it?'

'No. She said she wants to come back when you're here.'

'Did she now?' said Leonie.

Wanda raised her eyebrows and sipped her tea and said, 'Could it be that Karina doesn't like the look of me?'

'Could it be that Karina should find another travel agent?'

'I wish Karina the very best in her future endeavours.'

Leonie sighed and said, 'God, sometimes I feel so tired of this town. Or maybe I'm just tired.'

'Were they digging all night?'

'Not all night, but close to it. And even when they stopped I couldn't really sleep.'

'When do *they* sleep?'

'I think they do shifts. I see them come and go. It's just—I hear the digging and I think about what they're digging for. I can't believe that it's Ginny, even though I know it's Ginny.

But it feels like it's not really real. And then I half-expect Ginny to just pop over for a cup of tea.'

'Of course you do,' said Wanda, holding a cupcake. 'It's awful. It's unbelievably awful.' Leonie had covered the cupcakes in pink icing and hundreds and thousands for no reason at all. There was nothing to celebrate. Wanda said, 'You know, I was talking to Jenny about all this last night. We've never spoken about it before, but she brought it up because it was in the papers again and, you know, people are talking about it.'

'What does Jenny say?'

'Well, she has these opinions because of the police going into the restaurant.'

'The police go to Panda Garden?'

'Yes, they have big long lunches there once a month.'

'Golly,' said Leonie. 'Think of all that pineapple pork.'

Ha ha—laughter from Wanda.

Leonie split a cupcake in two. They were lovely moist little cakes. She said, 'So what does Jenny think?'

'Well . . .' Wanda looked at Leonie and said, 'I debated whether or not to tell you this, Lee. Because of everything. But I will tell you, because I think you'll want to know.'

'Of course I want to know.'

'Jenny thinks Ginny committed suicide.'

'She does not.'

'She does. She said that's what the police used to say, after a few Crown Lagers.'

Leonie sat back abruptly in her chair like someone had pushed her. She could have killed every policeman in Clarke. 'That is absolute crap.'

'I know it is.'

'Do we like Jenny?'

'Yes, but we're *terrified* of her.'

Leonie laughed. She said, 'Too terrified to ask her word for word what the police said?'

'I'll see how bold I'm feeling next time.'

Leonie nodded. Actually, she felt a little queasy. The smell of Verna had stuck to her somehow, fastened itself to her during their brief but firm embrace. Leonie recoiled at the smell, and at her own emotional outburst earlier at Fosseys. What was wrong with her? She set both halves of her cupcake back on her plate. '*Foof*,' she said. 'I think I'm still full from those pasties.'

Wanda looked down at the Fosseys bag.

'What did you get?'

'Just some clothes for Joe.'

'That's nice, Lee. I'm sure he'll like that,' said Wanda. And then: 'He's so lucky to have you.'

Leonie forced a smile. Affirmed by Wanda, she loved Wanda. But pained by the digging noises, which echoed inside her. Oh, *Ginny*. And pained by the smoky smell of Verna

Swan and the way she said *Maureen*. Leonie missed Maurie so much it killed.

She sipped her tea and stared at a snow globe of Vienna. *He's so lucky to have you.*

16

Barney could not park at his own house. Police tape sealed off his driveway. Police vehicles had taken up all the room on the street—outside his house, outside Leonie's house, outside number seventeen. Barney had to do a U-turn and park across the road, outside Earl's.

'This must be giving you the shivers, is it?'

This was Earl, sitting on his porch on a folding chair, holding a can of beer. This was the first time Earl had ever spoken to Barney. So how did Barney know Earl's name was Earl? Because EARL was the personalised numberplate of the orange P76 in Earl's driveway. And EARL was written on the side of the esky that sat permanently on Earl's shoddy porch.

'Something like that,' said Barney, who felt himself far superior to Earl.

Earl was in a tracksuit, his face was mostly moustache. He said, 'It's a shame what happened to her.' Yet there was an odd tone—like it wasn't a shame at all?

Barney stood beside his car and looked at the concrete statues on Earl's lawn, which were two 'Aboriginal men in hunting poses'. The statues wore red loincloths and held spears.

'Don't you like my Nevilles?'

'Is that what you call them?'

'*Kingswood Country.*'

'Sorry?'

Earl laughed! He laughed so much—*at* Barney—and Barney had no idea why. What Barney did know was that he was both far superior to, and quite afraid of, Earl. Earl's eyes had a certain blankness in them. Barney gazed at him dumbly.

'Oh, mate,' said Earl.

Barney felt the ghost of old Deb rise up inside him. He had always felt *Deb* was far superior. Deb wasn't afraid of anyone. Deb always said the only man she'd ever leave him for was Gough Whitlam, based on the strength of his convictions.

'I don't like your Nevilles,' said Barney, who felt like a flower in a nature documentary, blooming in time-lapse.

'Good for you,' said Earl coldly. He took a sip of beer and looked away.

Barney walked across the street to his own house, proud of himself and terrified of potential retribution.

•

Inside, Comfrey made excited circles around Barney's legs in the hallway. She nudged her sweet head against his shins. What a sight for sore eyes. Barney went to the kitchen and saw that Comfrey had left some breakfast in her bowl.

'Are you not hungry?' said Barney to his cat.

'Mr Clarke?'

Barney turned to see Detective Sergeant Levins on the back patio next to his impersonal plastic table. The detective was waving, his hand up above his head. Barney's father, Cal Clarke, had also been tall. Cal Clarke worked for Akubra and knew a lot about hats. But whenever Barney thought about his father—or his mother—he realised how little he thought about his father; he thought even less about his mother.

Barney went outside and closed the sliding door behind him, so Comfrey could not escape into the ether.

'My cats look very light—like that one—but then I pick them up and they're actually quite heavy,' said Detective Sergeant Levins.

'Is that right?'

'Burmese have heavy bones, they're very sturdy cats,' said Levins. 'Before that we had an Egyptian Mau. He was smaller but, even at four kilos, a very muscular physique.'

'I wouldn't imagine anything less.'

'How old's your tortoiseshell?'

'She's fifteen.'

'Geriatric,' said Levins.

Geriatric? Barney was offended on Comfrey's behalf.

Levins looked left, towards the side path, and said, 'It's not my pleasure to inform you that we're going to have to replace one of your pots. The terracotta one. O'Leary had a little accident.'

'That was my grandmother's pot,' said Barney.

'You're kidding.'

'I am kidding. The pots came with the house.'

Detective Sergeant Levins laughed. A very repressed laugh.

'So, Detective, I'm curious. If you were to find something, would you tell me?'

'Would I tell you? No, I would not.'

'So if you dragged an orange garment out of the ground in the middle of the night you wouldn't pass that information on?'

Levins smiled. He said, 'I wouldn't, no.'

'What was it?'

'Are you looking to switch careers, Mr Clarke?'

'It'd be nice to get superannuation.'

Levins paused, still smiling, and then he said, 'It's an item of clothing that we're going to keep as an exhibit.'

'How obtuse,' said Barney.

•

Leonie was almost done unbuckling Joe from his car seat when a voice said, 'Hello there,' and Leonie turned around to see Barney standing on his lawn, on the other side of the low brick wall that separated their properties. He was just beyond the long line of police tape.

'Oh, hi, Barney.'

If ever someone looked like they wanted to talk.

'A lot of action around here,' he said, hovering near the banksia.

'There sure is,' said Leonie.

Joe climbed out of the car, and Leonie gathered her handbag and Joe's backpack and the plastic bag from Fosseys.

'Hello, Joe.'

'Hi, Barney,' said Joe, and then, looking up at Leonie, 'Can we have mash potatoes for dinner?'

'Sure, sweetie. I think I have some potatoes.'

'I want to go in the house.'

Leonie closed the car door and said, 'Why don't we go inside and I'll get out your textas.' She turned to Barney. 'Just hold on a sec. I'll pop back out.'

Barney nodded. His skin was kind of grey and rough and reminded Leonie of an egg carton. He turned and faced the police cars on the street.

Leonie and Joe went inside and Leonie put the bags on the kitchen table and got the pencil case full of textas and the scrapbook Joe used for drawing. She set Joe up at the kitchen table, next to the pile of bags.

'I'm just going to go back out and have a quick chat with Barney,' she said, but Joe complained that he was hungry. So Leonie opened a Le Snak and set it on the table next to him, and he took a biscuit and dipped it in the soft pale cheese.

Barney was standing in Leonie's driveway now. He must have ducked under the police tape and then over the low brick wall. Leonie went down the concrete slope and stood with him in the shade of the carport.

'Well,' she said. 'I guess you weren't expecting all this then.'

'I really wasn't.'

'No,' said Leonie. 'Honestly, I never thought they'd come looking. So, you know, I didn't think to mention it in passing.'

'Of course,' said Barney.

'I mean, what can you say? A woman went missing from your house six years ago under suspicious circumstances and is probably buried in your backyard? It might have sounded a little morbid.'

'It might have.'

Leonie looked down at her feet on the concrete driveway, at her flats and sheer footlets. She saw a trail of ants disappearing into the grass. 'I don't suppose you know if they've found anything.'

'I do,' said Barney. 'I forced a confession.'

'What do you mean?'

Barney lowered his voice. 'I mean, they found an "item of clothing". But they don't particularly want me to know that.'

'Surely you haven't been spying.'

'I'd call it amateur surveillance.'

Leonie laughed. She said, 'I wouldn't know anything about that.'

'Given that I am not a clothing expert, all I can tell you is that it was orange. At first I thought it was a bag. But then I thought it was a cardigan.'

'Oh,' said Leonie. Her cheeks tingled. 'Golly.'

Barney—who was not an expert on clothing—was wearing brown shorts and a cream short-sleeved shirt and ancient lace-up boots from one of those outdoorsy stores. He looked like he was about to hand out religious pamphlets or go on a long-distance hike. He said, 'I imagine you knew Ginny?'

'Yes, I did.'

'Well. I'm sorry.'

'So am I,' said Leonie. 'She was a good person.'

Barney stood stiffly on his sinewy legs. He had a way of standing very squarely, without any lean.

Leonie said, 'For the record, all the things people were saying about Ginny, it was all a load of crap. I had people asking me if she was suicidal, or if I saw her consorting with other men, or if she'd run off with a cult. Like I might have failed to mention that a kombi full of hippies picked her up and whisked her off to Darwin. I mean, *really*.'

'A cult?' said Barney, and Leonie saw there was a gold wedding band on his finger. It was tasteful, understated. Not like that ridiculous thing Lou got Ginny.

'Lou started that one,' said Leonie. 'He told the police that some religious people doorknocked at the house and that Ginny was very interested. Well, they didn't doorknock my house, or any other houses that I know of.'

'A well-targeted attack,' said Barney.

'The attack of the invisible cult,' said Leonie. 'Meanwhile, Lou moved to Queensland and married an even younger woman called Janice, and he got Ginny's ring re-set for their wedding. Can you believe that? The same ring.'

'Jesus,' said Barney.

'Yes, well. Don't get me started on Lou Lawson.' And she gave a quick shrill laugh. 'Or Janice, who presumably manages to sleep at night while wearing a dead woman's ring.'

'Speaking of—'

'Leelee!'

It was Joe's voice from inside the house.

'I'd better go in,' said Leonie.

'Of course.'

And Leonie sighed and looked at Barney and said, 'An item of clothing.'

'Affirmative.'

'Well,' said Leonie. 'I'll see you later, Barney.'

Barney looked like he was going to say something more but he just said, 'See you later, Leonie.'

17

'Did Ginny wear cardigans?' asked Dorrie.

'She did,' said Leonie. 'And she had an orange one with embroidered flowers.'

'I don't remember,' said Dorrie, and Leonie could hear Clive's muffled contributions in the background.

'What's Clive saying?'

'He says he remembers Ginny wearing cardigans.' Dorrie raised her voice a little. 'I bet you wouldn't remember any of my cardigans. Do I wear cardigans?'

Background protests from Clive.

'What was I wearing yesterday?' asked Dorrie.

Background silence from Clive.

'See? You're unbelievable. What? No. I thought you were putting the rice on.'

Leonie closed her eyes and pressed the phone against her chin. She said, 'I'm going to go and practise amateur surveillance over the fence.'

●

Eunice had often made mashed potatoes for Leonie and Maurie. Before their father left, and after their father left.

Leonie remembered the last night she saw her father. She and Maurie were in a matching pair of flannelette pyjamas. The sound of fighting from the living room was familiar by then: Eunice in tears and their father's distant coldness. Leonie crawled into Maurie's bed. Creaking springs and blankets that itched. Their father walked into the room that night and looked at them heavily. In the doorframe he appeared a small man. Maurie knew he was leaving, but little Leonie wouldn't believe it for days, months, even years.

'When's Dad coming back?' she would ask Maurie of an evening, while they lay together in the dark.

Often they would hear Eunice beyond their closed door, carrying on to some friend about the injustices of her life. Then, by evening, some mashed potatoes and Eunice in one of her sulky moods. Or, some mashed potatoes and Eunice charming and wonderful! Those nights were a confusing joy. Leonie remembered the warmth of her mother as a heady storm that blew in fast but never stayed long.

When Joe had first arrived, those memories returned swiftly. It had been like Leonie was seeing herself as a child again, singing her sad refrain.

'When's Mum coming?' asked Joe, on his first night at Leonie's.

Leonie was dismantled by the question.

'She's not coming, sweetheart.'

'Why?'

'Because she died. And it's very hard to understand, but when people die they don't come back. We can't see them again.'

Leonie kept her voice steady, and Joe wept so hot and softly it was like he was scared of making any noise. Leonie held him. She said, 'I know,' to his weeping. She said, 'I'm right here for you, sweetheart. I'm not going anywhere.' And she remembered the way he heaved that night. It imprinted on her like a stamp—shudders of tiny wet breaths.

•

Joe and Leonie sat at the kitchen table now with the radio on, eating fish fingers and mashed potatoes. Leonie boiled some damp rounds of carrots too. She told Joe to eat his damp carrots and he complained.

After dinner they watched part of a video that Leonie had rented. It was *Charlotte's Web*, but the thing was terribly sad and Leonie began to feel overwhelmed by it. The little pig was so desperate for companionship, and Leonie was certain that things wouldn't end well for the spider. She felt herself heating up with sorrow, so she switched the movie off and Joe complained.

At bath time, Leonie hummed 'Hold On' by Wilson Phillips and watered the house plant that hung near the window—a gift from Dorrie. Joe played with his boats. But he wanted more things to play with so Leonie fetched him the plastic measuring cups from the kitchen. He took them and complained.

He complained about the bedtime book selection too. Those were extra loud and angry complaints. But he went off to sleep before Leonie had finished reading him the first story, and Leonie went to her own bedroom and stood in front of the mirror and undressed and looked at her body. She quickly averted her eyes. She sat up a while in the living room, watching television. Then she sat up a while in bed, reading *The Joy Luck Club* and drinking Ovaltine.

In the middle of the night, Joe called out. Leonie ached to stay sleeping. But Joe called again and Leonie groaned and got up and went across the hall to his bedroom where the bear light glowed and Joe was sitting up.

'What is it, sweetie?'

'I need you,' said Joe.

Leonie got under the sheet with him and Joe was so small—she almost forgot every time how small he was. He was as slight as anything, and he put an arm over Leonie and snuggled his chin against her soft shoulder. Leonie lay there and became awake. She thought of Barney, in his thick socks. She thought of all those policemen digging up his yard. And the specific feeling of disappointment Leonie felt when looking over the fence earlier. What was she expecting? An open grave? No, there were just the blue tents and the blue pool Ginny used to swim in, and Leonie had almost laughed at herself as a policeman began to wander over in order to tell her to please step away from her own fence.

An item of clothing, she thought, as she lay there in Joe's bed. Her eyes were adjusting to the dim light. She could see the Special Box of Maurie on Joe's shelf.

Oh, Maurie. Ginny. Maurie. Leonie had a vision of Maurie visiting with Joe that first time, lit from within by a triumphant glowing.

And where was Barney's wife?

She must have died, thought Leonie. Poor Barney. He's a widower.

Joe softly snored. Lying there against the sweet warmth of him, Leonie decided she would wait a little while longer before going back to her own bed. It was so nice to be of use to him. It consoled her to think of how she consoled him. She could feel his steady breathing. She would wait just a little longer with her eyes closed.

But the next thing Leonie knew there was morning light coming in the window. Joe was sleeping skew-whiff next to her, and she was still there in his narrow bed.

18

Barney lay awake and re-read a large section of *The Man Who Mistook His Wife for a Hat*.

Comfrey sat on Barney's chest, purring. She knocked her head against his elbow until he patted her, holding the book open with the other hand. He heard the occasional voices of policemen outside the window. He heard the sound of hand tools against earth. He looked up at the strange white light behind his curtains and then back to Oliver Sacks.

If a man has lost a leg or an eye, he knows he has lost a leg or an eye; but if he has lost a self—himself—he cannot know it, because he is no longer there to know it.

Barney underlined this passage with a biro and drew an asterisk next to it in the margin.

Comfrey's sweet crackly purr. Barney had grown so fond of her. But he knew it was because of Deb, and how much Deb had once loved Comfrey. Comfrey was a proxy. Sometimes the action of patting her would restore a vision of Deb on the couch in the evening, Comfrey on her lap, reading something from her pile of books. *Companion Planting in Australia* by Brenda Little. *The Organic Garden Doctor* by Jackie French. *Mayi: Some Bush Fruits of the West Kimberley* by Merrilee Lands. Deb was a true conservationist, and so Comfrey was an indoor cat, in order to preserve the life of birds. Deb said, 'Cats should be either inside or attached to a resonate bell.' So Barney built an elaborate cat run for this cat he had never really wanted and had no part in acquiring. Enclosed with wire mesh, the structure allowed Comfrey to climb up and play solitary cat games on various furry ledges and carry a stuffed bear along the fence line for a distance of three metres. Deb would look up from her spot in the garden and laugh, and then get back to her task of forever mulching.

That Deb rejected Comfrey was as astonishing to Barney as Deb's rejection of him.

'You take her,' she'd said, when he came to pack the last of his things.

By then Deb was so cold. She was the icy temperature of the creek. And Deb's sister was there, kind of hovering and making frittatas.

'Why would I take her?' Barney had asked. 'She's your cat. She's always been your cat.'

'Because I don't want her anymore,' said Deb.

'Can't you just take the cat, Barney?' said Deb's sister, exhausted by him. Her name was Irene and she was a physiotherapist. And of course Barney had heard via Helen Last that Irene lived there now, in the house. In *his* house. She'd made her bedroom in his old study.

What had Dr Prakash said?

Dr Prakash had said: 'You should try to avoid always comparing her to how she "used to be".'

Sure, sure.

'I don't want a cat,' Deb had said again, in their old living room. She was becoming agitated.

'Barney, please,' said Irene.

Barney had felt like the living room was a sinking ship and they were all going under. He could hear an aggressive type of music coming from behind Ben's closed door. Ben's door was always closed. Irene sighed loudly. Deb began pacing. And Barney went out to the shed and fetched the cardboard cat box they used for trips to the vet. He went to the back sunroom and collected Comfrey from her favourite spot on Deb's armchair and set the old cat inside the box and closed the lid. Then he drove her to his new house, on the front seat of his car, and Comfrey made that guttural yowl that she always made when she was enclosed in the box. She yowled for all of the short drive to Calboonya Avenue, South Clarke.

•

In the morning, when Barney woke, his lamp was still on and the book was open next to him on the bed. Where was Comfrey? This was unusual. She must have already got up.

Barney heard activity in the yard. There was an exciting monotony to it now. He could hear the familiar tones of Detective Sergeant Levins.

Barney rose and went to the window and opened the curtains. The policemen had all moved. What was the collective noun for police? A *force* of police was now next to his washing line, over near Leonie's fence. There were Barney's stiff beige briefs. And there was Levins, crouching, and the others, standing.

Barney watched for a few moments before closing the curtain. He went out into the hall and into the kitchen, where he found Comfrey—his unmuscular cat. She was sitting under the kitchen table, a place she never usually sat, staring intently through the glass at the police people.

Barney had read in an article once that cats have incredible intuition. He had scoffed at the time. He thought it was an example of very questionable science that an enormous percentage of cat owners believed their cats had a sixth sense about imminent bad news. Barney watched Comfrey watching the police for a moment. He contemplated her feeble, protruding spine. He wished he had brought in his washing. Barney went across to the bench and pressed the button on his shiny kettle.

•

Leonie lay Joe's damp new pyjamas and his damp new shorts and t-shirts over the Hills Hoist and attached them with faded plastic pegs. She slung his bedsheets over and, more carefully, his pillowcase. His socks were the length of her finger. She would laugh to herself with delight sometimes at the size of his clothes. But this morning she did not laugh so much as she looked at the backs of a huddle of police people who had moved from the blue marquee to the patch of grass near Barney's washing line.

There they all were, so close. And her acquaintance from yesterday gave her what she read as a warning nod while she watched them.

Yes, yes.

There was nothing to see anyhow. Except for them all being in this new position, and the industrial-sized tin of Nescafé over there on their picnic table, and the fact that Barney needed new underwear.

Inside, Joe was playing with Lego on the living room floor. He had made a tower of Lego that was almost as tall as the coffee table.

Leonie set down the washing basket near the back door and picked up his breakfast bowl and Peter Rabbit cup. She went over into the kitchen and put them in the sink. It felt to her that there were always some dirty dishes in the sink. It didn't seem to matter how often she washed them.

The phone rang and of course it would be Dorrie. Leonie picked it up quickly and said, 'They've moved to the washing line.'

A pause.

'Okay.'

And another pause and then, 'Can I speak to Leonie, please?'

Leonie flushed with embarrassment. 'I beg your pardon. Speaking.'

'Leonie, hi, I thought that was you. It's Eileen.'

A sensation of cold air arrived in Leonie's chest.

Eileen waited and then, when Leonie didn't speak, said, 'Eileen Swan. Verna's daughter.'

'Yes,' said Leonie. 'Of course. Hello, Eileen.'

'I know it's been a while,' said Eileen. 'But, I don't know, I just wanted to call and see how you're going. Mum said she bumped into you at the Plaza.'

'I'm fine, Eileen, I'm just *fine.*' Leonie swallowed hard, with some difficulty.

'Mum was a bit worried about you, Lee. And I thought, wow, I haven't seen you since that time at the church. Time really flies, doesn't it? Joe must be getting big.'

'Oh, he is,' said Leonie, and she giggled for no reason. Eileen had always made her nervous. 'How's Nathan and the girls?'

'They're fine,' said Eileen, whose voice had a husky quality to it. And Eileen went on pleasantly with that kind of catch-up small talk that Leonie found so difficult to concentrate on. The names of the girls flew past. Something about kindergarten at Clarke Primary. Oh, Clarke Primary. Leonie's world was propelled by memories. And then: 'Listen, I was thinking. Why don't we meet up at the park sometime? The kids can have a play.'

'Oh,' said Leonie. 'Well. Sure.'

'How about Saturday? We usually go to the big playground near the statue around nine.'

'Oh, well, okay,' said Leonie, and she was overwhelmed by the thought of it. And then Eileen said her goodbyes, and Leonie hung up and stood by the toaster. She realised she was grinning like a maniac, alone there in her kitchen, not in the least bit happy.

Eileen Swan! Of all people.

Maurie's old friend.

•

'Good morning,' said Barney to the police guard, who was a boy of barely twenty.

'Morning,' said the police boy.

'You bored yet?'

'Just quietly.'

Barney and the police boy stood near each other for a moment, but it seemed the exchange had reached its natural conclusion. Someone started up a leaf blower nearby. Barney went across the lawn to retrieve the newspaper, warm under the *Banksia integrifolia*. What a sensational tree.

Oh, and Earl was on his front porch again. In fact, from Barney's lawn he had a direct view of Earl's porch, and presumably vice versa. Earl was no doubt over there plotting his revenge. Though, in fact, Earl was reading. What would Earl read? Not a book, was what Barney thought. Barney was glad that his house was crawling with police people for the moment. He imagined that, when they left, Earl might egg Barney's car. Earl might put an explosive device in his letterbox. Earl might throw through his window a brick with a menacing note attached.

Barney unfolded the newspaper and looked at the front page.

Well, there you have it, he thought. Prime position, right under the masthead, biggest news in town.

Barney wanted to tell Deb!

But instead he said, quietly to himself, 'Good for you, Janice Clifford.'

•

Next door, *Play School* was on the television now and Joe was standing in front of it.

Leonie kneeled on the carpet and pulled a t-shirt over Joe's head, and she got one of his arms through and then the other.

Hello. I'm sticking some cord on this block of wood to make a stamp.

'Benita,' said Joe.

'Yes,' said Leonie, glancing sideways at Benita in a white smock. 'Now, pants.' Leonie held up Joe's old shorts and he held on to her shoulder to steady himself as he put a foot in.

Do you know what my stamp is meant to be?

Benita was looking at the camera, holding up her block of wood.

Joe looked so shy, he hid behind Leonie with his shorts around one leg.

'Leelee, can she see me?'

'No, sweetheart,' said Leonie. 'She can't see you.' Leonie got another leg in and pulled Joe's shorts up and smiled at him. Joe sat down and crossed his legs and watched the TV.

When the phone rang in the kitchen, Leonie startled. She had considered taking it off the hook. Eileen Swan! She hadn't stopped thinking about it. Whoever would have thought?

'I'll just see who that is. Can you go find some socks?' And Leonie went nervously now to the kitchen, like the phone was some scary new thing, a bringer of voices out of the woodwork.

'Hello, this is Leonie Wallace speaking.'

'Oh,' said Dorrie. 'Well, hello, this is Dorothy Little speaking.'

Leonie laughed. 'It's you.'

'It's always me.'

'Well, you never know.'

'Lee.'

'Dorrie.'

'You need to get the newspaper on the way to work.'

'Why?' Leonie's heart went all aflutter. 'Is it Ginny?'

'It's Janice,' said Dorrie. 'She's left Lou and I'll put money on it that she's the one who's dobbed him in.'

19

Deb and Barney had an address book at the old house that sat on the hallway table, next to the phone. It was a black square book that was falling apart with overuse. Deb had written the numbers of everyone they'd ever known in that little book. But Barney no longer had the book. So he ran his finger down the M's in the White Pages until he found William Murrow of Clarke Hill, because he couldn't quite remember the number anymore, even though he had dialled it so many times.

In the past couple of years, Barney had noticed that a lot of information from his past life had left him. Yet other memories from his past life were so vivid he wished he could forget. It would be fantastic to be able to choose one's memories. It would make life so much more bearable.

Barney picked up the phone and dialled, checking the number as he went. He listened to the ring tone and was inexplicably nervous.

'Hello, Murrow residence.'

'Hi Rita, it's Barney.'

'Oh, Barney, hi. How nice to hear from you.'

That was nice. Rita was so warm. Did she pity him? Maybe, but Barney tried his best to think otherwise. They had a brief chat and then there was a pause while Rita fetched Bill. Morning television came through the phone line. A woman's voice was talking excitedly about a new type of exerciser for the thighs.

'G'day, Barney. How are you, mate?'

'I'm good, Bill. How are you?'

Fine, fine. Rita and Bill were fine.

'Bill, do you remember that business with Ginny Lawson?'

'I'm just reading in the paper about Ginny Lawson.'

'They're digging up my yard, looking for her body.'

A pause.

'You're kidding me.'

'I wish I was.'

'The house you've rented.'

'Yes, my new house is *that* house. They've dug up a slab of concrete and now they're over in a different spot. There's a small army of them.'

'Jesus Christ. Rita will have a conniption.'

The television had been turned down and Barney heard Rita say: 'Rita will have a conniption about what?'

Barney sat there at his new kitchen table, watching Comfrey carefully lick her paw and rub it over her eyes and face, while Bill and Rita carried on their own conversation on the other end of the line. Comfrey's paw went over once, and then again. And then the other paw. And then both paws, in quick succession, all the way over her ears.

It's going to rain, thought Barney.

Rita had taken the phone from Bill now and was telling Barney how she had followed the case since the beginning.

'And we were just reading it in the paper! And I'm *relieved*, for the minute, because I always had this awful feeling that the new wife would wind up dead too. I've never believed those people who say she topped herself. And I certainly don't believe those people who say they've seen her.'

'Seen who?'

'Ginny Lawson,' said Rita. 'There was an article in the paper a couple of years ago saying that she'd been seen in Sydney by some woman, at a concert. I can't remember which concert it was, but a big crowded thing in the city. And this woman had bad eyesight is what the article said. I don't even know why they printed it. And I have a friend whose friend thinks she saw Ginny in Lismore when they were there on holiday. But my friend isn't really *good* friends with that friend—more like acquaintances.'

The sound of Bill—a moan.

'And who else?' asked Barney.

Rita waited a moment before answering and then said, 'Sandy. You know—from Combing Attractions?' Rita said this softly, because Sandy had always cut Deb's hair.

'Oh, sure,' said Barney, trying to sound unmoved. 'Sandy.'

'Well it wasn't Sandy per se,' said Rita. 'But one of Sandy's clients is in the police, and this policewoman said there'd been some report that Ginny was in Darwin. That someone had seen her in Darwin with some religious people.'

'Who?' asked Barney.

'Oh, I don't know. Someone with a big imagination,' said Rita. 'I don't believe any of it, Barney, I really don't. Even Sandy thought it was rubbish. Ginny Lawson's not in Darwin or going out to concerts.'

'No.'

'And she didn't run off with some other man or whatever people were saying years ago.'

'No, it doesn't seem like she did.'

'Before I started power walking, I used to do aerobics with this woman called Dorothy something, who lived opposite Ginny. Opposite *you* now, Barney. Do you know Dorothy? She used to be a counsellor or a psychologist or something like that, before she retired, so she's a smart woman. She

knows people. She knows about human nature and that sort
of thing. And do you know what she told me about Lou
Lawson? She told me that Lou Lawson is a vile man. The
whole street used to hear them fighting and whatnot else.
They'd have these big ugly rows, and they'd hear him abusing
Ginny. Dorothy said Ginny was a nice, quiet person. She
loved her little boy. She loved her husband. And what did
her husband do? He murdered her and buried her in her own
backyard, plain and simple.'

•

Leonie read the newspaper on one of the metal benches in
the Plaza, next to a discarded McDonald's drink container
and an artificial plant.

There, on the front page, alongside an article about a tiny
lamb that was born at nine hundred grams and survived:

EX-HUSBAND OF GINNY LAWSON
CHARGED WITH DOMESTIC ASSAULT.

Leonie gasped and could have gasped all day.

Janice Clifford, thirty years old, had been granted a
restraining order against her husband, Lou Lawson, in the
state of Queensland. After an incident at their Bribie Island
home in January, Lou Lawson had been charged with three
counts of common assault and one count of destroying or
damaging property—ugh, he was disgusting—and then

Leonie skipped forward, sensing Ginny's name approaching in the next paragraph.

> Mr Lawson's first wife, Ginny Lawson, disappeared six years ago. On Monday, police began a 'forensic search' at the South Clarke home she and her husband shared in the 1980s. A senior police source confirmed that the search, which is expected to last five days, is based on new information.

> A Detective Sergeant Levins from Clarke Police was quoted:

> 'It's a complex block of land because there was a lot of concrete and the ground is very compacted, so digging is not easy. But it is an extensive search and we will be digging in several areas.'

Leonie read this quote twice, and then she stared blankly at the disposal store opposite, at the selection of military fatigues and Swiss Army knives in the window.

New information, she thought. Janice *Clifford*, she thought. And honestly, how many times could the *Gather Region Advocate* reprint this photo of Ginny and Lou on their wedding day? Leonie had seen it a thousand times. Surely she was immune. And yet she looked down at Ginny again now—this grainy smiling bride—and her eyes filled with fresh tears.

•

The police had all moved now to the area near the washing line. A new marquee was installed. It was not entirely blue, but blue and yellow, which was a nice change. The edge of the canvas roof flapped sporadically in the light wind. Barney could see the string line designating the new site, and he watched as two policemen took up at least six square metres of turf.

Imagine if Barney were someone who cared about the sanctity of his lawn. He wasn't. He had never understood the men of Clarke and their obsession with lawns. And of course Deb would have appreciated any act of grass removal. 'Lawns are for retirees,' she would say. Deb preferred weeds! *Weeds have tremendous purpose.* The ghost of old Deb spoke to Barney, her voice was in his head so often. She was offering a spirited discourse on the myriad uses of dandelions, or reading aloud from *Food for Free* by Richard Mabey.

Barney watched the turf now as it formed a discarded pile. These lawn-removing policemen wore their regular uniforms, but with gloves and face masks. Two red wheelbarrows had appeared and Levins was eating a packet of Twisties. Another officer was taking photographs of this new spot by the washing line. Sadly, Barney's undergarments were quivering in the breeze.

20

'What *I'm* wondering,' said Varden, 'is did he tell the new wife that he killed the old wife? Or does the new wife just guess it?'

'Guess it on account of being half-killed herself?' said Leonie, who had the newspaper plonked on her desk. Wanda was next to her, at Wanda's desk, and Varden was standing, gesticulating, holding a can of air-freshener.

'Yes,' said Varden. 'Because they have this *new information*. And so we think: Well, what is this *new information*? Is it that the new wife *knew* that he killed the old wife? Like she has some actual piece of evidence? Or does she just *think* he did?' Varden's arms were really flapping around. He continued: 'Or do the *police* just think he did, because of how he's beaten the new wife?'

'It's Janice,' said Leonie. 'It's Janice and it's Ginny.'

'Yes, and do we think Janice knew?'

'Well, we certainly hope Janice didn't,' said Leonie.

Wanda made a kind of grimace and sipped her Garfield tea. Then she said: 'But what say she had her suspicions. And then this whole thing's made it finally dawn on her. Like with the wedding ring. She must have thought something. What type of man *recycles* the ring of his missing wife? She probably told herself for the first few years, you know, surely *not*.'

'Yes,' said Varden. 'She tells herself everything's fine. She convinces herself.'

'Denial ain't just a river in Egypt,' said Leonie.

'Ha!' went Varden.

'Look, I think this is probably not the first time he's had a go at Janice,' said Leonie. 'Given that he's Lou. But I'd fall off my chair if he'd actually confessed to her. I think he would have been all charming and grieving for Janice. And, you know, *You're the only woman who really understands me*, and all that crap. Until he wasn't.'

'Until they find his ex-wife's clothing buried in his old backyard,' said Wanda.

'Well, yes, except that Janice wouldn't be privy to that information,' said Leonie.

'Unless she knew all along and she's the one who told the police where to look!' said Varden.

'I just don't see it,' said Leonie, and she turned the newspaper to page two—a picture of a sturdy local woman whose son had been sent off to the Gulf War. Leonie peered at an adjoining article about the oil spill clean-up and a photo of a doused seabird. Wanda slurped her tea. Varden's tape of duduk music reached the end of side one. And Leonie drifted elsewhere . . . Eileen Swan had called her! It had made her feel so *special*. And Leonie felt embarrassed, for feeling so special.

But 'Verna's daughter'? That's what Eileen had said on the phone. Which was true, of course; she was Verna's daughter. But didn't Leonie know her much more as Maurie's friend? Could Eileen not say Maurie's name either?

And that she hadn't seen Leonie since *that time at the church*.

Could Eileen not say 'Maurie's funeral'? Maurie. Maureen. Maurie's funeral. Was it that hard to say?

It was. It was so hard.

Leonie closed the newspaper and sighed.

'I think you're right, Lee,' said Wanda. 'I think Lou would have lied till the end to protect himself.'

'Well, you know what they say,' said Varden. He stood up, raised the aerosol bottle and sprayed a mist of lily-white flowers. 'Lies have short feet.'

•

At Maurie's funeral, Eileen Swan had worn an oversized shirt done up to the top button and a pair of maroon velvet slacks. After the service, she had stood with Verna

133

while Verna smoked on the neat lawn outside the Anglican church. Verna looked like an elderly whippet. Skeletal, with skin like crinkled paper. And Eileen, as always, was just so put together.

Maurie's city friends and her work colleagues from the State Library, they were all there, in little groups, these very impressive people. Eileen and Verna didn't mingle. And god, it was lucky that Eunice had not lived to see that day. Lucky for Eunice—and lucky for Leonie that at least she didn't have to deal with Eunice too. These were life's tiny mercies.

Leonie had held Joe in her arms inside the church and, when he began to cry at the end of the service, she took him outside and rocked him and spoke to him quietly. Joe was two, and small for his age, and Leonie felt she might die of her sadness. And Eileen Swan was over there with Verna on the lawn. Leonie saw Eileen cover her face with her hands and weep. She saw Verna put a gaunt arm around Eileen's shoulder.

•

Decades ago, Eileen Swan would walk through the front door of the Wallace family home without knocking. She would stay for dinner and Eunice would be such a charming host! Eunice was so likeable in company, and Leonie would glow with reflected glory.

One evening, when Eileen and Maurie must have been seventeen, Eileen came out of Maurie's room fast and blinking.

'Something's wrong with Maurie.'

Eunice and Leonie were in the living room watching television, and Eunice shot up like the room was on fire.

'She's having a fit or something.'

Young Eileen Swan was the calmest panicked person Leonie had ever seen. She stood in the living room, close to crying but totally holding it together. Eunice went quickly to the back of the house. Leonie had sat awhile and then said, 'It's okay, Eileen,' which was quite the case of role-switching, on account of Eileen being older and more authoritative in general. Even as a teenager, Eileen seemed in charge of her own destiny. And Leonie had found her beautiful to the point of being almost mystical.

Leonie left Eileen in the living room and went after Eunice to Maurie's room.

And by then Maurie was sitting on the floor blankly, with Eunice crouching down next to her. Eunice had one arm around Maurie's shoulders, and with the other she held Maurie's hand.

Leonie watched this tender moment from the doorway: Maurie's unusual absence, Eunice's unusual presence.

'You're okay, Maureen,' said Eunice. 'You're just *fine*.'

Maurie was off wherever it was that Maurie went. And Leonie was fifteen years old, her eyes full of envious, worried tears.

'Mum—' said Leonie from the doorway.

'*Shoosh*, Leonie.' Eunice gave her such a look. Then Eunice stroked Maurie's arm and said, 'Not to worry, Maureen. Mum's here.'

21

In his study, at the front of the house, Barney made a structural change to the Duncan article for *Aboriginal History
Journal*, volume 15 ('Aboriginal Influence on Archaeological
Practice'). He managed to tend to a small tranche of admin-
istrative matters. He wrote a cheque to *Southerly* to renew
his subscription. He wrote a cheque to *History* to renew his
subscription. He opened a week-old letter from the RTA and
contemplated his car registration documents and sticker.

Oh, but the car. Of course it made him think of Deb. Deb,
who would never consider getting a second car, because she
hated driving and because of the ozone layer. Deb had thrown
away all of their aerosol cans and everything squeaked at the
old house due to a lack of WD-40.

Barney opened his filing cabinet and slipped the renewals
into the *SUBSCRIPTONS* folder. He glanced, just for a

moment, at the file tab that said *DEBORAH* and flinched at the horrors of memories contained within. Then he leaned back in his chair and looked out the window onto the street, where the adolescent policeman was standing in the driveway and the police cars had become a fixture. It was so difficult not to go and check on the progress in the yard. And it was then that Barney realised he hadn't searched the microfilm for 'Lou Lawson', only 'Ginny Lawson'. He should return to Rosamie and search for 'Lou Lawson'.

Barney looked back at the registration papers and reached over to his wooden in-tray, sifting through the pile until he found the unopened envelope from the NRMA. He would write a cheque for his green slip, and then he would need a pink slip. Barney was not in charge of his memories. He did not want to be there in his study, recalling that most awful day. Yet here he was, thinking about the day when he didn't pick up Deb from work.

'But you hate taking the car,' he had said.

'Yes, but if I drop you off early then you can get the most out of the day.'

'That's true,' said Barney, and he had been very pleased to be dropped off early so he could get the most out of the day.

•

Dr Prakash had asked, only two months later, 'How would you describe her now?'

Barney had said, 'Like a stranger.'

'Can you say more?'

'It's like it's not Deb who's come home,' said Barney. 'She looks like Deb, but she's not Deb.'

'How much have you spoken with her about this?' asked Dr Prakash.

'A little.'

A more truthful answer would have been: *Not really at all.*

Dr Prakash said, 'As you know, Dr Daniels and I have spent a lot of time with Deborah. But have *you* really asked her how she feels?'

'Not in so many words,' Barney said. 'I have so much to take care of at the house.'

'I would suggest that you ask Deborah how it feels for her, Barney.'

•

'What are you doing here?' asked Leonie, looking up from her desk as Dorrie came through the glass door of Harvey World Travel, holding a takeaway coffee.

'I want to book a trip to Bali,' said Dorrie. 'Isn't that where everyone goes?'

'Oh, stop it.'

'How are you, Wanda?' said Dorrie as she sat down in Leonie's customer chair.

'I'm good, thank you, Dorothy. How are you?'

139

'Intrigued,' said Dorrie.

'Aren't we all?' said Wanda.

And Leonie said, 'You have about six minutes before Varden gets back from lunch and issues a formal complaint.'

'It smells very floral in here,' said Dorrie.

'Lily-white flowers,' said Leonie.

'Varden just sprayed,' said Wanda.

'Well I just got a mani-pedi,' said Dorrie. 'Every nurse from Clarke Base was there on some sort of nurses outing.'

'Which reminds me—' Leonie began, but Dorrie kept on going.

'I saw that you were quiet so I thought I'd just pop in. I can't stop thinking about Janice! You know, Lee, if she knew, then she's an accomplice—to *murder*.'

'I think she'd be an accessory,' said Leonie. 'After the fact.'

'Did you learn that on *Columbo*?' said Dorrie.

Wanda laughed. She had leaned sideways to be part of the conversation. And Dorrie sat in the customer chair as if she owned the place. She sipped her coffee and swallowed. 'But what if she was in on it?' she said.

'Like she helped?' said Leonie. 'Dorrie, I don't think she helped.'

Dorrie sighed. 'No. I think I'm just a bit overexcited. It must be this disgusting cappuccino.' And then to Wanda, 'I mean not *excited* excited, like if I was actually going to

Indonesia. Oh, and did Leonie tell you about the item of clothing? Of course she did.'

'Of course she did,' said Wanda. 'But wait—did Janice ever come to Clarke? I thought Lou met her up in Queensland and she never actually came here.'

'Who knows?' said Dorrie.

'I've always assumed she didn't,' said Leonie.

And Wanda nodded and said, 'Well, you'd probably have noticed her if she was hanging about next door. She has quite the look. Remember those pictures in that Queensland newspaper? In the social pages?'

'Oh god, yes,' said Dorrie. 'Janice with her fluffy hair and her fluffy little dog.'

'That was the best client gift you ever got, Lee,' said Wanda. 'A page from a newspaper!'

'Better than a snow globe,' said Leonie.

'I guess Lou likes women who like little dogs,' said Dorrie.

'What was the name of Ginny's little dog again? Was it a sausage dog?'

'Yes, Peaches,' said Leonie. 'She *adored* that dog.'

'She really did,' said Dorrie.

'And it was all a bit funny, that whole thing with Peaches,' said Leonie. 'Someone left the gate open one day and off went Peaches. Ginny was absolutely devastated.'

'She really was,' said Dorrie.

'And so I said, *Well, let's put up signs! Let's doorknock.* I said we should at least doorknock our street and the streets leading up to the highway,' said Leonie. 'But Ginny didn't want to do any of that. She just said she'd called all the vets and reported it, and that someone would hand in Peaches if they found her. And that was that. And no one ever handed in Peaches.'

'That's sad,' said Wanda.

'Ginny was such a don't-make-a-fuss kind of person,' said Leonie, and she tapped the table with her fingers.

The atmosphere turned oddly flat. Dorrie didn't look quite so excited anymore. She sighed. 'Well.'

Wanda nodded and then Leonie nodded.

And Dorrie stood up and hoisted her bag onto her shoulder, a whiff of nail polish to her. 'On that note, I'll love you and leave you,' said Dorrie. 'Before we all get clinically depressed.'

'Good to see you, Dorothy,' said Wanda.

'I'll see you later on,' said Leonie.

'Come at five thirty,' said Dorrie.

And after the door had closed behind Dorrie, Wanda turned to Leonie and said, 'Dorothy's so funny.'

'Yes, she's a real thigh-slapper.'

'How many grandchildren does she have now?'

'Four. Her daughter brought the youngest two down to visit last month actually.'

'That's nice,' said Wanda. 'It must be nice having an older friend.'

'Oh,' said Leonie. 'I guess it is, I've never really thought about it.'

•

Just ten minutes away, at the library, Barney was hovering near the new releases section, looking expectantly at the front desk. No Rosamie. A bereft feeling rose in Barney as he stood under the low fluorescent lights. The new releases section seemed only to offer crime novels in large print. There was a different and inferior librarian behind the front desk, sitting on a stool, reading a crime novel in large print.

Barney went through the low doorway and down the stairs to the Local Heritage Room where, it seemed, no one ever was.

Do you have old photographs of the Gather Region? asked a laminated sign. *Contact Rosamie P. at the front desk to be part of this exciting project.*

Rosamie *P.*? As if she needed to be differentiated from all the other Rosamies?

And well, yes, Barney had a lot of photographs of the bushland of the Gather Region, dating back at least twenty years. He had the loveliest photo of Deb with Helen Last at Clarke Point, in matching blue jeans and flannelette shirts. Perhaps Rosamie P. would like a photo of Deb and Helen and

Phil and Rae, swimming at the base of the Wibung waterfall? Or of Deb and Norma next to a goanna on a tree on the Birrung Track?

Barney suspected Rosamie P. would prefer something slightly more historical, like an image of when Colonial Road was still a big field of cows.

It was musty in the Local Heritage Room and a central table displayed a collection of arcane publications. *Scenes From Our Streets: A pictorial history of Clarke*; *The Gather Region and its Pioneers*; *Grant's Lake: A social and natural history*. Barney had the latter book at home, still packed away in one of his boxes. He flipped through this copy and saw the old grey photos of the big lake. There was vegetation on the west side in those days, where the road now was. He stared at old-fashioned wooden boats and an image of a man holding a tremendous fish.

Barney put the book down and collected his thoughts.

He had read all the articles regarding the disappearance of Ginny Lawson from 1985 to 1988. That just left 1989 and 1990, but Barney would get to those later. Right now he wanted to know more about Lou Lawson. He wanted articles that mentioned Lou Lawson before Ginny went missing and Lou's name became synonymous with the mysterious fate of his wife.

Barney typed in 'Lou Lawson', and a short while later he carried one box over to the annexe. He spooled the film through as Rosamie P. had showed him. Rosamie was probably married. All those groceries he'd seen her carrying. She was probably keeping Con's Convenience and Deli in business. Those groceries spoke of a woman dripping with children.

From the *Gather Region Advocate*, 17 March 1983: a photograph of Lou Lawson among the various members of the Clarke Hunting Club. Even next to these burly men, Lou looked enormous. Barney read the accompanying article, which was about the landowners around Clarke being inundated with feral animals.

'The farmers here are fighting with one hand tied behind their back,' says local physiotherapist and hunting enthusiast, Lou Lawson.

Local physiotherapist and hunting enthusiast! Barney wasn't sure what he'd expected, but it wasn't that. Lou had been speaking in reference to hunting rules and regulations. Lou had felt there was too much red tape between him and all those animals. Barney looked again at the photo, which was of seven men holding rifles next to a barbed-wire fence. One of them was in a camouflage outfit. It was all very hairy-chested. Barney wondered if any of these men cared about the impact of introduced species on native vegetation and fauna.

Vost, Stallan, Scotting, Marrel, Lawson, Finch, Hickey. These were the surnames of the men in the photo. What was

Barney looking for? He wasn't even sure. But it was true that part of him had expected to find a trove of information about Lou Lawson's past life, which he could then dissect for clues of future murderous intent. He should have just borrowed a crime novel from upstairs, in whatever font size he could find. Barney wanted to laugh at himself. Lou was just a very large physiotherapist.

Barney thought of that old photograph he had of Deb and everyone on that walk, swimming at the base of the waterfall. That was such a fantastic day. For the first time in a long time, Barney allowed himself to feel a little shiver of how much he missed those walks. But he had told himself that he couldn't go anymore—not without Deb—because that would be too painful, and Barney didn't want to feel any more pain.

22

L eonie was folding the washing. Which meant neat piles on the couch. The big blue couch was for Leonie's clothes. Work things made of synthetic materials. Comfortable things for around the house. She had always had this sense that her clothes were enormous. Big, billowy things with too much fabric to them. What a wasteful amount of fabric she required! These were thoughts that occurred to her as she folded, pushing the garments down so as not to take up so much space.

But on the smaller blue couch: smaller piles of smaller things. Joe's socks in miniature sock balls. Joe's white singlets, which required an astonishing amount of stain remover. Joe's new pyjamas, new t-shirts, new shorts.

'I got you some things,' said Leonie.

'What?'

'Some new clothes.'

Joe crawled across the carpet on his hands and knees and then stood up and gently put a hand on the folded pile of shirts.

'Is there a picture?' asked Joe.

'On the t-shirts?' said Leonie. 'No, they're just plain.'

Joe kept his hand on the pile of shirts and stared at them, so clean and new, and said, 'I'm wishing there was a picture.'

•

At 5.30 pm Leonie and Joe, holding hands, went across the street to Dorrie's.

Clive opened the door and said, 'Here's trouble,' and Leonie giggled, and then she heard herself giggling and stopped and sighed. How ridiculous she was. She held out the bottle of Jacob's Creek she'd bought at the bottle shop in the Plaza, and Clive took it and said, smiling, 'I guess we'll just have to drink it.'

Leonie smiled. '*Foof*,' she said, as she sat down at the outdoor table, as if walking across the road was such an effort.

'I've got some of that apple juice you like, Joe,' said Dorrie, standing on the patio.

Joe smiled and buried his head in Leonie's soft bosom.

'What a lucky duck,' said Leonie, and Joe made an agreeable noise.

Dinner was roast lamb and mashed potatoes and a salad with sun-dried tomatoes in it. Leonie cut Joe's meat into tiny portions and he asked for tomato sauce and Leonie had some too, and she helped herself to some salad.

'Delicious,' said Leonie. 'What's in the dressing?'

'Balsamic vinegar,' said Dorrie, and Leonie had never used any of that.

'Golly,' said Leonie. 'This is all so delicious, Dorrie.'

Dorrie said, 'It's like falling off a log, Lee,' and she ate a sun-dried tomato.

Always such humility from Dorrie, who was such a good cook. Dorrie was good at everything. And Clive was in a fabulous mood, very talkative, which wasn't always the case with Clive. He could be moody and reserved, on account of serving at the shop all day and being so naturally charming. Natural charm can really take it out of you was what Leonie thought. It was like a trim lawn—such an effort to maintain.

Leonie changed Joe into his new space pyjamas after dinner and he was permitted to watch *The Land Before Time* on the couch, where Leonie could see him through the open back doors. She said, 'Oh, yes,' as Clive offered Aerogard for her ankles and a second glass of wine.

'Clive thinks Janice has some sort of damning evidence,' said Dorrie.

'Like what?' asked Leonie.

'The bracelet,' said Clive. 'I bet you she's got Ginny's bracelet.'

'She wouldn't have the bracelet,' said Leonie. 'Ginny literally couldn't take it off. The gold was so thick, and Lou had squeezed it so tight around her wrist. It was like a cattle tag.'

'Yes, but,' said Clive, 'he might have taken it off her—you know: after.'

'Oh god,' said Leonie. 'What, like he chopped off her hand?'

'Clive thinks like a butcher,' said Dorrie. 'It's an occupational hazard.'

'I guess it just depends on if he was in a hurry or not,' said Clive.

'Or if he's enough of a psychopath,' said Leonie.

'But if Janice has it—like, if she's found it among his things,' said Clive.

'Then at least they've got him in a lie,' said Leonie.

'They'd be able to say that, at a minimum, he lied,' said Clive. 'And if he lied about that then—et cetera.'

'Hmm,' went Leonie, who was horrified by the image of Ginny's darling wrist. She thought of Clive effortlessly deboning a leg of lamb. The sheer size of Lou Lawson's meaty hands. Leonie took a sip of wine and turned to look at Joe, who was snuggled up on the couch, holding Rabbit. He was small and quiet and concentrating on the movie. The back room of the house glowed about him. Leonie loved to be at

Dorrie's, where something nice was always cooking and there was a warm feeling to every room.

Leonie looked back at Dorrie and said, 'I wanted to talk more to Barney. He seems very interested in the whole thing. But it's a bit impossible with Joe.'

'Of course,' said Dorrie. 'Joe shouldn't be hearing that.'

'He shouldn't, and yet he's desperate to watch what the police are doing all the time and he asks a hundred questions.'

'Joe loves a question,' said Dorrie.

'He has a wedding ring on,' said Leonie.

'Who?' asked Dorrie.

'Barney.'

'Oh. And no sign of a wife.'

'No.'

'I wonder what happened there,' said Dorrie.

'Maybe he killed her and buried her in the backyard,' said Leonie.

Clive laughed.

And Dorrie smiled and said, 'You might have to go back up to the station in your best dress.'

•

Joe fell asleep on the couch, and they moved inside to the kitchen and Dorrie made tea and sat down on one of the barstools. Leonie had almost finished rinsing the dishes and stacking the dishwasher, despite Dorrie's protests, and Clive had disappeared to the front of the house, where they had a second sitting room and a second television.

'Guess who called me?' said Leonie.

'Who?'

'Eileen Swan.'

Dorrie said, 'Huh.'

'We're meeting at the playground on Saturday so the kids can have a play,' said Leonie.

'Well,' said Dorrie on the barstool, holding a cup of tea. 'Do you feel okay about that?'

'No,' said Leonie, as she rinsed the tomato sauce from Joe's plate. It had dried in a big smear and she rubbed at it with her thumb under the warm water until it came away. She put it in the dishwasher and said, 'But it might be good for Joe. He only really plays with Ben and Milo outside of preschool.'

'I like Milo,' said Dorrie. 'He's always counting everything.'

'Milo can count to a hundred and twenty.'

Dorrie smiled. She said, 'Clive sees a bit of Nathan these days. I hear Nathan's been buying a lot of sausages.'

'I've only spoken to Nathan maybe once in my life. But Maurie used to say that Eileen was way too good for him.'

'Who knows what goes on behind closed doors.'

'Exactly.'

Leonie spooned the powder in the tray and pressed the buttons on the Dishlex.

Dorrie said, 'It's nice of Eileen to call.'

'It's only because I ran into Verna at Fosseys.'

'I can't believe Verna's still alive.'

'I know, it's like she's eternal,' said Leonie. 'I think she thinks I'm a big mess.' And Leonie had that feeling again like she would cry. That if anyone were to comfort her she would surely cry. The embrace with Verna had stuck to her like so much cigarette smoke.

'Do you want me to come with you to meet Eileen?' asked Dorrie. 'We're supposed to be going to the lake with the McDonalds on Saturday, but I can easily cancel. Or Clive could still go, and I could come with you.'

Oh, unbearable kindness. Leonie turned to her friend and smiled and said, 'No.'

Dorrie nodded. She looked quite worried now. 'You're not a mess to me, Lee. And I know you don't want to hear this, but it might be good for you to talk to someone. I mean, specifically, it might be good for you to talk to someone about Maurie.'

23

In the grey evening, Barney sat at the kitchen table with the window open, watching the marquees. He could hear digging sounds and murmurings from within. Trowels hitting small rocks? Something with a higher pitch than dirt. Barney had prepared a sad dinner of boiled eggs.

He hadn't seen Levins for hours, but that other one, O'Leary, was out there. Did O'Leary have a cold or was it some structural issue with his adenoids? An enlargement of the tonsils? Barney had gleaned a lot from editing medical papers. He had read so much in his life, and yet it had taken him this long to realise that there were no women among these police and forensics people. There was just this troupe of men, looking for this woman.

He put his second egg onto a piece of buttered toast and used a knife to squish it down, flat and even. He added a lot of salt. Barney took a bite and chewed and heard O'Leary laughing nasally from inside the marquee.

•

An hour later Barney had finished the crossword. He switched on the television. A David Attenborough documentary was on the ABC. He watched as a digger unearthed piles of limestone in a former bay in some region of Germany.

And the processes of decay, which depend on oxygen, could only move very slowly.

David Attenborough was always an affable presence. Barney stared at the images on the screen. Fish in dark waters and a white floor of sea. He took a sip of beer. (Home brew batch: December 1990—a bit flat. Beer and priming sugar not adequately mixed in brewing bucket? Needs more time to condition?)

So if the corpse of an animal that was living in the waters above slowly drifted down here, it could settle on the bottom and remain entire, undecayed and undisturbed by scavengers, until mud settled down upon it, and buried it.

Oh, for god's sake. Barney snorted out a laugh. Here was David Attenborough, tonight of all nights, talking about corpses. Deb loved a good coincidence. Barney wanted, so much, to tell Deb about all of this. He could sense Deb nearby so often. She was in the opposite chair, or pottering about in the kitchen while he read his journals.

David Attenborough's voice was authoritative and calm, and Barney's mind flipped to Dr Prakash—another calm voice. But the content: so uncalming.

Ask Deborah how it feels for her.

Barney had been too terrified of the answer, so he did not ask.

Be consistent, don't confront her.

These were easier requests.

Only when Deb and Barney had attended Dr Prakash's office together had it been said so plainly.

Deb was off in her own world at the appointment. She couldn't focus, she wasn't interested. She spoke only when asked a direct question, and she looked at her lap while she did.

If Barney hadn't been so traumatised, perhaps he would have been embarrassed. His wife, who had been so warm and sociable! His caring, thoughtful wife!

'What is it like for you now, Deborah?' asked Dr Prakash. 'Could you describe for Barney and I how you feel that things are different for you?'

Barney and *me*, thought Barney.

'I feel fine,' said Deb.

Dr Prakash said, 'Could you say more? Like what we've spoken about before, when you were still in the hospital?'

'Oh that,' said Deb. 'Well, I guess I feel like I've lost my soul.'

Dr Prakash looked at Barney—sympathetic, composed—and Barney felt as if his chest was constricting around his heart, tight enough to choke it.

Deb stared at her hands in her lap. She seemed so bored, like having to be there was such a drag. She said, 'I feel like nothing in particular, really. Just sort of hollow. But it's okay.'

Barney closed his eyes now in the living room. Then he opened them again and saw, on the television, a man showing David Attenborough the upper arm bone of a flying dinosaur.

•

Next door, Leonie lay on the big couch watching television. She watched the end of *Murphy Brown*. Every now and again the sound of digging would disturb her concentration. Leonie was very tired. Thankfully Joe was asleep. Clive had carried him across the road and laid him gently in his bed, and given Leonie a silent thumbs-up as he crept out.

Leonie switched to the ABC, where David Attenborough was talking about pterodactyls, holding up a bone. Ugh, bones. It gave Leonie a shiver to see a bone. She didn't want to think about any of that tonight.

And she didn't want to think about Maurie either. But now David Attenborough was on a dusty plateau, talking to a man in a legionnaire's cap about fossils. The things that made Leonie think of Maurie were just endless. She was instantly transported to the Clarke Plaza food court, to a rare occasion when Maurie was not only in town but had come in to meet Leonie for lunch. They had one of the metal tables outside the Oasis Café and toddler Joe was asleep in his stroller, making gentle snores.

'Mum is trying to set me up with Marshall Farmer,' said Leonie.

How Maurie had laughed! Leonie loved cracking Maurie up more than just about anything. Maurie said, 'Does he still collect fossils?'

'I think his whole collection consisted of four fossils. It's just that he spent all of primary school talking about fossils.'

'Didn't Marshall Farmer lose a foot?'

'Marshall Farmer lost the bottom half of his leg from type two diabetes. He has a prosthetic.'

'I'd be more concerned about the drinking,' said Maurie. 'Why would Mum want you to date an alcoholic?'

'Because Carmel Farmer has convinced her it's actually just rosacea and a speech impediment.'

Maurie grinned and took a sip of iced tea. She looked at Leonie a little warily, and Leonie knew that look well enough to take a nervous breath. Maurie said, 'I saw Clayton.'

Leonie's eyes went to the metal table, which was not particularly clean. 'Oh.'

'I ran into him at the Hoyts in the city.'

Leonie nodded. She saw that the table had scratches on it and a drop of something that could have been dried egg yolk.

'He said he goes by "Clay" now.'

Leonie wanted to scratch the maybe-yolk off with her fingernail. That would be satisfying, potentially diverting.

'Lee.'

'What?'

'Well,' said Maurie, who had her foot on the stroller wheel and was moving it back and forth, to keep Joe sleeping, 'just because the only man you've ever loved and trusted broke it off and disappeared from your life without any care or explanation.'

Leonie looked up from the table and broke into a smile, and Maurie smiled back.

Leonie said, 'Don't be an arsehole.'

'I just think it might be good for you to talk to someone.'

'I do talk to people. I talk to Dorrie all the time.'

'You know what I mean.'

'Dorrie comes with the added bonus of being a trained professional.'

'Dorrie's not your psychologist, though—she's your friend.'

'Why would I want to pay a stranger sixty dollars an hour to talk about Clayton?'

'Oh, Lee,' said Maurie. 'It's not all about Clayton.'

Leonie fake-coughed. 'What?' she said. 'So it's all about Dad?'

'It's about Dad for a minute, and then it's all about Mum.'

Leonie felt a dreadful sting in one of her eyes, like someone had thrown a sharp stone in there. She winked and a single tear fell out and rolled down her pink cheek.

'Are you crying?'

'I have something in my eye.'

'Lee,' said Maurie.

'Maurie,' said Leonie, wiping her eye with the back of her hand. Leonie felt very claustrophobic. They should have sat outdoors on the terrace. Neither of them had finished their lunch, which was very unusual for Leonie, and not at all unusual for Maurie. Leonie said, 'Just because you're on a journey of self-discovery.'

Maurie opened her bag, which was a big brown corduroy thing full of nappies and tiny Tupperwares of mashed foods. Leonie was flushed now and half-weeping while Maurie wrote something down in a notebook and then tore out the page and handed the piece of paper across the table.

'I just happened to come across it at work, and I actually found it very helpful,' said Maurie.

Leonie took the paper, one eye full of stupid tears, and read what Maurie had written: *Healing the Shame that Binds You by John Bradshaw*. Leonie laughed at her sister and said, 'Oh, come on.'

Now, on the couch, Leonie sat up and stretched her back. She pressed the off button on the remote and the television became a blank grey screen. Then she stood up and went across the carpet to the mantel, where she had her collection of framed photographs: Eunice; Joe; Joe again; Maurie and Joe; Maurie.

The picture of Maurie was in an expensive brass frame that Leonie had bought especially at the one-hour photo place in the Plaza. She had put the photo in the frame and then had tried, for almost two years, not to look at it.

Leonie stood in front of the mantel now, gazing at her bare feet on the carpet. She wiggled her toes around. She would raise her eyes in a moment and look at Maurie. It was just stupid, really, how much she couldn't stand to look at her own sister. But then, she was so tired.

She heard a loud clinking sound from next door, like metal against metal. The floodlights spilled over into her yard, she could see the shine of them down the hallway, through the glass pane of the back door.

Leonie really was very tired. It might be best to just go straight to bed. Perhaps tonight wasn't the right time to look at a photo of Maurie after all.

24

At first light, Barney opened his eyes and felt the warm ball of Comfrey wedged behind his knees. He heard a tentative kookaburra, then another kookaburra. Then a full chorus of kookaburras. Their laughter filled the streets of South Clarke. Barney thought, It's going to rain.

A man's voice said, 'Make this the access route.'

And then someone responded. Laughter? Again, this laughter. Why would anyone—doing this job—ever laugh?

A spade creaked into hard earth.

Barney wandered into the kitchen in his shorts and t-shirt. The blue marquee where the shed had been was gone, and now there was just a string line and a large rectangle of redistributed soil. The original marquee and the blue-and-yellow one by the washing line were still in place. A mound of dirty turf sat beside it. Barney could see Levins, and he could see O'Leary, and he could see three others whom he had come to know the faces of, if not the names. Levins had his hands on his hips and his back to Barney. He was on a bit of lawn, between marquees.

Barney let himself outside onto the patio and saw that that a policeman was taking photographs of the ground in front of the lemon tree.

•

'Uh-oh, dear,' said Joe.

Leonie was in the bedroom getting dressed. All three polo shirts were in the wash. She buttoned her back-up blouse in front of the mirror, the navy blouse she was so unfond of.

'Hold on, sweetie,' she said loudly, attaching her name tag. She straightened herself, straightened her clothes. 'What is it?' she said, as she came into the kitchen.

'I spilled,' said Joe, and there was puddle of milk on the red formica table.

'That's okay,' said Leonie. 'I'll get a sponge.' And she went to the sink and fetched a sponge, and she cleaned up the milk and rinsed the sponge under the tap until the water ran clear.

'I'm sorry,' said Joe.

'It's fine,' said Leonie. 'It was just an accident.'

Leonie rinsed her tea mug and set it on the drying rack. She went back to the table and collected Joe's milky bowl. 'Uptown Girl' was coming softly out of the radio.

'I want to see my mum.'

'Sweetheart,' said Leonie, holding the bowl.

'I want to see her now.'

'Of course you do.'

Joe's face crumpled and he let out a wail. The tears could come so fast with Joe. Leonie set the bowl on the table and went to him. She crouched down in front of his chair. 'Sweetheart,' she said, as he heaved and wailed. She put her arms around him, and he pressed his wet face into her chest, her awful blouse. She looked down and saw the top of Joe's head, the top of her name tag.

'Of course you want to see your mum.'

Joe made a long noise that resembled *yeah*, but was mostly wailing.

Leonie closed her eyes. She had a steely determination in her not to cry, not a drop. But, oh, how it went on. It felt like a forever of Joe's sobbing. But it was only a minute—or it was five. And then it turned into those staccato sniffles that happen when crying stops, and Leonie held on tight and said, 'Why don't we go get the Special Box from your room and we'll look through it together. We can look at all the pictures of your mum and all her special things.'

Joe sniffled.

After a while he said, 'Okay,' into Leonie's chest. Then he said, '*Bug* and *rug* rhyme.'

•

The fourth-last time Maurie had visited—not that Leonie had counted—she'd come to Leonie's house first and then they'd gone on to see Eunice a while later, after catching up just the two of them.

Eunice was waiting in her room at Sunset Gardens, tingling with anticipation. The sight of Eunice's needy intensity was like a punch in Leonie's belly. That room at Sunset Gardens whiffed of talcum powder and Eunice's sour perspiration.

'Maureen! Oh, Maureen.' Eunice embraced her and then let go, stepping back to take in all of her oldest daughter, that full up-and-down appraisal. Did Maurie wince through it? Probably. It was excruciating. And Eunice said, 'Boy. Maureen. You look very . . . healthy.'

A sideways look from Maurie, and Leonie stifled a smile.

Eunice wanted to hear every detail of the trip. Like Maureen would want to sit there and give her mother an intimate re-enactment of six months of travel. And then, when Maureen did begin a broad-brushstroke review, Eunice interrupted. 'When I was in France, I felt such an affinity with the people.'

Maurie hadn't been in France. She had been to various parts of South America, a place Eunice would not have dreamed of going to. So *ethnic*. Not the *right* kind of foreign. But to have Maurie there for any amount of time at Sunset

Gardens was a gift to Leonie. To have Maurie see what Leonie saw, to feel what Leonie felt.

'Honestly, there isn't a day in my life when I don't think about Paris,' said Eunice, after they'd each had scones. Eunice took a sip of tea and said, 'It really is funny, Lee, how you're a travel agent and you've never travelled.'

'It's funny how you keep reminding me of it,' said Leonie.

'Not everyone wants to travel, Mum,' said Maurie.

'No, I know,' said Eunice. 'I just wonder, you know, now that you've done this big trip.'

Leonie said, 'Well, I need to pee like a racehorse.' She got up and left the room and, in Eunice's lavender bathroom, she stared at herself in the mirror and practised smiling on cue. Smile, release. Smile, release. *I can't bear it*, was what she felt.

Back in the living room, Eunice had risen on her swollen ankles, holding the plate of remaining scones. 'I'll put the rest of these away. You won't have any more, will you, Lee?'

Maurie's eyes went to the floor. And then she looked up at Leonie and winked—comforting, private solidarity—and Leonie sat back down in the armchair where she always sat.

'I'd like another scone,' said Maurie.

'Oh,' said Eunice.

'I'm hungry,' said Maurie. 'Are you still hungry, Lee?'

'I'm fine,' said Leonie, who was still hungry.

Eunice had set the plate back down and forced a smile.

'And so, Mum,' said Maurie, 'the big news is that I'm pregnant.'

Well, golly. Eunice looked like she'd just walked into a glass door.

•

Joe was dressed now in a new t-shirt and new shorts. He sat on the carpet and packed Rabbit in his backpack and zipped it up and hugged the bag.

Leonie watched him from the kitchen, his eyes not even puffy. 'How are you feeling about going to preschool?'

'Good,' said Joe. 'Kaye said we have dance.'

'Well, that sounds fun.'

Joe unzipped the backpack and pulled Rabbit out and hugged Rabbit and whispered, 'You're very sad, Rabbit,' and then zipped Rabbit back in the bag. Leonie burst a little inside. The Special Box of Maurie was on the coffee table. Leonie went over to the kitchen window and peered out and saw that Dorrie's car was back. Good. Dorrie would call any minute.

Leonie fixed her hair anxiously in the bathroom—she could hear Joe speaking softly to Rabbit. She could hear the police noises from next door through the bedroom window. The phone rang. Leonie went out to the kitchen. Through the window she could see Dorrie standing in Dorrie's window, in her blue leotard, holding the receiver.

'Is Clive insufferable?' asked Leonie.

'Absolutely insufferable,' said Dorrie. 'He left a note on the table that says, *Call Lee. Lemon Tree. I TOLD YOU SO.*'

Leonie laughed.

'*I TOLD YOU SO* is in capital letters,' said Dorrie.

Ha ha ha from Leonie.

'Can you see much?'

'Not really. They're putting up another one of those tent things there now. You can sort of see it through a gap in the fencing.'

'Just some minor loitering then?'

'Well, putting out the washing has taken on a leisurely quality.'

'I can't believe it,' said Dorrie. 'Seriously. If she's under that bloody tree.'

'I know.'

'I'll have to murder Clive and bury him under *our* lemon tree, he'll be that annoying.'

Leonie laughed and Dorrie laughed and their laughter was of a very sad variety.

'I have to go to work,' said Leonie.

Dorrie said, 'I know—you go. I look like an ancient beetroot, I'm going to go wash off aerobics.'

25

Tony's Automotive Repairs was between a fishing tackle shop and a bright yellow building that sold fencing supplies and gates. Barney wandered down an aisle full of lures, hooks and a selection of locally made blackfish floats. He read from a chart about the broad range of fish species available in the estuaries, beaches and blue water fisheries of the Gather Region. He stared at a shrine of photos near the entrance showing local men holding their catches. Lloyd McCallum of Clarke, dwarfed by a blue marlin. Roy Murray of Goodwood, with what a small printed caption described as an eighty-seven-centimetre dusky flathead from Grant's Lake (*Town Record, Biggest Catch, 1989*). And, for god's sake, would you look at that? Barney couldn't believe it. There was Lou Lawson, standing at the boat wharves, holding up a long, fat fish.

Lou Lawson, 1984, monster King George whiting! Grant's Lake. 1.51 kg, 520 mm long.

'Do you need a hand with anything?' asked a sunburnt man from behind the counter.

'I'm just looking,' said Barney.

He stared at the photo and shook his head. A big fish, sure, but in the hands of Lou Lawson did any fish look big? Barney wanted to make a complaint to management. This man on your shrine murdered his wife! Then he almost murdered his second wife! Barney wanted more than anything to tell Deb. Wait till Deb hears about this! And yet he merely went on to ponder a display of blue-and-white eskies. He thought about Lou Lawson's enormous hands around Janice's neck. And after a further ten minutes in Clothing and Apparel, he returned to the mechanic and leaned against a wall, next to a tin can of cigarette butts in old rainwater.

'All done,' said Tony the mechanic.

Finally.

Tony was not his usual, old mechanic, but a new person in this new location. Barney could not bear to go to his old mechanic anymore. His old mechanic, of twenty-five years, was so chatty. What if he had said something about the old Subaru, or about Deb? Barney could not think of anything more unbearable than to talk with his old mechanic about the Subaru; or about Deb.

Barney paid for his pink slip and made small talk with Tony about his newish car, which was a blue Corolla station wagon. And then he drove his Corolla along the highway towards the Plaza, past Furniture 4U, the tiling shop, a yard full of used motorhomes and RVs.

Barney wondered what there was to find under the lemon tree in his backyard and how long it would take to find it.

He was driving through familiar territory now. Dangerous territory. Blocks of units, Clarke Stockfeeds, the big car wash, the Seventh-Day Adventist church.

Barney could see the corner of his old street up ahead. He would not turn. Too many times he had destroyed himself by turning, by driving past his old house and seeing it there so painfully the same. He would not do it again.

I will not turn. I will not turn.

His old street got closer. His heart raced. Barney gripped the wheel tightly. And—a victory—he did not turn.

•

Everyone sang 'Happy Birthday' to Varden while he bowed and smiled self-consciously. And after the hip-hip-hoorays, Leonie led a brief round of applause, along with Wanda, who'd just arrived, and Varden's wife Anush, who had come in for cake. There was also Pat, who worked Thursdays and Fridays, and Elena, who usually worked Mondays through

Wednesdays but who had taken long service leave and was about to depart for Cyprus.

'Thank you, thank you,' said Varden, standing next to a proud vanilla cake with chocolate flakes and *Happy Birthday* in Ice Magic. Leonie had ordered it from Hot Bake in the food court and picked it up on her way in.

'There'll certainly be enough cake,' said Pat.

'You shouldn't have,' said Varden.

'We should have and we did,' said Leonie. 'You only turn fifty once, Var.'

Varden was a modest man. He had modestly been to thirty-six countries, including all seven Stans, and kept a list of them on his office wall, next to his wedding photo and a portrait of Soghomon Tehlirian.

'No, no,' said Varden when Leonie told him to cut the cake.

So Leonie cut the cake, and she issued a slice to Varden on a white napkin, and then one to smiling Anush. Anush had dark eyes and curly black hair that made Leonie think of Cher.

Niceties regarding the cake. Wanda went to the kitchenette to make tea while Pat and Elena chatted near the fax machine.

'I hear you've had the police around next door,' said Anush.

'I sure have,' said Leonie.

'And it's about time, yes?' said Anush. 'It seems that before now the police have only looked at it through the space of their fingers.'

Leonie nodded and swallowed a piece of cake. 'Well,' she said. 'Sure.'

'That they haven't taken it seriously,' said Varden, 'is what Anush means.'

'Oh, *yes*,' said Leonie. 'No, they haven't.'

Anush nodded. 'Varden said you went up and talked to the police when it happened and they weren't very receptive.'

'That's a nice way of putting it,' said Leonie. 'And yes, I went up there several times, and I called several times. I told them how Lou was. How Ginny was. I told them: that woman would never have just up and left Tobias. Ever.'

'No,' said Anush.

'People don't just pick up and disappear,' said Leonie. 'And we were all a bit naive about it. We all assumed that the police were doing all this work behind the scenes, and it took a while to work out if their response was sloppy or intentional. But let's just say that Lou moved up to Queensland scot-free and the police probably helped him load the van.'

Wanda wandered over with a mug in either hand. She set them on the desk next to Leonie and went back to the kitchenette for the others.

'And they accused the man across the street?' said Anush.

'You mean Earl?' said Leonie. 'They made a song and dance about Earl for about one minute. And to be fair, Earl's foul, he really is. But it was just because Lou hated Earl and

Earl hated Lou, and Lou probably told the police to go look at Earl.'

'Because Earl had been leery,' said Varden. 'To Ginny.'

'Earl's as leery as they come,' said Leonie. 'He just sits on his porch and watches. If ever I look at Earl's porch of a night-time, he's just sitting there in the dark, smoking and watching. It's the wrong kind of Neighbourhood Watch.'

'But you don't think it was Earl?' said Anush as Wanda returned with more milky-white teas. Wanda picked up her slice of cake-on-white-napkin and took an enormous bite.

Leonie said, 'I think Earl's a leery racist who deals pot from his garage and trades in stolen car parts, because he's actually been arrested for both of those things. But I don't think he killed Ginny. I don't think he has the energy.'

Wanda smiled, as much as a person can smile with a mouth full of cake, and Varden said, 'It's good there's this new lot of police now. For some fresh eyes.'

'It's even better that there's no sign of Senior Constable Marrel,' said Leonie.

Wanda finally swallowed, an errant chocolate flake at the edge of her mouth. 'Earl's a red herring,' she said.

'Exactly,' said Leonie.

26

The car park under Clarke Plaza smelled of fried foods and urinals, and Barney held his breath as he walked alongside a row of still cars and thick pylons in the dim light. He went up the ramp and entered the too-bright plaza. He passed the booth where a bald man cut keys and engraved pet tags. There were novelty numberplates and a beer cooler with a pair of breasts in relief.

Woolworths, barbershop, the virulent fumes of the nail salon. And moments later, butcher smells, fish shop smells and there was the RTA. Barney hated the Plaza. He found it so banal and depressing. But he did stop briefly outside Harvey World Travel to look through the glass.

There she was—his neighbour, Leonie. She was towards the back of the shop, eating a piece of cake and talking. It was some kind of party. Barney watched on a moment. Leonie was so animated. She was chatting with this group of people, throwing her head back in a laugh, and Barney found himself smiling there watching her. What a funny, pleasant woman.

In the RTA, he dealt with the business of registration renewal. The tall, healthful man at the counter wore a name tag that said KERRY. Barney leaned on the counter and felt a kind of deadness in the task. The administration of his life, which didn't feel like a life anymore.

Kerry asked, 'Paying by cheque?'

And Barney nodded and wrote the amount down and signed his name.

'Barney Clarke, of Clarke,' said Kerry.

Barney handed the cheque across the counter and found a smile and said, 'No relation.'

•

Anush left, and Elena stayed a while longer, during which discussions ensued about Elena's replacement. Elena was moon-faced and beautiful and had dressed solely in black for almost four years, since the untimely death of her husband. It was only a slight adjustment to the uniform—a black polo shirt instead of a navy one—which Varden graciously allowed. Then there was Pat. Tiny Pat. You could fit her in a suitcase if she got down in it and hugged her knees. Pat reminded Leonie of Eunice, on account of the way Pat made little comments regarding the size of Leonie's lunch portions and her tendency to over-cater.

Oh, Eunice. Poor old Eunice.

Varden leafed through a pile of résumés. 'While you're all here, ladies, I could do with some input.'

'What about the one who's married to that nice electrician?' said Wanda.

'I liked her,' said Leonie. 'Someone Roberts.'

And Varden found the résumé with surname Roberts and read over it. 'I'll call her,' he said.

Shortly after Elena left, promising postcards, and Leonie announced her intention to use the bathroom, the closest of which was situated between the bookstore and the Fosseys.

'Take a half-hour,' said Varden, as Leonie hoisted her handbag over her shoulder.

'I should throw you parties more often,' she said. And, speaking of Eunice, Leonie thought about her mother all the way to the bathroom.

•

Eunice Wallace had sat in her reclining armchair at Sunset Gardens and said, 'I don't know how I'm supposed to tell her to change the duvet cover if she can't speak basic English.'

'I think she can,' said Leonie. 'I've had conversations with her.'

'She can't,' said Eunice. 'Yesterday I asked her to heat up my soup and she came back five minutes later and it was still lukewarm. There's three of them here now who can't speak English.'

'I'll talk to her,' said Leonie, and she closed her eyes for a moment, facing the bench where Eunice had a kettle and a toaster and a Johnson Brothers Devon Cottage tea set.

'It's so lonely here, Lee.'

Leonie felt like she was dying inside, and she tried to focus on the kettle as it boiled, the steamy loudness inside, the switch popping to the off position all by itself. She moistened a sponge and wiped down the cheap bench.

Eunice said, 'Merta across the hall watches *Mass for You at Home* every Sunday at six am. Every Sunday. And then she talks about it until Tuesday.'

Leonie rubbed at her neck, which was stiff and sore.

'I really am so lonely,' said Eunice. 'And all this business with Maureen.'

'I think Maurie seems happy.'

'Come on, Lee, it's a shocking situation. And I'm just so surprised that she's let it happen like this. Maureen, of all people. Not a day in my life have I ever known Maurie to be careless.'

Leonie poured the boiled water and said, 'Maybe she wasn't being careless.'

'She doesn't even know his last name,' said Eunice, scandalised in her recliner. 'So the baby will have this whole Mexican family on the other side of the world that doesn't even know it exists. *And* the baby will be completely estranged from its own father. I just don't think that's right, for the child not to have a father in its life.'

Leonie brought the tea over and set it on a coaster on the cane side table, where there was a Maeve Binchy novel and a tube of haemorrhoid cream.

'He's not Mexican, he's Chilean,' said Leonie. 'And Maurie and I have been estranged from our father since we were children.'

Eunice blinked and paused and then said, 'Oh, but that's different.'

•

As she passed Fosseys, Leonie considered going in to browse, but the sale was over and she decided on the bookstore instead. She had always loved the look of books arranged in a window. And now she had this unexpected time to browse, unhurried. Leonie loved the Plaza. She found it so familiar and soothing.

A perusal of new releases. She read the blurbs on the back of *Wild Swans, How The Garcia Girls Lost Their Accents* and a new thriller by Ann Cleeves called *Murder in My Backyard.*

But here she is, murdered in her own backyard on a bitter St David's Eve.

No, thank you. Leonie put the book down. She thought of the lemon tree next to her fence. She thought of Ginny's lovely, cautious expression. She thought of Joe and his aching sobs for Maurie. And then, in her mind, Maurie became Ginny; Ginny became Maurie.

Oh look, a new Bill Bryson—that'll be helpful for work. Leonie picked it up, she'd buy it. Then she meandered leftwards a few metres and found herself in a different section, staring at a book that was sitting face out: *Healing the Shame that Binds You* by John Bradshaw.

Leonie gasped. This *book*. It's *here*. A vision of Maurie, in the food court, handing her that scrap of paper. Leonie looked over both shoulders. There was no one nearby. She popped the Bill Bryson under her armpit and picked up the John Bradshaw. There was a profile of a face on the cover—presumably a very ashamed face. Leonie flipped through the pages.

Toxically shamed people tend to become more and more stagnant as life goes on.

Golly, thought Leonie. And had her heart started racing? Of course it had.

'Hi, Leonie,' said a deep voice, and Leonie turned around and went as red as a wheelbarrow.

'Oh,' she said. 'Hi, Barney.'

'Anything good?'

Leonie closed the shameful book and said, 'Not really,' and she let out a high-pitched laugh. She was like a big silly bird. 'What are you doing here?'

'I had some errands.'

Leonie stood there with one book under her arm, another pressed against her polo shirt, cover facing inwards. She noticed Barney was holding a Fosseys bag and felt certain that there would be new underwear in there. Clean white briefs. Her hands were quivering softly. 'Well. Errands. That's great,' she said.

Barney smiled.

Leonie remembered herself and said, 'I saw that they've started looking around the lemon tree.'

'Yes,' said Barney. 'It's their last day today apparently. If the weather holds out. I must say I've been quite preoccupied with the whole thing. When I left earlier they'd started in on the new site, under the tree, but I don't think they've found anything since the *item of clothing*.'

'Right,' said Leonie. 'Well, my friend Clive across the street has a strong feeling about the area around the lemon tree, so you never know.'

'Why's that?'

'Because of some woodchips. I mean, it sounds crazy. Woodchips. But a lot of people have had a lot of theories. Clive thinks Lou's new wife, Janice, must have some damning piece of evidence, and that's why the police have come looking after all these years. Or come digging, I should say. I'm sure you saw the article in the paper yesterday about Janice.'

'I did, and I was going to tell you when I saw you on Wednesday that I read the application for the search warrant. The police have to apply to the local magistrate to get a warrant, and they put their evidence in the application. And I was allowed to read it because I'm the occupier, as it were.'

'What did it say?'

Barney lowered his voice. 'It said that Lou almost strangled Janice to death.'

Leonie was briefly speechless. Janice! All that fluffy hair and her young children and her little dog. Of course Leonie knew that it was all real and serious. But she couldn't believe it was all so real and serious! 'God,' she said.

'Yes.' Barney was holding his Fosseys bag in both hands now, hugging it against himself like a pillow, like Leonie was hugging her shameful book. 'It went so far as Janice losing consciousness, and she spent a few days in the hospital. She had broken ribs and I think a broken collarbone. And then in her statement to the police she told them that she now believes that Lou murdered Ginny.'

Why was Leonie shocked to hear the word *murdered* said out loud, and not some euphemistic other expression. 'Golly,' she said. 'But does she have any actual evidence? Like something of Ginny's? Or a weapon?'

'It didn't say anything about that,' said Barney. 'But I think Lou's the weapon, all by himself. I've seen pictures of the guy. He looks like he plays professional rugby.'

'Do you mean league?'

'I don't know what I mean.'

Leonie laughed. She liked Barney, she really did. She said, 'Lou's built like a brick shithouse.' And what the heck. 'Barney, I've got to get back to work, but why don't you come over for a cup of tea on the weekend and we can compare notes.'

He looked quite touched. He said, 'I'd like that.'

27

'**B**ut why?' asked Joe.

'Because Varden was in a terrific mood and I got to leave work early, and I thought we'd do something fun together,' said Leonie. 'Something different.'

'Oh,' said Joe. He ate a hot chip, and then another.

Leonie took a bite of her Junior Burger and a sip of her Coke and looked around. There were only a few other people sitting down at tables, on account of it being the afternoon and not lunchtime.

'How're your chips?' asked Leonie.

'Good.'

'What was your favourite thing about preschool today?'

'I don't know,' said Joe. 'Dance.'

'That sounds fun. I'd like to see you do some dancing. You could dance at home sometime.'

Joe did not smile. 'Okay.'

There were three people behind the counter, none of whom looked old enough to have finished high school. They wore matching striped shirts and little visors that said *McDonald's*. When Leonie leaned on the table it was sticky, as if covered in a mist of oil. But it was nice here, with the air conditioning and the smell of fried foods.

The boy behind the counter was lanky and somehow familiar, and Leonie smiled when he made a joke with his co-workers—two girls—and they all laughed. But then an image of Lou popped into her head, his huge fleshy hands around Janice's throat until the poor woman passed out. Leonie looked down at the patty in her burger and decided against finishing it.

'What about after this we go to the playground?'

'Okay,' said Joe.

'Okay,' said Leonie, and she picked up two long golden chips and ate them. She said, 'I don't know what it is, but these don't taste as good as they used to.'

•

Barney heard kookaburras again on the drive home from the Plaza. He went over the railway crossing at Horsham Street, because he never crossed at Albion Street. Out his car window, he saw three kookaburras up on the wire and the sky covering with cloud.

The old sign up ahead said CLARKE HILL, and for a moment he thought he would turn. He would turn and head back around the park and north towards his old street. At his old house, he would pull into the driveway like it was no big deal. He would be home.

The kookaburras began to laugh again—they were somewhere behind him now. He glanced at the rear-view mirror and saw the corner receding. He had not turned.

It is possible, he thought, to feel pride and disappointment at the same time. Barney had learned that it was possible to feel a great many different emotions all at once.

According to Deb, signs of imminent rain were: cats cleaning behind their ears; black cockatoos flying from the mountain towards the sea; cows sitting down in a field; sighting an echidna; an increasing number of indoor ants; and kookaburras laughing, especially in the day.

•

In the McDonald's car park, Joe pointed and said, 'What are they?'

Leonie said, 'Those blue things? They're milk crates.'

Joe climbed into his car seat and Leonie buckled him in. She opened the passenger door and threw in her handbag. The car smelled like pasties.

'What are they for?'

'They're for milk,' said Leonie. 'But people do other things with them as well. Clive has those two on the back of his ute for his fishing stuff. They're quite useful.'

Joe was quiet in the back seat and Leonie pulled out of the car park and headed past the newsagent, past Noble Meats.

'I wish I was a milk crate,' said Joe.

Leonie smiled and said, 'You're very useful just the way you are, sweetie.'

'No, I want to be something that doesn't die.'

'Oh,' said Leonie. She slowed to a stop at the lights outside the library. It had become overcast. The sky was white and also grey. In the rear-view mirror, she could see Joe looking out his window. 'But you couldn't do anything. You couldn't dance or play or anything like that. Don't you think it'd be a bit boring being a milk crate?'

'No, because I'll be a milk crate. I won't know anything.'

Leonie turned up the air conditioning. Was it awfully hot? She felt hot. It was the humidity, really, that's what gets you. The light went green and she forgot what gear was what. When she vroomed the Magna, nothing happened. Oh, she was in neutral. She pushed the clutch down and found first and they hopped slightly forward. She said, 'I guess I've never thought about it like that. But I sure would miss you if you weren't Joe.'

They drove a while, almost to the park, and Joe said, 'I don't want to die.'

'Me neither,' said Leonie.

•

When Leonie was a child, she found one of her father's shirts. She and Maurie were playing in the garage, and the garage smelled of damp cement and a type of glue. This was a few years after their father had left and Leonie had moved a never-used beach umbrella that was leaning up in a dank corner. The umbrella was bright yellow and her father's navy shirt was hanging behind it on a hook. Leonie remembered that her father used to spend a lot of time in the garage doing solitary things that she wasn't to interrupt. He mostly smelled fumey. For his private garage work, he wore this navy shirt.

Maurie had run back inside the house, carrying an armless doll, and Leonie stood looking up at the shirt as if it were a mirage, a trick. She reached up and unhooked the shirt and held it to her face. Then she sat down on the slab floor and sobbed into the shirt, until Eunice came in.

'Stop it, Leonie, you're being ridiculous.'

Leonie kept sobbing and cradling her father's shirt. But Eunice reached down and took the shirt away; Leonie never saw it again.

'Leonie, stop crying,' said Eunice. 'Come inside and have a mandarin with Maureen.'

•

At Clarke Park, Joe said, 'What playground is this?'

'This is the Clarke Park playground. It's bigger than the one we normally go to, isn't it?'

'This is the best playground in my whole wide world!' said Joe, and he ran off across the grass, past the big statue, and disappeared up a ladder into a red plastic hut.

Leonie walked along, her handbag over her shoulder, stinging with guilt that she always took Joe to the same old playground in South Clarke. She was so stagnant! Look at him running ahead with excitement. Actually, it was getting quite windy. There were other children at the swing set, some mingling parents. There was a very young woman with a stroller. Leonie sat on a bench and watched as Joe went down a silver slide, and up the ladder, and down the slide again.

They were to meet Eileen here in the morning, and what was Leonie doing? She was doing a dry run. She was turning into Eunice. Eunice used to go on dry runs to make sure she knew the parking options. Eunice used to say she'd never been anxious *a day in her life.*

Joe was now running away from a little blonde girl, who had begun to chase him, and he laughed hysterically while he ran. He squealed! Leonie grinned, watching him. She glanced at the woman with the stroller and thought of Joe as a baby.

Tiny fresh Joe.

That feeling she had when Maurie had passed him to her that first time. The tender bundle of Joe. He was so small that Leonie had gasped at the lightness of his body, wrapped in a cotton blanket.

Eunice had said, 'He's not as dark as I thought he'd be,' and Maurie didn't even flinch. She was so serene.

Leonie had looked down at this baby—Joseph Carlos Wallace—and she felt like a cracker had gone off inside her heart. It exploded in beautiful colours.

'Joe!' she yelled now.

He ran over, pink-cheeked, and Leonie said, 'Looks like it's coming over rainy. Just ten more minutes.'

'We should come here so much often,' said breathless Joe.

'Well, we're coming back here in the morning to meet Eileen and the girls.'

'Good,' said Joe, and he ran back to where the girl was waiting and they began to run and squeal and soon some rain began to fall. Leonie just sat there. The other people left and Leonie let Joe run in the rain until it began to get heavy.

28

There were so many police cars that Barney couldn't even park in front of Earl's. He had to park outside the house next door to Earl's. The rain was heavy now and Barney hadn't brought his umbrella. Just crossing the street would drench him. He sat in his car a moment, watching the water on the windshield. Was that movement on Earl's porch? There were policemen up there. And Earl, of course, with his handlebar moustache and no doubt a cocky expression.

Barney switched off his wipers and watched through the rain-streaked glass. Earl's house became indistinct with rain, but Barney could make out blurry Levins and blurry O'Leary, conducting what looked like an interview. Levins was standing, O'Leary was sitting on Earl's esky. And Earl was leaning back in his folding chair with his hands behind his head, as relaxed as a sunbaker.

Huh, thought Barney. The plot thickens. He wanted to sit and watch longer, but he felt too obvious.

He got out and crossed the street quickly in the rain. Under the police tape, up the soggy hill to the letterbox. Barney had this ludicrous expectation of finding Ben's instant reply to his letter. He found instead a moist catalogue and an electricity bill.

Inside, Barney said, 'Hello, Comfrey,' and Comfrey geriatrically meowed.

The hallway was cooler and, as usual, dim. Barney went through to the kitchen and put his disappointing mail and his Fosseys bag on the table. Outside, pools had formed around the pool. The police had packed up the marquee next to the washing line, but there was still a marquee by the lemon tree and tarpaulins covering the ground all around it.

Barney watched through the window as Levins and O'Leary appeared, just returned from Earl's. How long had they been at Earl's? Why would they be talking to Earl? Another policeman in face mask and gloves was standing under the awning on Barney's patio, holding what looked like a dust brush.

Barney stood in the kitchen and removed the tags from his new pairs of underwear. He went through to the laundry, which was off the kitchen, at the back of the house. He put the underwear in the machine with the rest of his washing and added a half-scoop of Deb's favourite phosphate-free detergent and pushed the button to start.

'I thought it was a cat,' said the nasal voice of O'Leary.

Barney could hear this through the open laundry window, which was high up on the wall.

Someone laughed.

And then the distinctive voice of Detective Sergeant Levins: 'That's why you won't be making a career in forensics.'

Barney stood listening, stone-still in the laundry.

'Poofy little dog then,' said O'Leary. 'I don't get the point of a dog like that.'

•

The phone rang while Leonie was at her dresser, changing out of her wet clothes.

'Can I answer?' yelled Joe from the kitchen.

'Sure.'

'Hello? This is Joe?'

Leonie heard this from her bedroom and smiled. She pulled on her comfort pants and soft house shirt and went out to where Joe was standing, bare feet on the kitchen lino.

'It was good,' said Joe, and then a stretch of silence. 'Yes. We were at my best playground.'

'I'll take it, sweetie. Say bye to Dorrie.'

'Bye, Dorrie,' said Joe. He passed over the receiver and went back to the table to eat sliced banana.

'This rain can't be good for an exhumation,' said Dorrie.

'My thoughts exactly.'

'Did you get an early mark?'

'Yes and we went for a little outing,' said Leonie. 'I'm trying to be less stagnant.'

'Well, speaking of stagnant, guess who the police were just talking to?'

'Who?'

'Earl.'

'Oh, for god's sake. They have no imagination.'

'Or do they?' said Dorrie.

'I don't know.' Leonie was irritated now. She looked over and saw Dorrie in the window, but the rain had fogged up the windows at both their houses and Dorrie was just a smudge.

'Anyway, Clive will be back in an hour and then the real suffering begins.'

Leonie laughed. She looked up and said, 'Sweetie, do you want to watch cartoons for ten minutes?'

Joe nodded and left a piece of banana on his plate. He went across to the living room, switched on the television and sat down on the carpet.

Leonie lowered her voice and said, 'I've had this weird feeling, Dorrie, of it all being so unreal. Like all of this is happening, but it's not happening—it *can't* be happening.'

'Yes,' said Dorrie.

'It's like I never thought they'd come looking for her, but at the same time I always knew they would, and I've just been waiting.'

'Yes.'

'And I've had this other weird feeling too: that I don't know if I want them to find her or not. I can't tell anymore.'

Dorrie said, 'Well, if they find her, it'll be absolutely horrible. It'll be devastating, Lee. And if they don't find her, it'll be horrible in a different way. It'll be like a continuation of the horrible it's been since she went missing, but worse.'

'Yes,' said Leonie.

'Do we need to go through this again?'

'Maybe.'

Dorrie said, 'Okay. What would you want for Ginny?'

'I want her to be alive.'

'Yes, but realistically.'

'I want Lou Lawson to be in a jail cell for the rest of his life,' said Leonie.

'Exactly,' said Dorrie.

•

At the kitchen table, Barney sipped his tea and skimmed an article in *Australasian Science* about the various asteroids discovered by Masahiro Koishikawa. He learned that Finland and Poland had both joined CERN. He read about a new thing called WorldWideWeb and found it difficult to understand precisely what it was. It was difficult to concentrate on much at all.

The noise of footsteps amid rain. Detective Sergeant Levins was coming over the back patio towards the sliding door.

Knock knock.

Barney got up and went across the kitchen. Levins took off a sodden raincoat and set it over the back of an outdoor chair then wiped his boots on the rubber mat.

'Couple of things.'

'Come in,' said Barney.

Levins stepped inside and stood drippily on the tiles. He said, 'Bit of weather.'

Barney said, 'I might end up with more than one pool.' He closed the sliding door and sat back down at the table.

Levins said, 'We're going to have to leave it until it clears up.'

'I thought as much.'

'The forecast is for more of this tomorrow and Sunday, so we've sealed it all off.'

Barney felt tired and deflated. The rain was loud on the roof of the awning, beyond the back door.

Levins said, 'Mr Clarke, I've been wondering if you're a descendant of the man they made a big statue of over at Clarke Park.'

'No, I'm not,' said Barney. 'I'm a descendent of murderous bushrangers who terrorised innocent people from here to Braidwood from 1865 to 1867.'

'You've used that line before.'

'It's come up a few times over the years.'

'Have you ever had a dog at this house, Mr Clarke?'

'No, I have never had a dog at this house or any other.'

'Okay then,' said Levins. He nodded, and turned to leave.

'You found a small, pointless dog?'

Detective Sergeant Levins smiled and said, 'What dog?'

29

Bill Murrow—Barney's old friend—said, 'Another for you, Barn,' and set down a schooner of Reschs on the table.

'Thanks, Bill,' said Barney. He put his hand around the glass to feel the blessed coldness of it.

Bill put a round tray to one side and sipped his own beer, and Bill's wife, Rita, sat back in her chair with a fork in her hand. She said, 'We were just discussing the relevance of dogs.'

'I think they found a dog,' said Barney.

'Or something dog-related,' said Rita.

'Which sounds completely irrelevant,' said Barney. 'But the detective in charge came and asked me if it was my dog—if I'd ever had a dog. Which makes me think that it might be relevant.'

'It might be relevant,' said Rita.

Barney tilted his head. He said, 'The more I think about it, though—I mean, if you dug up every yard on the street you'd probably find several dogs.'

'We had a graveyard of little birds when I was a kid,' said Bill. 'My mother kept budgerigars.'

'There you go,' said Barney.

'I suppose,' said Rita, and she cut neatly into her schnitzel.

'It's taken me fifty-eight years to realise how weird my mother was,' said Bill.

Barney stared at the penguin logo on Bill's polo shirt. He took a sip of his beer and set it back down on a coaster that said *Clarke Bowling Club, Since 1914. 'Clarke's Friendly Bowlo'.* Barney's hand was cold and wet. He could hear ABBA on the stereo, there in the bistro, and it made him obscurely sad.

'The police just say very little, which I find frustrating, as you could imagine,' he said.

'You in particular,' said Bill.

'I do like information,' said Barney.

'I believe Deb used to use the word "exhaustive",' said Rita.

'Not "exhaust*ing*?"' said Barney, and Rita smiled.

That was nice. Traumatically nice. Barney hadn't been sure if anyone would say Deb's name, and it was a relief now that someone had, so he could stop worrying so much about hearing it.

'Do you think it's a bit suspicious that Lou Lawson was in the hunting club? Like that it speaks to a violent nature?' said Rita.

'Only if he shot her,' said Barney.

Bill laughed. Bill's steak was covered in a mushroom sauce that made Barney think of the lake on a cloudy day. Bill said, 'Sweetheart, if that was a common thing, like if every man who joined a hunting club killed their wife, we would've heard a lot more about it.'

'But maybe there are women who are killed that we don't hear about,' said Rita. 'You don't know.'

'We *do* know,' said Bill. 'We read the paper. We watch the news. We know.'

Rita raised her eyebrows and sipped her chardonnay. She said, 'Well all *I* know is that Lou Lawson is no boy scout. Even though he actually was a Boy Scout.'

'Was he?' said Barney.

'He really was,' said Rita. 'My friend Lynette, the one whose friend thinks she saw Ginny in Lismore—which is ridiculous, but anyway—Lynette's dad was the Scout leader at the Clarke Scouts. Apparently Lou Lawson was in the Scouts. He got some big medal for—what's it called?'

'Orienteering,' said Bill.

'Orienteering,' said Rita.

'Huh,' said Barney. He had ordered a steak too, no sauce, and he had eaten just the smallest portion of it. It sat in front of him, taking up so much of the plate, and there was a tiny 'salad' next to it, of lettuce and red onion.

'There's something off about Lynette's dad,' said Rita, glancing down at her plate. 'He's too smarmy.'

'Well I'm glad Dean didn't do Scouts then,' said Bill. 'Or . . .'—and Bill awkwardly stopped mid-sentence.

Rita looked to Barney and smiled tentatively. She said, 'You know, I hear a bit here and there from Dean, about Ben. It sounds as if he's happy with his new arrangement. But you know what boys are like. Sometimes I think I'd be better off if I didn't ask any questions at all.'

Barney felt that his heart had stopped.

What new arrangement did his son have? How to respond? Oh, discomfort and pain.

'Yes,' said Barney, and he coughed into his fist.

Rita paused and shot a look at Bill, and then she said cheerily, 'You know who loved Scouts? Phil Last. He *loved* being a Scout.'

•

Leonie and Joe played hide-and-seek for half an hour, even though there were so few places to hide. Leonie hid in the sunroom, behind the sewing table, and when it was Joe's turn, he hid in the sunroom, behind the sewing table.

Then Leonie hid in Joe's room, behind Joe's door. And, right after, Joe hid in his room, behind his door. Leonie pretended to look for him in every other room of the house, and then Joe squealed when she found him, his body pressed flat against the wall.

'Okay, enough,' said Leonie, and she went out and lay on the couch, where Joe climbed all over her like she was the play structure at Clarke Park.

The rain was unending. Biblical rain. Joe pushed his face against the kitchen window and asked if he could float leaves down the gutters. Leonie said no, and he was crestfallen and cried. The police cars had departed, save for one, which presumably belonged to the lone guard who would watch over the site in case of—what? Newspaper reporters? Grave robbers?

Leonie had a shower and put dinner on and Joe danced in the living room to Eurythmics.

Then, after dinner, they each ate a slice of Varden's leftover birthday cake and Leonie told Joe a little about her day.

Joe asked, 'Is all of the world called Australia?'

'No. The world is called the world. The country we live in is called Australia.'

'Oh,' said Joe. 'Is Sydney in Australia?'

'Yes, it is,' said Leonie.

'Are the big tunnels in Australia?'

'Everywhere you've ever been is in Australia. Everywhere *I've* ever been is in Australia.'

'Why?'

'I don't know. Just because that's how it's been.' Leonie licked her plate and set it down on the table. She wished for more whipped cream. She said, 'Should we get out the *Junior Atlas* and have a look?'

'Okay,' said Joe.

•

Barney took his time washing his hands. He stared at himself in the dirty mirror and the man who stared back was old and could do with a new shirt. Had his complexion turned slightly grey? It must be the lack of sun. He used to get so much more sun. He used to always be out walking with Deb, and with Phil and Helen Last and the rest of the club. God, he loved those walks. But he mustn't think of that now; it wasn't helpful to think of it.

Barney went the long way back to the table, through the bar and around the other side of the bistro, where there were a few tables that looked out onto the green and a small area of play things for children.

The pleasant loudness of families, several lively tables. Up ahead was a couple with three young children. The woman had the loveliest long black hair. Very poetic hair. She laughed at something one of her children had said, and she put a hand on the child. *Rosamie!* It was her.

Barney didn't know where to look so he looked at the floor. The carpet was a relentless pattern of triangles. Orange triangles inside blue triangles that just went on and on. He turned his head to the window and looked out at the rain pouring on the green in the dwindling light. He passed Rosamie's table, pretending to be interested in the view. He was somehow humiliated. Did she see him? He didn't know. At that first glance of her she had seemed consumed by the children—and the man she was with, presumably her husband. Barney had seen the back of his head and the back of his jacket.

He walked another few metres. There was a wall of framed portraits of bowlers and a large wooden board covered with gold letters. *Ladies' Achievements*. He would not turn his head. But he couldn't help it. He couldn't help but turn.

Barney looked over his shoulder to see what type of man Rosamie would have dinner with, have children with, marry.

You've got to be kidding me, thought Barney.

It was Dr Prakash.

•

Joe and Leonie lay side by side on Joe's bed, and Leonie read *Morris's Disappearing Bag*. The story involved a rabbit who feels left out when his older siblings are playing with their gifts on Christmas morning, until he receives a bag that makes him invisible, and then all of his siblings want a turn of Morris's disappearing bag. Joe listened earnestly, as always, and Leonie loved Morris almost as much as she loved the idea of a disappearing bag.

Joe said, 'You know Jeremy? At preschool?'

'Which one's Jeremy?'

'The one with the pimples.'

'You mean freckles?'

'Yes, freckles.'

'Then, yes, Jeremy.'

'Jeremy's dad's in jail.'

'Is he?'

'Yes.'

'Oh,' said Leonie. She set the book on Joe's bedside table. 'Do you know what being in jail means?'

'Yes,' said Joe. 'It means he's locked up by the police and can't come home.'

'Well, that must be very hard for Jeremy.'

Joe kicked his legs up and down on the bed. Then he said, 'Jeremy's five,' and rolled over onto his side. He had Rabbit under his armpit. Leonie stared at the ceiling, at the constellation of glow-in-the-dark stars. She felt a little hand begin to play with her earlobe. A moth circled the lamp. Leonie switched the lamp off and watched the stars begin to glow. Within five minutes, Joe fell asleep holding her ear.

Leonie watched television for a half-hour, dozy on the couch. She went to her bedroom to the sound of rain. She was filled with relief at the rain, because it would be too wet to meet Eileen Swan at the park in the morning. They would have to cancel. Thank *god*.

It was all too much for Leonie. And it wasn't that she didn't like Eileen Swan. It was that Eileen Swan made her feel so self-conscious and uncomfortable that it just wasn't pleasant. Not to mention that Eileen would talk about Maurie. Which meant Leonie would have to talk about Maurie—and she would completely collapse if that happened. She would perish. Leonie would not bear it; she would need a disappearing bag.

Leonie got into bed and there was still a little light outside, coming through the thin curtains. *Healing the Shame that Binds You* was on the top of her book pile. She picked it up and almost laughed at herself. What was she doing? And why would Maurie read this book? She imagined Maurie breezing through the aisles at the State Library—and this was what took her fancy? Maurie, of all people. Leonie was struck by an awful feeling of being so separate from her sister. Mysterious, complex Maurie.

Hell, in my opinion, is never finding your true self and never living your own life or knowing who you are.

Leonie had just opened the book at a random page. She read this passage twice. Then she glanced up at the ceiling—the old fan, the frosted pendant light—and wondered if she knew who she was.

'I am Leonie Anne Wallace,' she said aloud to the room.

And yet. This odd feeling of being so much more than she had allowed herself to be. Or so much different?

Maureen Ida Wallace.

Leonie wouldn't permit herself to say Maurie's name aloud. Instead, she flipped ahead several pages, very uncommitted to the whole thing. She read paragraphs here and there and, really, the book made her feel very anxious. It's just that it had seemed like some kind of sign—seeing it there at the bookstore and remembering how Maurie had written the title on that scrap of paper for her in the food court. Leonie felt ridiculous as she read a whole page about blushing and its relationship to shame. Actually, that part was quite interesting. She put the book down in her lap and stared at the dresser, reciting names in her head.

Leonie Anne Wallace.

Maureen Ida Wallace.

Virginia Rose Lawson née Cayley.

Janice something Lawson née Clifford.

There was Eunice's vase on the dresser. There was a texta portrait of Leonie, by Joe, blu-tacked on the wall. Leonie pictured Janice and wondered what it would feel like to be strangled. She wondered what thoughts would come before everything went dark. She thought about Eileen Swan a moment and her mind went kind of still. Then she set the book on the bedside table, switched off the lamp and pulled the quilt over her chest.

Leonie felt sad and absurd, and she covered her face with her hands. Oh, for god's sake. It was just her—Leonie Anne Wallace, alone in her bedroom—and she was blushing.

●

Back at the table, Bill lit a cigarette. He said, 'So you think they were questioning this Earl guy, like as a suspect?'

'They were certainly questioning him, but I'm not sure why,' said Barney. 'I haven't read anything about there being any other suspects. That wasn't in the papers.'

'I never heard anything about any other suspects,' said Rita.

They'd stacked their plates in a pile and set them on the edge of the pinewood table. The talking in the bistro had got louder as people had got drunker. It was dark outside now. Barney could see the darkness from where he was sitting, through the big windows that faced the car park.

'He looks like a real piece of work, though, this guy Earl. He just has that look about him that makes you want to cross the street.'

'I know the type,' said Rita.

Rita had her hair in a bun and it looked good like that, so you could see more of her face. She was a pretty woman, and looking at her in the bistro reminded Barney of old times in a painful way. There was a sadness there too, in her eyes, because Rita had been through a lot, as Deb used to say.

Bill blew out a thick line of smoke and said to Rita, 'It's a big town. I'm sure if you ask around, you'll find out if he's a suspect or not.'

'It's a big town that feels like a small town,' said Rita.

'Clarke was actually declared a city in 1979,' said Barney, his eyes twinkling.

'Says the man who's not even a proper local.'

'I've lived here for twenty-nine years, Mrs Murrow.'

Rita ginned and said, 'And you'll always be a blow-in.'

That Rita. She was sharp as a tack and just as pointy. Barney smiled at his old friends. He said, 'Just let me know if I start to look too comfortable.'

30

When the phone rang at 8 am, Leonie thought, That'll
be Eileen. She went over to the kitchen in her nightie
and her dressing-gown. It was cooler now, with the rain.
Joe was watching Saturday morning cartoons, lying on the
carpet on his belly.

'Hello?'

'Hi, Lee. It's Eileen.'

'Hi, Eileen—I thought that might be you. Can you believe
this rain?'

'I know. It's not really park weather, is it?'

'What a shame.' Leonie could hear the theme song from
Gummi Bears.

'Why don't you and Joe come over here instead then?'
said Eileen. 'For morning tea.'

'Oh,' said Leonie, who had not expected this.

'I might bake something with the girls.'

'Well . . . sure,' said Leonie. 'Okay then.'

Eileen gave Leonie her address, and Leonie wrote it down on the top of her quarterly rates instalment notice from the Gather Region Council. A logo of a green mountain, blue lake, yellow sun—even though in real life the lake was brown, at best a very murky green, and never blue at all.

'See you in a bit then,' said Eileen, and Leonie hung up the phone and stood in the kitchen.

'Crap,' she said softly.

'What's crap?' said Joe's little voice, from all the way over on the carpet. He had the hearing of an owl.

Leonie looked over at him and said, 'I guess we need to think about getting dressed.'

•

Barney lay in his bed with Comfrey on his chest. Comfrey was so close to his face, he could feel the air of her breaths against his chin. A whiff of Whiskas. Ocean Platter in Jelly. Yet this was not gross, but comforting. Dear, comforting Comfrey. Sometimes he felt that Deb manifested as his beautiful elderly cat and was here with him.

Still, the rain. Still, a policeman in his yard, the one who had been here most of the week and always looked like he was about to be found out for doing something naughty and get in trouble from his superior officer. Barney could hear the policeman's radio, tuned to something FM. He could hear a very modern song. Then the rain heavied and he could hear only the rain. Then a little time later, a song welled up again.

Last night, when Barney had returned home, the policeman was sitting on the patio, under the awning, in a raincoat and police-issued hat. He had given Barney a look through the sliding door as if to apologise, and Barney had felt bad for him. Also, Barney was tipsy. He had opened the sliding door and said, 'Don't worry, it's just a sorry situation all round.'

The policeman had said, 'Sorry?'

Barney put his hand up now in bed and ran it along Comfrey's bony back. Her purring grew more crackly and loud. Barney had read in *National Geographic*, just last week, that the low frequency of a cat's purr causes related internal vibrations that lessens their pain and heals their wounds. As soon as he read it, he had thought, Wait till Deb hears this. Deb'll love this.

Ben went through a stage, when he was about five, of conducting endless surveys. Barney was surveyed on his favourite plant (*'Banksia ericifolia'*), favourite day ('Sunday'), favourite season ('Autumn'), favourite smell ('Whatever that oil is that your mother wears').

But Deb was Ben's favourite surveyee. Deb endured a thousand questions, often the same ones over and over. Ben would write the questions and answers in a lined notebook called 'Ben's Remember Booklet'. Barney would hear them in the kitchen, while Deb was frying onions, or making moussaka or sauerkraut, and Comfrey was just a tortoiseshell kitten.

'What's your favourite food?'

'Pesto.'

'What's your favourite plant?'

'Comfrey.'

'What's your favourite animal?'

'Comfrey.'

Ben's high tooting laugh. 'Not a pet, a *animal.*'

'I'd argue that cats are animals.'

'Mum.'

'Okay, blue-tongue lizard.'

'What else?'

'Frogs.'

'What else?'

'Lyrebirds.'

•

Dr Prakash had said, in his suffocating office: 'You might need to explain to Ben that, yes, Deborah used to be the person who took care of the meals and the running of the house and perhaps attended to most to his needs, but now *you're* the person who is in charge of all that.'

'I think he's gathered that his mother is no longer attending to his needs.'

'Of course,' Dr Prakash had said. 'But just to make it clear that *you* are. That someone is.'

Why had Barney taken it out on Dr Prakash? Because there was no one else to take it out on? Because Dr Prakash only seemed to deliver bad news? Barney didn't know. But in the horrid office he had cleared his throat and thought: What in hell does this man across the desk in his blue tie know about my son?

And now he thought of Dr Prakash, flagrantly spooning Rosamie while their three children slept in safe, adjacent rooms.

Eighteen months ago, Dr Prakash had said to Barney, 'Has Ben been witness to the agitation, the volatility? These new behaviours?'

'We all live in the same house.'

'Directed at him, though?'

'No. But he's certainly seen it directed at me.'

Dr Prakash had nodded and sat back in his swivel chair. 'What's most difficult for the child of the person, I think, is the lack of affect. Not so much the big emotional outbursts, but more the change in day-to-day interactions. That "monotone" we've talked about.'

Barney had said, 'Ben's not a child.'

•

When the phone on the hall table rang around 9 am, Barney thought, That'll be Ben.

214

Always this silly, illogical hoping. Barney was in the kitchen and he stepped over Comfrey and went to the phone, which never rang. Had it ever rung in the time he had lived there?

'Hello, this is Barney speaking.'

'Hi, Barn, it's Rita.'

Disappointment, reality. Rita was not Ben.

'Good morning,' said Barney, wondering why he was speaking to Rita again.

'I know. Bill says I'm overthinking it, but I just felt like I wanted to check in.'

'Oh,' said Barney. 'Here I am.'

'Barn, you know I love a good worry. But I hope I didn't say the wrong thing last night.'

'About what?'

'About Ben. Or about anything. I was so glad you could join us, and I guess being there at the Bowlo again, and thinking about all the other times we were there together, I just felt like I didn't know how to be *normal*.' Rita sounded so sheer. Like the way she used to talk with Deb. Rita and Deb talked so candidly and often.

'You don't need to be normal,' said Barney. 'I mean, I don't know. I don't know.'

A dreadful pause. Barney could feel his heart in his chest again. This organ that he'd paid so little attention to in his previous life. Now, in this new life, it just kept making itself apparent.

'We really loved seeing you, Barn. I just . . .'

Barney heard Rita exhale audibly. And her voice went all wobbly when she said, 'I just miss her so much. I think about her all the time. And you must miss her *so* much more.'

Barney closed his eyes and swallowed. He endured the wretched thumping inside. He managed to say, 'Yeah,' with his eyes still shut.

'Yeah,' said Rita, and then the sound of Bill kind of reprimanding her in the background.

Barney said, 'Consider me checked in on.'

Rita laughed, or perhaps cried. She said, 'Okay. Job done.'

•

Leonie wasn't sure which one was Bridge Street so she consulted her street directory and ran her finger along the page until she touched it.

'Okay, so we go left at the river, then at the third street after that we go left again, and that's their street. You got that?'

'No,' said Joe, looking out the window.

Leonie watched him in the rear-view mirror for a moment and then she set the street directory on the passenger seat, open at the relevant page, and reversed out of the carport with the wipers running front and back.

'What's the name again?' said Joe.

'Her name's Eileen. Her husband is Nathan. And the girls are Annie and Patty.'

'I wish we could go to the playground,' said Joe, as they began to drive along their street.

'I know.' Leonie put her blinker on and waited at the Give Way sign and watched three cars pass, water whirling off their tyres. She turned right and drove along the wide road that led to the highway. A flock of cockatoos was up ahead on the verge, eating at the grass in the beating rain.

'Wet day to be a bird,' said Leonie.

'Yeah,' said Joe.

Leonie kept glancing at him as he stared out the window. She had tried to be very unfazed about this visit to Eileen's. So normal! Just off to see some friends! Privately, Leonie was so nervous she thought she'd burst. She took a deep breath. Honestly, what was Eileen going to do? Be too lovely? Leonie was making a whole lot out of nothing. It'll be fine. It'll be just *fine*.

Joe said, 'The person who put the numbers on all the letterboxes would be very tired.'

•

Where was Ben?

Barney had a headache and couldn't recall the last time Ben was not working on a Saturday. Often Ben didn't work on a

Wednesday or Thursday, but he was always there on Saturday. And yet it was Saturday morning, and where was Ben?

Barney sat in the car park under the dripping tree. The waifish girl was absent too. Just that other boy, and those other two girls—these adjunct people, these imposters—serving so many hash browns.

Barney sat in his car and recited the meanings of as many acronyms as he could think of: NATO, QANTAS, ASEAN, UNESCO. CERN was in French. *Conseil Européen pour la* something. It didn't work. Barney could not distract himself. He wanted to see his son, and the absence of Ben sent his mind to that terrible day when Barney didn't pick up Deb from work. Specifically, the way Ben had looked at him in the corridor at Clarke Base Hospital. Ben had said, 'Why didn't you pick her up like you always do?'

Barney sat in his car and watched the rain on the oblong of windshield. He recalled the concerned nurse who'd given him a pamphlet entitled *Helping Young People After Loss*. For some reason, he'd kept it in the glove box of his then-new car, with his logbook and torch. The pamphlet was probably the reason he hadn't opened his glove box for two years.

But *nineteen* years ago, there was a wonderful time when baby Ben finally learned to sit up. Barney could still see, in his mind, Ben's perfect posture. Deb would plonk him on the rug to play with his Montessori toys, and she'd go and potter about. Then, every so often, a soft thud and a silence and a cry. Barney would come in to find Ben toppled over. Barney was always so unconfident in his ability to comfort his son. But what did it matter, at the time, if Deb was always there to do it?

Barney stared now at the glove box. He looked up at the McDonald's. He felt a futile resentment towards the young boy at the cash register for the crime of not being Ben.

It wasn't clear at what precise moment Barney lost all resolve. It was like a landslip, after a lot of rain. It pelts down endlessly until, at some point, the fragrant earth gives way. Barney started the car and made a bold right turn onto the highway. He headed north towards his old house in Clarke Hill.

31

Eileen Swan's house was set back off the street behind some frangipani trees, and there was an old mulberry tree too, next to the carport. Leonie could see mulberries hanging off the low branches as she and Joe went along the front path to the door.

It opened before she knocked. Eileen must have heard them coming or been hovering in the hall.

'*Lee*,' said Eileen Swan, who was standing in the doorway with her arms open as if a hug was imminent, and yet she was too far away.

'Hi, Eileen,' said Leonie, finding the look of Eileen Swan to be overwhelming in its loveliness. 'Here we are.'

Eileen said, 'And Joe! Look how big you are.'

Joe hid behind Leonie's legs.

Leonie shook her umbrella off over the path, and she set it against the weatherboard wall next to the front door.

A doormat said *Welcome* on it, and there was a cactus in a pot, and at least four pairs of small shoes strewn in a pile.

'Well,' said Leonie, as awkward as she'd ever felt.

'Come on in. I think the girls are hiding. Maybe you can help me find them, Joe.'

So Leonie and Joe followed Eileen Swan into the house, out of the rain. Eileen looked different from two years ago. She had a bowl cut and a grey singlet and blue jeans with a waist that went up to heaven. The whole ensemble made Leonie think of Demi Moore in *Ghost*.

'Golly, something smells delicious,' said Leonie, regretting her own choice of attire: a spotted cotton dress from the sale at Fosseys.

'We've just made oat and peanut butter cookies,' said Eileen. 'Do you like oat and peanut butter cookies, Joe?'

Joe was pulling on the back of Leonie's dress, pulling it down in a way that made her even more embarrassed, this time about her body. She reached around and grabbed his hand and held it tight in hers.

'I don't know,' said Joe.

Leonie put her jolly voice on. She said, 'I guess I've deprived us of oat cookies for too long.'

•

Barney could see the corner of his old street approaching up ahead. It drew closer and closer as he drove past the nursery, past the car yards, past the Kennards. Here comes the corner, he thought, to the squeaking sound of the wipers. Tony—the new mechanic—should have put in new wiper blades. These ones sounded like the old swing set at the Clarke Park playground, where little Ben had wanted to be pushed forever.

I mustn't turn, thought Barney as he turned.

And here he was again, in his old street. Here he was, in the past. It was only months since Barney had been here, and yet he was flooded with a stinging rush of memories that made him nauseous. How he had missed that row of bottlebrush trees. How he had missed the Murrows' house and Rita's sweet arbour. He slowed down and imagined he was arriving home. His old house was up ahead. He saw the edge of it as he approached and then there it was, nestled behind Deb's beautiful bush garden, where she had planted five varieties of banksia, just for Barney.

But now the garden looked unpleasantly overgrown. There'd been an infiltration of onion weed and oxalis and kikuyu. There was yellowed foliage and no one to spray on iron chelate.

Barney felt a little dizzy when he pulled up out front and left the engine running. Deb's sister's car was there, but not Ben's car. Where was Ben? He had expected Ben's green Mazda to be in the driveway.

Leaning over the passenger seat, Barney could see that the house was the same. The weatherboards were still that olive green that Deb had chosen. The eaves still pink and peeling. Even through the rain, Barney could see the furniture in the front room was unchanged. Those bamboo blinds, that bookshelf, that couch—it was such an indecency for him to be here. His cheeks began to burn. The engine was running, he should just drive away. What was he thinking? Barney cursed himself.

But just a moment longer. He would count to ten and then he would go. He would begin counting soon. Barney stared at the front window and—there—a flash of her. Her form going past the big open lounge room, where the windows all faced the front garden. He could see her walking towards the kitchen. Deb.

He squinted, wanting more of her. Deb? Come back from the kitchen, Deb. And it was as if she heard him! For here she was, returning to the lounge room with a mug. She stopped and took a sip, as if she'd forgotten what she was doing. Then she wandered across to the couch, where she sat down and he lost sight of her through the rainy window.

Tears came to Barney's eyes. He had a clammy hand on the passenger seat, looking out for just one more glimpse of her.

Oh, Deb. Deb!

And then the jolt of a knock on the driver's window—*tap tap*. Barney almost left his own body with fright.

Here was Deb's sister, Irene, bespectacled under a golf umbrella. She must have come out the side gate, behind his car. Barney rolled down the window.

'What are you doing here, Barney?'

'I was just—I wondered where Ben was.'

'He moved out,' said Irene. The rain was dripping down from the edges of her umbrella. 'He's living with his girlfriend.'

'Where?'

'Near the uni.' Irene stared at Barney, but her glasses had fogged up in the weather. Irene's eyes were lost in the mist. And so it seemed that she was staring at Barney, but really it was impossible to tell. Barney stared back anyway and there was a moment of silence.

Until Irene said, 'I want you to know, I tried talking to him. I advocated for you.'

'He thinks I should have stayed.'

'I know he does. And I told him that would have been impossible. Of course you couldn't stay. But I think he's just dealing with everything in his own way because he's a nineteen-year-old boy and he's been through a heck of a lot.'

Barney nodded.

'Barn, you really shouldn't be here. You know it's best if she doesn't see you.'

'I know,' said Barney, nauseously. He felt so dehydrated. He couldn't remember the last time he'd had any water. The engine was still idling. He put the car into first.

Irene said, 'You look thin.'

'I'll go.'

'And pale.'

'Sorry, Irene.'

'*I'm* sorry,' said Irene. She looked damp and sad and eyeless, and the sight of her—so like Deb in that sisterly way—nearly undid him. Who knew which way she was looking, but she said, 'I really am sorry, Barn.'

32

Annie and Patty laughed for days when Joe and Eileen 'found' them in the pantry. Imagine having a walk-in pantry. Leonie thought that was wonderful. And chickpea, buckwheat, spelt, rice—she had no idea there were so many types of flour.

Aiiiiiieek! Hahahaha!

The girls squealed and laughed and, to Leonie's surprise, Joe squealed and laughed too. Then the girls chased Joe down the hall and Joe ran and squealed some more, as if they were kin and did this every weekend.

'They've been so excited,' said Eileen, spooning tea-leaves into a metal pot.

'That's very sweet,' said Leonie. 'Joe's not usually so forthcoming.'

Eileen went over to the fridge for milk, still chatting to Leonie, but Leonie found it difficult to follow what she was saying over the happy shrieks coming from the bedroom down the hall. The clamour of children, seeing Eileen again, being in Eileen's house—it was all a bit distracting. Leonie nodded and said, 'Yes,' a few times, about the preschool. She tried to concentrate as Eileen listed the pros and cons of modern-day Clarke Primary.

Leonie was sitting at the kitchen table by then, which was a heavy wooden thing that looked like it belonged on a farm. 'Nathan's still working at Stockfeeds then?' she asked. 'I guess they do good business on the weekend.'

'You know, Lee, he is. He's probably there right now. But Nathan and I are separated.'

'Oh. I didn't know that.'

'That's okay. How would you?' said Eileen. 'And it's fine. I'm fine.'

'I'm glad to hear it then,' said Leonie. 'I mean that you're fine. Not that you're separated.'

Eileen smiled and said, 'I know what you mean.'

'Not everything works out. Is what I meant to mean.'

'It doesn't. And don't get me wrong, Nathan's a good guy. But he just sits around, Lee. He never does anything. He never wants to do anything. He just goes to work and then he comes home and sits in front of his big TV. He'll play *California Games* all day of a weekend. He's like a child.'

'Is that a video game?'

'Yes,' said Eileen. 'He moves a cartoon person around on a skateboard.'

'That's a shame.'

'And I wasn't going to spend the rest of my life just watching him sit. So I told him to go sit someplace else.'

Leonie looked up at Eileen from her rustic wooden chair. She said, 'Well, good for you. People need to get up every once and a while, at a minimum.'

'Yes, they do,' said Eileen. 'And he loves the girls, which is all I really care about. He has them every second weekend, and he takes them Tuesdays and Thursdays after school. I mean, I think he's miserable, but he'll be fine. I'm sure he'll find someone else to sit for eventually.'

'Of course he will. Some woman out there will be thrilled to watch him sit. And you can send her your condolences when that time comes.'

Eileen laughed. She said, 'Gosh, it's good to see you, Lee.' And she tilted her head and said, 'I've always found you so—'

But whatever Eileen had found Leonie was left unsaid, because Joe came running into the kitchen, pursued by Annie and Patty. They ran an exuberant ring around the table then disappeared back down the hall.

Eileen watched Joe. She said, 'He's gorgeous.'

'He is.'

'He looks like Maurie.'

Leonie's throat went tight. Here it goes. She's going to speak about Maurie, ask about Maurie, and I'll perish. I'll die. Leonie said, 'He does.'

'And the father too, I'm sure, with that colouring. Although I never saw a picture.'

'There is no picture.'

'Is that right?'

'That's right.'

Eileen looked rather serious now and Leonie wondered if Eileen would cry, but Eileen didn't cry. She said, 'He's so lucky to have you, Leonie.'

'Well.'

Leonie's discomfort—it was intolerable.

And when the buzzer on the oven went off, Eileen just looked at her warmly and said, 'Saved by the bell.'

•

Eileen, Annie, Patty, Leonie and Joe sat up at the kitchen table and ate oat and peanut butter cookies. Joe ate four. His cheeks were flushed from all the fun he was having.

'I like them, Leelee.'

'I'd better get the recipe,' said Leonie.

'They're so easy,' said Eileen.

'They've been police next door at our house,' said Joe.

'Why?' said Annie, who was in kindergarten and had on the most adorable striped overalls.

'They're working there,' said Joe.

'Yes,' said Eileen. She sipped her tea from an old brown mug with white daisies on it and gave Leonie a knowing look. 'I was going to talk to you about that, Lee.'

•

Barney drove home, watching the road through rain and tears.

But in his mind he was in the old house again, half-reading on the couch, and Deb and little Ben were in the kitchen.

Ben's voice, so high: 'Okay, so. What's your favourite colour?'

Deb's voice, so warm: 'Greenish brown.'

'What's your favourite thing to do?'

'Go on a family bushwalk.'

'What's your favourite thing?'

'Friable humus.'

'What else?'

'The mountain.'

'What else?'

'The coffee pot.'

'What's your favourite sound?'

'You breathing.'

•

'Patty, hold the big one up higher,' said Eileen loudly. 'It's almost on Annie's head.'

Patty, god love her. She was all of eight years old and coordinating two umbrellas. One small one above her head and one big one over Joe and Annie, while Joe and Annie picked mulberries.

'My arm's sore,' said Patty.

'You're doing great,' said Eileen, and she turned back to Leonie on the front porch. Leonie was standing next to the potted cactus, in her poor choice of dress.

'So you actually talked with Ginny about it,' said Leonie.

'I was in sub-acute at that time and I was with her after she saw the doctor. And I just said to her that the injuries she had didn't look like a fall.'

'Good on you.'

'But that's already well beyond my job description. It's just that we have so many, Lee. We have so many women come in—and you can just *tell*.'

'What did she say?'

'She was evasive the first time and evasive the second time. But the second time, I sent another nurse in to talk with her—my colleague Judy, who has a bit of a sixth sense for these things. So Judy spoke with her.'

'And what did Judy say?'

'Judy said: You've got to get out. She said: You can't just wait for it to escalate, which is what it does.'

'And what did Ginny say?'

'I don't know. This was, what, six years ago? And even if she agreed, in her situation, it probably wasn't as easy as just getting up and leaving him. It's never as easy as that.'

'You should tell the police.'

'I did,' said Eileen. 'When she went missing, I read about it in the paper and I recognised her. So I called the police and told them.'

'What did they say?'

'The policeman said he'd look into it.'

'And?'

'And I never heard from them again.'

'Fucking hell.'

'Yes,' said Eileen.

'Leelee, can we eat some now?' yelled Joe.

The rain was misty at that moment and not too heavy and the grass sparkled white with water. The children came quickly up the path. Joe was holding an ice-cream tub full of mulberries.

Leonie crouched down and smiled and said, 'Don't they look delicious? Of course you can.'

33

Leonie thought about Eileen, on-and-off, for the rest of the day. Which is to say that she thought about Eileen, which always made her think about Maurie, which often made her think about Eunice.

That evening, Leonie wiped down the kitchen table after Joe went to bed and thought about the week after Eunice died, when Leonie and Maurie had sat at this very table. That was when Joe was still a baby. He was having a rare moment of sleep in his travel cot in the spare room. Baby Joe was quite the patchy sleeper. That was the third-last visit and Maurie was looking far less luminous.

Leonie had asked, 'Are you going to go see Eileen?'

Maurie said, 'I don't think so. She has three children, if you include Nathan. She seems very tired.'

'Why is she with Nathan anyway? I always thought Eileen was more in charge of her own destiny.'

'You always thought Eileen should be put up on a little pedestal.'

'I did not.' Leonie blushed.

'I think Eileen is probably just biding her time.'

'Well you didn't seem to talk to her much yesterday.'

'There were a lot of people to talk to, Lee.'

Maurie was not herself. She was irritated and she looked exhausted. That pallid, drained kind of exhausted.

Leonie said, 'I got stuck with that woman from Sunset Gardens: Merta—the one who wears the blue visor. She told me that Mum was the funniest person she'd ever met. She used those actual words.'

Maurie rolled her eyes.

The house was festooned with flowers. Leonie had used up all three of her vases and several old jars. There was a bouquet of carnations in the sink that she had no idea what to do with.

Leonie took a bite of leftover cake. Eunice would have been appalled at the amount of cake at her own wake. It had been a ghastly amount of cake for a woman who thought that the most impressive thing a person could do was eat very little.

'I'm so fucking tired,' said Maurie.

'Maybe you should do a Lou Lawson and offer Joe a temazepam.'

'Did you know humour is a defence mechanism? I'm sure Dorrie can explain it to you.'

Leonie grinned. Then a murmur had come from the spare room, where baby Joe was sleeping. He'd not been down long. Maybe twenty minutes was all. *Gyaah, gagagaga*, went baby Joe.

'Oh, Maur,' said Leonie.

'*No*,' said Maurie. She closed her eyes and looked like she might cry.

•

On the actual night Eunice had died, Leonie had gone across to Dorrie's.

Dorrie had opened the door and opened her arms and said, 'Oh, Lee.'

They went down the hall to the kitchen.

'When's Maurie coming?'

'Tomorrow.'

'Good.'

'At least I get to see baby Joe.'

'Seeing baby Joe will help.'

'Maurie has to go back for work though. She and baby Joe are going home again before the funeral and then coming back.'

The kettle whistled and Dorrie turned off the gas. She told Leonie it would be chamomile, to relax her, and the tea was made in silence. Then Dorrie set a steaming cup down and said, 'Have you eaten?' and Leonie began to sob.

'I'll make you a sandwich.'

'I was awful to her,' said Leonie, sobbing.

'Lee.'

Dorrie's kitchen was all wooden cabinets and yellow tiles and laminate benchtops. A profusion of hanging pots. Leonie sat on a stool next to a maidenhair fern. She cried and cried. 'She was my mother and she was so old and I was so impatient with her. I was hostile. Sometimes I felt like I couldn't stand her, Dorrie. I was like a child.'

Dorrie looked at Leonie squarely and said, 'You did all you could. You did what you could reasonably manage.'

'But she hated it in there. She made me feel so bad about it I thought I'd die.'

'I know she did.'

Leonie put her head on the bench, lousy with guilt. She bawled, and Dorrie stood and companioned her quietly. Leonie had this sense, amid her bawling, that Dorrie was really holding back, and that Dorrie had much more to say.

'I should have had her move in with me,' said Leonie, lifting her head. She must have looked a fright.

And Dorrie looked rather beautiful. She had the roundest angel face and her hair was this great big grey cloud. Dorrie said, 'What, and killed yourself in the process?'

'Wanda's mother lives with Wanda and Mickey. Wanda gave her the main bedroom.' Leonie was weeping when she said this.

'Well, you're not Wanda and you couldn't have done that. You had to keep something for yourself. Look at Maurie. She hasn't done all the things you've done.'

'But Maurie left.'

'Yes, she did.'

'Maurie's free.'

'Well,' said Dorrie.

Leonie was a bit ranty now. She said, 'I feel like I was always at Sunset Gardens. Every time I turned around I was like, *Here I am again, at Sunset Gardens.* And it was never enough. She just made all these little comments about how I never visited. She told me how lonely she was all the time. She was so lonely, Dorrie.'

'Leonie.'

Leonie nodded and blinked out tears.

Dorrie left the room and returned with a roll of toilet paper. 'Clive used all the Kleenex for his stupid hay fever,' she said, and she went to the fridge for a Tupperware of cold chicken, and to the cupboard for a fresh jar of mayonnaise.

Leonie wiped her face as Dorrie assembled a sandwich in silence. Leonie watched as Dorrie spread the mayonnaise and laid on the pieces of chicken. Dorrie added thinly sliced celery and crushed walnuts and continental parsley. She sprinkled some salt flakes and she ground some pepper. Dorrie set a slice of bread on top and cut the whole thing into two neat halves. Then she set the sandwich on a plate on the bench in front of Leonie and said gently, 'Your mother was so out of tune with you, Lee.'

34

On Sunday morning, Leonie woke up in Joe's tiny bed. He must have called out in the night. She must have fallen back asleep there, wedged between Joe and the edge of his mattress. Some nights were a blur to Leonie. If she were called to testify on the nocturnal movements of her own household, she would make an unreliable witness.

She felt Joe sit up now, beside her.

No, she thought. Leonie would have traded a kidney for more sleep.

'Leelee,' said Joe brightly, as if he'd been awake for an hour. 'It's still raining.'

Leonie made a pained sound.

Joe said, 'Whenever I wake up the birds sing a little song for me.'

•

'It's just me,' said Dorrie, shaking out her umbrella on the porch outside Leonie's screen door.

'Hi, Dorrie!' said Joe.

Joe and Leonie were finishing their breakfast of pancakes with sliced banana and maple-flavoured syrup.

Dorrie closed the screen door behind her and kicked her shoes off and walked barefoot across the linoleum. 'Good day for ducks,' she said.

'How was the lake?' asked Leonie.

'Wet.'

'No kidding. I thought you'd cancel, but then your car was gone all day.'

Dorrie sat down next to Joe and said, 'We went to Bart and Flora's for lunch instead and it turned into a long lunch, and then it turned into the pub because Clive and Bart were in a mood.'

'The Wicko?'

'It's such a charming pub, Lee, we should all go together some time. And suffice to say Clive's a bit under the weather from trying to keep up with Bart McDonald.'

'I thought Bart McDonald gave up drinking after the heart attack.'

'For about five minutes.'

Leonie forked her last piece of pancake and pushed it around in the syrup on the plate. 'So did Clive sing opera all the way home then?'

'Relentlessly for forty minutes,' said Dorrie.

Leonie smiled. She said, 'I regret to inform you that these are of the packet variety, but would you like a pancake?'

'I'm fine. Clive made eggs Benedict, which was disgusting. I'm having a bit of a time digesting it.' Dorrie turned her attention to Joe and said, 'Now, Joe, what is that puzzle over there on the carpet?'

Joe bowed his head and smiled shyly. 'Smurfs,' he said. 'It's got one hundred pieces.'

'One *hundred*,' said Dorrie. 'And isn't it good puzzle weather? Do you want to finish it together?'

'Okay,' said Joe, and Dorrie and Joe went over to the carpet and sat down, next to Joe's toy rabbits.

Leonie picked up the sticky plates and set them in the sink and filled the kettle with water. She looked out to the street. More water; endless rain. Leonie was so frustrated by the rain. And she flinched when she heard Joe say, 'I wish I had a train set, but Leelee said I'm not allowed to get a train set.'

'Well,' said Dorrie, without missing a beat. 'I guess you'll have to make do with your cars. And your rabbits.'

'Dorrie, how much pieces can you do in a puzzle?'

'As many as you got,' said Dorrie, and she found a knees-up position on the carpet, her back against the couch. She said, 'Aw, look how comfortable that Smurf looks there, lying against the tree. That Smurf is not going to have nearly as much trouble getting up as I am.'

•

Milo's mother dropped Milo off and didn't stay and chat, on account of she had to drop off Milo's sister to a different playdate in Mulamang, the next suburb along. Leonie considered for a moment the idea of having to care for more than one child. Milo's mother in fact had four children. All their names started with M. It exhausted Leonie to think of their unique and numerous needs.

Leonie went back to the living room where Dorrie was sitting, now on the couch. The house was so small. Small in the sense that Leonie could plainly hear Milo already counting something in Joe's bedroom.

'You did know Ginny,' said Dorrie. 'You knew Ginny as much as Ginny wanted to be known.'

'But I didn't,' said Leonie. 'I mean, here's Eileen Swan telling me that Ginny was in the hospital, all beaten up, at least two times, and I had no idea.'

'Yes, but.'

'I lay awake last night thinking how much I *thought* I knew Ginny.'

'But who else knew her? Who else was her friend?'

'He cut her off from her friends! She wasn't allowed to have friends. You know that.'

'But even her sister didn't really know.'

'If her sister lived in Clarke, she would have known. If her family lived here, and not in Victoria.'

Dorrie looked at Leonie and said, 'What's the point of this conversation?'

'The point is that the only reason Ginny and I were able to talk like we did was because I was next door. I was proximate. I could've been anyone.'

'But you're not just anyone. Ginny had two next-doors you know, and she didn't go confiding in Doug and Sandra at number seventeen.'

Leonie felt a pain at her temples. She was just anyone. Or she was no one. She wasn't sure what she was. Dorrie was so kind—even when somewhat irritated. And Ginny was one of the kindest people she'd known. Or not known. Leonie said, 'It's not like I didn't know she was leaving stuff out. I mean, Jesus, the things I heard Lou say.'

'The things you heard Lou do.'

'But if I'd known just a bit more,' said Leonie, 'I just think, you know, if I'd known he'd actually put her in the hospital . . .'

'Then what? You could have saved her? Come on, Lee.'

Leonie was on the smaller couch, the one with texta on the armrest. She was sitting on something—it was digging into her left buttock. She reached around and retrieved a Hot Wheels.

She turned it over and read the chassis: '67 *Camaro*. She said, 'I let him get cars. Just not a train.'

'I don't think you're depriving him of anything, Lee.'

Leonie nodded. She turned the red car around in her hand. She said, 'I just wish Ginny had trusted me enough to tell me.'

'I don't think it was about trust.'

'What was it about then?'

Dorrie said, 'Being terrified?'

'Oh,' said Leonie. 'Right.' She sighed and rolled the little red car slowly along the armrest of the couch.

●

In the bathroom, Barney cut himself shaving. It didn't hurt as much as it bled. He dabbed his chin with a square of toilet paper. He stared at the blood on the paper, which was almost perfectly in the shape of a heart. Barney Clarke did not consider himself a poetic person, but he stared at the blood-heart for a number of seconds and felt it heavy with significance. Then he brought the armchair out from the bedroom and set it in front of the sliding glass door in the kitchen.

From there he had a good view of the yard. He sat and watched the rain fall on the pool. It was mesmerising, watching water go into water. Barney had read that the tallest waterfall in the world was Angel Falls in Venezuela. It was over nine hundred metres tall. It was so tall that, in a very hot summer, the water turned to mist before it reached the stream below.

Comfrey had come out of the bedroom too, much like the armchair. She stood now at Barney's feet, and Barney lifted her up and put her on his lap. She kneaded his thighs and turned around in circles and sat down. Dear Comfrey. Barney stroked her longways, down her bumpy spine. He saw that there was still food in her bowl, covered with ants. An increasing number of indoor ants, because of the rain.

The young police guard was out there somewhere, sitting out of sight. Last time Barney checked, the guard was on a white plastic chair, under the awning near the side path. He was playing with an electronic device that did not seem relevant to policing.

Why had Barney driven to the old house? Why had he ruined himself like that?

He recited softly to himself: *Never again, never again.*

Yet he knew that he would go again.

He sat in the chair for half an hour. He repeated his mantra. He closed his eyes and opened them and read over an article he had edited several years ago for *Australian Journal of Forensic Sciences*, volume 20, issue 4. His red pen marks were all over the copy paper.

He'd forgotten this: a story about a woman who was shot in rural New South Wales in the early 1980s.

The minimum possible age of the oldest maggots found on her corpse had been used to establish time of death and, as a result, arrest her killer. Apparently insect access was a key determinate in the rate of decomposition in pigs' cadavers. Domestic pigs were currently recommended as analogues for humans in forensic entomology research.

Barney's legs were stiff, perhaps slowly decomposing. He touched his chin and then checked his finger—no blood. God, he hadn't been walking in such a long time. How was it possible to miss something so badly and yet be terrified of ever doing it again? Barney wondered about this. And about what, and how many, insects had access to Ginny Lawson's body.

'Down you get.'

He lifted Comfrey off his lap and placed her gently on the floor.

She arched her back up in a half-moon stretch, and then sat down and stared at a spot on the tiles. Comfrey made him think of Deb, and how Deb walked so robotically now across the living room in the old house. She moved like a much older woman. Only three years ago, she had danced lithely in the old kitchen to her Ethiopian piano music.

Deb had looked so thin. Did Comfrey look thin? Barney watched his beloved frail cat and thought that a breeze could blow her over. Barney felt so lonely. He went to the sliding door and opened it, and yelled along to where the young policeman was sitting, 'Wet enough for you?'

'Just about,' said the young policeman.

'What've you got there?'

'This? It's a Game Boy.' The policeman said it like Barney was an absolute moron. The policeman looked the same age as Ben.

Barney nodded and couldn't think of anything else to say.

'Barney!'

Someone was calling his name. Was that his name? *Barney.* It sounded odd when someone else yelled it. It was a woman's voice, but it wasn't Deb. Of course it wasn't Deb! Deb had a low, husky, wonderful voice. She could have had a career in radio. Barney wondered if she'd ever got around to changing the answering machine message at the old house.

'Bar-ney!'

His name was ridiculous. It should be the name of a cartoon horse. The voice was coming from the front of the house. He went up the hallway, opened the front door, and peered into the misty rain. The street was all washed out and white. There was no one on his verandah, no one on his lawn.

'Hi, Barney!' said the voice, and he turned to see Leonie on her front porch, waving.

'Oh. Hi, Leonie!'

They were yelling at each other over the rain. Barney felt like one of those old people who yell at the sky.

Leonie yelled, 'Sorry to be so yelly! I didn't want to get drenched! Do you want to come over for that cup of tea?'

35

At Leonie's kitchen table, Barney sat with Joe and Milo, eating mulberries.

'This is Rabbit,' said Joe, holding Rabbit.

'What about those rabbits over there?' said Barney, pointing to two other toy rabbits, lying face down on the living room carpet.

'That's More Rabbit and Another One Rabbit,' said Joe.

Leonie was at the bench near the window. She'd decided on a pot of tea, as opposed to two separate cups, because Barney had never been over for tea before and he might like things a touch more formal. She put two teabags in the pot and poured the water in.

'Have you seen *Pinocchio?*' asked Milo.

'*Pinocchio,*' said Barney. 'I think so. A long time ago.'

'The boy turns into a donkey and it's really scary,' said Milo. 'Do you like mulberries?'

'Yes, I do,' said Barney.

Milo said, 'You've eaten nine.'

Leonie brought the teapot over and set it on the table, then she brought the sugar and the milk and two mugs and a spoon.

'Knock knock,' said Joe.

'Who's there?' said Barney.

'Police.'

'Police who?'

'Puh-lease let me in.'

Milo and Barney laughed. As in, Barney really laughed. He had a deep laugh and it went for a while and Leonie found it so endearing—a generous laugh—and Joe looked very satisfied.

'That's a good one, Joe,' said Barney.

'Have you kids had enough mulberries?' said Leonie.

Joe and Milo nodded.

Leonie said, 'Why don't you go finish your Lego mansion.'

●

On the back pavers, Leonie and Barney watched the rain from under the awning. The rain was falling on the Hills Hoist and the fence and the blue marquees beyond.

Barney said, 'You can see quite a lot, really. The big marquee and the smaller one at the lemon tree.'

'Or you can see not much at all,' said Leonie. 'Which is how it feels.'

Leonie was holding a mug that said *Call Your Mother!* in red letters, next to a drawing of an annoyed old lady. She wished she had chosen a different mug. She could feel the weather inside her dress. The fabric stuck to her in that certain way with the humidity. Not to mention what this kind of climate did to her hair. She was like a moist terrier.

Barney said, 'If it makes you feel any better, I can't see much more than this. Just a different angle. I see them going in and out of the marquees to do their digging. I see them take a pie break. Then they go back in to do more digging.'

'Is it mainly little spades?'

'And those big round sieves, to sift the soil.'

'No wonder it's taking so long. I guess they have to look at every little thing.'

Barney was holding a mug with blue stripes on it. Leonie noticed a small cut on his chin. He took a sip of tea, which he'd taken with milk and one spoon of sugar.

And Barney didn't say anything so Leonie went on: 'It's just good that Senior Constable Marrel isn't in charge anymore. And that, as you say, this Levins fellow seems thorough. Ginny deserves thorough.'

'The name Marrel sounds familiar.'

'From where?'

'I don't know.'

'Huh.'

Leonie closed her eyes a second and opened them again, and she saw a flicker there, beyond the fence. Ginny was walking in the rain. Ginny was in her orange cardigan with the flowers on it. She must be getting so soggy. Leonie would fetch her a towel.

But Ginny wasn't there at all.

'It's funny,' said Barney. 'Having them here all week and watching them setting up their marquees and using their radars and trowels and everything. Day after day.'

'I know,' said Leonie. 'It's all just theoretical until someone turns up with a shovel. And then it's just bizarre.'

'I was going to say it's amazing how anything can start to feel normal.'

•

Inside, Leonie made a second cup of tea because the first one didn't hit the sides.

'For one thing, I found out that Lou Lawson was in the hunting club,' said Barney.

Leonie said, 'He sure was. He liked to fish at the lake and he liked to hunt on the mountain. The hunting club shoots up on the mountain. There's a lot of deer up there, apparently, which is a surprise to some people. Actually, that's how Lou met Janice. That's the theory anyway. The hunting club goes on trips and they went on two trips to Queensland before Ginny went missing. I have a client at work whose husband is in the hunting club. My client—Di—said that on one of the nights they were up there, some of the boys went out drinking and Lou was on the prowl. Next thing, Lou marries a woman in Queensland who used to work at a titty bar—by which I mean Janice. Biscuit?'

'Sure,' said Barney.

He was sitting at the table again. Leonie could hear the boys playing. She took four Coffee Scrolls out of the packet and put them on a plate, and she stood at the bench a moment wondering if that looked too formal. Like she was trying too hard. Could a person try too hard with Coffee Scrolls? God, she was ridiculous. It's just that Barney was obviously a highly educated person, on the verge of being intimidating. She went across and put the plate on the table and said, 'Anyway, you don't need to look at the library for any of the articles about Ginny. I kept all of them.'

Barney picked up a Coffee Scroll and examined it as an exoticism. He took a bite and chewed neatly and he looked around the kitchen. 'You have a very nice home.'

'This old thing?' said Leonie. 'Are you from around here, Barney?'

'My wife and I used to live in Clarke Hill.'

'Well. Clarke Hill's nice. There're probably less dead bodies in the backyards of Clarke Hill.'

'You never know,' said Barney, holding a Coffee Scroll.

'I guess not.'

'My wife and I are separated. Obviously.'

'Oh. Well. You never know,' said Leonie.

'I guess not,' said Barney, and he even briefly smiled.

Leonie leaned back in her chair. *Separated*. The word put her in mind of liquids left too long in the fridge. Joe and Milo were hysterically squealing down the hall. Leonie said, 'It's amazing how much noise two boys can make.'

'They could drown out a concrete saw,' said Barney.

'Just about.'

Barney smiled at the squeals. He said, 'It must be nice having someone to tell you jokes.'

'I've only heard them all a hundred times. But I do love a joke. That's what you need in a good tragedy: a good joke.' And Leonie laughed in that way she was prone to do, when nothing was particularly funny. Then she sighed and said, 'I mean, honestly, if you don't laugh you'll cry.'

'I guess that's true.'

Barney had eaten neatly around the entire biscuit, leaving just the centre circle with the pink icing. And now he ate this small pink circle. He wasn't intimidating, really. Leonie had begun to feel quite at ease. She said, 'Do you have children, Barney?'

Barney was generally a grey colour, but he went a pink colour. He said, 'Actually, yes. I have a son who won't speak to me.'

●

There were no two ways about it—little Joe reminded Barney of his own son. When Ben was a child he had that same curly hair and Deb always let it grow long, like Joe's was. Ben looked like he was raised on a commune some days, scooting around the garden after Deb, 'helping' her with her jobs. Deb had been extraordinarily patient. She would instruct serenely and then stand aside and let Ben do it all himself. She would let him get it all messy and wrong. But then, by kindergarten, Ben knew how to sheet mulch and make a weed fertiliser tea.

Barney, in his own pursuits, had been focused on efficiency, and having Ben 'help' was never efficient. He had an image now of Ben at the baby gate, which blocked the doorway to his study. Ben, the poor kid, would hold on to the bars like he was in a cell. He was there at the baby gate at eighteen months, at two, at three, four, five. Barney left the gate on for so many years it became an indignity to his son.

'Dad, will you play with me?'

It made Barney wince to think of Ben's tiny voice.

Or it made him wince to think of his own perennial reply: 'I'm busy. Go ask your mother.'

And now here was Joe, with such a similar voice! It was so weirdly familiar. Discomfiting, for sure, but also lovely, and Leonie's house was just as cosy as anything. Even on a rainy day, it was full of natural light. Full of friendly clutter.

Barney could hear the boys having the most fantastic time down the hall. He realised now, in Leonie's kitchen, just how depressing his place next door was. It was dead in there, and not just because it was the scene of a murder. He should buy something to put on a wall. He was beginning to forget all the slowly collected artworks that Deb had hung at the old house. He and Deb had gone on a dozen daytrips to Cedar Valley, so she could find yet another treasure at the big antique store on the main road.

Leonie was sitting back in her chair, talking away, so convivial, and Barney had momentarily lost the thread of the conversation. What had he missed? Leonie said, 'Some people just think that because Earl is a criminal and he lives across the street then it must have been Earl. But Clive's cousin works at Clarke Wreckers and he knows a bit about Earl. From what I hear, Earl is both sloppy—as far as being a criminal mastermind goes—and a big wuss. Clive's cousin just can't believe that Earl has sold that much pot and stolen that many cars, and yet somehow he's not serving a lengthy prison sentence for either. That's the mystery of Earl. It's not whether he killed Ginny or not; it's why is he not in jail? So I don't know why the police were over there talking to him—again—but it makes me worry that they just don't have a clue what they're doing. Again. Or that they're deliberately *not* doing what they should be doing. Again.'

Barney nodded and looked about at Leonie's kitchen area, which opened onto the living area. She did not have artworks so much as needleworks and prints and framed photographs on the mantelpiece. Deb would not have hung any of these things. But Deb could be a little superior when it came to art and culture. Barney blinked and said, 'And so. Hold on. What about Ginny's family?'

'Ginny's from Victoria,' said Leonie. 'She didn't have any family here and her mum had only come up a few times to see Tobias. I think Carol wanted to come more often, but Lou had this way of keeping Ginny to himself. Like it was always too hard for Ginny to go down to Warrnambool, and it was always too hard for Carol to come up here and stay, because Lou needed the spare room for his fishing gear, or Lou needed it for his physiotherapy equipment. Or Lou had a headache. Or Lou needed to sleep, so they should just slip Tobias a sleeping tablet! Honestly. That was what he wanted to do. He wanted to drug his own child so he could sleep better. Of course, Ginny wouldn't let him do it, and she just ended up sleeping in Tobias's room, but then Lou didn't like that either. Lou didn't want anything to get in the way of whatever Lou decided that Lou needed at the time.'

'He sounds like a real piece of work.'

'He's my least favourite person of anyone I've ever met.'

Barney smiled. He couldn't tell if Leonie was a very unusual woman or a very normal woman. What was normal anyway? Leonie had a dusting of freckles over her nose. She said, 'Families fight their whole lives for justice on this kind of thing. I got a letter from Carol a few years ago. She said that she appreciated how I'd "agitated". Which I did. I agitated the Clarke police no end in 1985. And by 1986 I was just exhausted and sad. I can't imagine how exhausted and sad Carol is.'

'Leelee, we're hungry,' said Joe, who had appeared next to Barney's chair. He was like a trick of the light, that Joe. His friend, Milo, was hovering in the living room, hopping from one foot to the other.

'I'd better get going,' said Barney, who didn't really want to go.

'Don't leave on my account,' said Leonie. She looked up at a big round clock and said, 'Milo's getting picked up in half an hour and then I'll be trying to think of suitable indoor activities. I hate it that the library's closed of a Sunday.' She got up and went to the fridge and began taking out the makings of snacks.

Barney said, 'The forecast for tomorrow is good, so I'm assuming they'll be back first thing to finish up.'

'You let me know if you surveil anything else of interest.'

'I will,' said Barney. 'In fact, I think they did find something, even if it's completely irrelevant. After they'd been over at the lemon tree for a while, Levins asked me if I've ever had a dog.'

'A dog?'

'Yes, they found a dog. A dog the size of a cat, as I understand it. Which is not really the objective, but a curiosity nonetheless.'

Leonie went white in her pretty cotton dress. She was holding a family-size block of cheese. 'Oh my god,' she said. 'Peaches.'

36

'So what's your theory?' said Dorrie.

'Well obviously that Lou murdered Peaches.'

'To show Ginny what he was capable of, you think?'

'To terrorise her.'

'Yes,' said Dorrie. She was stir-frying vegetables and strips of beef in a wok on her gas stove. 'What else could it be, really.'

Clive was standing. He had a hand on the benchtop, a hand on his hip. The whole lot of him was askant. 'I hate to be boring,' he said, 'but what if Peaches just died and they buried her?'

Dorrie scoffed. It was a windless evening and the rain had lessened. Leonie could hear just gasps of it. Drips from the gutters and drips from the awnings. Dorrie said to Clive, 'Do you not remember the whole thing with Peaches? Peaches went missing was what Ginny said. Not that Peaches died. As far as we knew, Peaches was never found. And it has to be Peaches. There has not been another dog living at that property in living memory, except for Peaches.'

'No wonder Ginny didn't want to put up posters,' said Leonie. 'If she knew Peaches was already dead. I mean, that makes more sense now.'

'And no wonder she was so upset about it. Not to say that people aren't upset when their dog goes missing, but if your husband murders your dog that has to be a whole new level of distress,' said Dorrie.

Clive took a sip of beer and said, 'I'd forgotten the saga of Peaches. The ballad of Peaches. Actually, now that you mention it, I think Ginny used to say that Peaches loved lamb chops. Ginny bought a lot of chops back in the day.'

Dorrie turned the gas off and the aroma in the kitchen was like the one time Leonie went to Panda Garden. Delicious. Dorrie was such a good cook. The wok was steaming, and Dorrie was holding a wooden spatula thing. She said to Clive, 'If you make light of this, I'll hit you.'

Clive grinned. He set his Heineken on the bench and the bottle was wet with condensation.

'Do you think he would have done it in front of her?' Leonie lowered her voice, even though Joe was over on the couch, re-watching *The Land Before Time*.

'I think we might be better off not thinking about the particulars,' said Dorrie.

•

At the table, Dorrie held a pair of chopsticks and said, 'So there was a message from Flora McDonald on the machine earlier, when we got home from the nursery.'

Leonie held a fork and said, 'And?'

'Well, we had a long talk about Ginny yesterday at their house. They know about the case, of course, they're very informed people. And because Bart's on the council, he comes to town a fair bit. *And* he knows a policeman. Quite well apparently.'

'A Clarke policeman?'

'I think a Goodwood policeman. But the police people all know each other. Flora said in her message that Bart made a call and found out some "very interesting things".'

'What things?'

'I don't know,' said Dorrie. 'I left her a message. I'm waiting for her to call back.'

Leonie set her fork down. She'd finished her impromptu second dinner of stir-fry. She said, 'When it rains it pours.'

'Literally,' said Clive, who was in a droll mood. He was sitting opposite Leonie. 'So they just cover everything with tarps and wait for the rain to stop.'

'That's what Barney said.'

'And what's Barney like?' asked Dorrie.

'He's a very nice man,' said Leonie. 'I thought he was very serious at first, but he's actually quite funny, in a dry kind of way.'

'We like funny,' said Dorrie.

'We do,' said Leonie. 'And he's interested in absolutely everything, which really makes you feel like a good conversationalist.'

Dorrie laughed. She said, 'Is he retired? He looks retired.'

'No, he's an editor. He said he used to be at the university, but now he works at home editing academic journals and textbooks and that kind of thing.'

'Sounds riveting,' said Clive.

Leonie sat back in her chair and looked at Dorrie. 'He said that he and his wife are separated.'

'Oh, so she didn't die,' said Dorrie.

'She didn't die,' said Leonie. 'And he implied that his son had taken the wife's side in the separation. I think that's what he meant. I couldn't really tell. He said his son won't talk to him. It all sounds very difficult. You know when a person's whole demeanour changes when you ask about something?'

'I do,' said Dorrie, who was very good at demeanours, and very good at chopsticks. She picked up the thinnest slice of capsicum, just a wisp of it, and said, 'That must be very painful for him.'

'Oh, come on,' said Clive. 'The wife left him and the son won't talk to him? Maybe your new friend Barney ran away with his secretary and it didn't work out as planned.'

•

Barney let himself under the police tape and put the garbage out in the bin in the driveway. What a cloudy, muted night. A brief break in the rain. He stood for a moment under the streetlight, which lit up the front of his house. It lit up Leonie's carport and her maroon Mitsubishi.

Distant sounds of cars on the highway, gutters dripping, someone's television. Barney stood listening a moment, until he sensed that Earl was over there on Earl's porch, smoking in the dark. The form of Earl was only just discernible. Barney wondered why Earl did not make use of his porch light. So Earl could watch everything incognito?

And now here was Barney, bright under the streetlight, like he was an actor in a suburban one-man show. And over there was his audience: Earl. Barney felt so exposed. He turned to face his own house—the dark lawn, the ghostly banksia—and went quickly back inside.

Barney shut the door and deadlocked it. He went down the quiet hall. He wanted to make a cup of tea and sit down, somewhere comfortable with Comfrey.

'Comfrey,' he said, in the kitchen.

Barney had removed her anty food from the morning and replaced it with fresh food, but the food had not been eaten.

'Comfrey.'

When Comfrey didn't come, he checked in the study, where she would often sleep under his desk or lie on the rug near the door. She was not in his study, so he checked in the laundry, where he would sometimes find her asleep in a basket of his clothes.

He checked the bedroom and there she was, asleep on Deb's old armchair, lying on her side. Barney went over to her and laid his hand on her tufty fur. When he found her body as stiff as a board he must have jerked back a metre. Barney heard himself make a yowling sound. He saw that Comfrey had, at some point, soiled herself on the velvet. Barney went down on his knees, he put his forehead on the floorboards, he sobbed like a levee breaking.

Oh, Comfrey! He thought, Oh, Deb! I need to tell Deb!

37

In the early hours, Leonie lay awake ruminating. Outside, it was still dark. This was very early, before the birds, just the steady sound of rain and the clock ticking. It was unusual for Leonie to be awake at this hour, but normal for her to ruminate. Today was for agonising over the last time Maurie visited—if only Leonie could take it all back.

In the living room, two years ago: Maurie and Leonie and Joe—who was toddling around and in love with his mother. And why wouldn't he be? Maurie was wonderful with him. She breastfed him for what seemed like a decade. How she managed to nourish him like that when there was so little of her, Leonie did not know.

'It's probably about time,' Leonie had said, when Maurie told her that Joe was weaned and drinking cow's milk from a cup.

'I know, it's better,' said Maurie unconvincingly. 'I did feel guilty about my medication going into my breast milk.'

'I thought they said it was only a tiny amount.'

'Yes, but I didn't want any amount.'

Leonie had screwed up the paper bag from her spinach and cheese pasty and put it on the coffee table. It was a brown paper ball. Joe wandered over to the kitchen and Maurie looked drawn and tired. 'So you felt guilty about the medication when you were breastfeeding, and now you feel guilty about not breastfeeding.'

'Not as guilty as I feel when I'm so tired I forget to take my medication altogether.'

'That's not funny.'

'Have I even taken it today? I need one of those plastic pill boxes that Mum had with the days of the week on it.'

'Seriously?' said Leonie.

Maurie said wryly, 'What could possibly go wrong?'

'A whole new level of guilt? You know you're very good at guilt.'

'*We're* very good at guilt.'

Leonie flashed a smile and said, 'I don't know what you mean.'

'Do you know that people find you frustrating?'

'Do they?'

'They can't figure you out.'

'I don't think anyone's ever tried.'

Maurie had picked up the paper bag ball and begun throwing it up and catching it. She said, 'Don't you see how it's confusing when someone's warm and funny and like-able, and so people try to be friends with that person, but that person just hides away in their house and hardly goes anywhere and never lets anyone get close?'

'Who are we talking about here?' Leonie was grinning.

'Oh my god, Lee. Don't be so defensive.'

'I like my life just fine how it is.'

'No, you don't,' said Maurie. 'Come to Chile with me and Joe.'

'Because you think I'm depriving myself by not coming?'

'I think you're either depriving yourself or you're scared.'

'I've never been scared *a day in my life*,' said Leonie, in the voice of Eunice.

'Oh, fuck off. You're impossible.'

'You fuck off.'

'No, *you* fuck off.'

Leonie had been giggling as Joe tottered back to the carpet and began circling the room in his miniature overalls. And Maurie had smiled and thrown the paper bag ball at Leonie so it hit her on the breast and fell to the floor. Maurie said, 'Your Aunty Leelee is impossible,' and she picked up Joe and took him off to the spare room for a nap in his porta-cot.

Leonie had sat on the carpet, her back against the couch, and stared at the lint and pasty crumbs.

But none of this was what Leonie wished to take back. What she wished she could take back was what happened just after, when Maurie had said, 'Joe should sleep for another forty-five. I might go to the shop and get some peanut butter. Do we need milk?'

'Don't get Sanitarium.'

'Fine. I'll get Kraft.'

'It's never oily or dry,' said Leonie.

Maurie laughed. 'Do you mind sitting with him while I go?'

'Sure. If he wakes up and seems too happy I'll show him photos of Mum.'

'Leonie.'

Golly, Maurie really was tired. Leonie said, 'You go. We'll be fine.'

And so Maurie had gone.

•

Joe got up first and took himself out to the living room. Leonie could hear him from her bed, pottering around. She'd been awake for hours. She heard the television come on and the sound of cartoons. Joe's growing up, she thought. He had slept through the night again—good for Joe. Now he was getting up and starting his day without her.

When had the rain stopped? Leonie hadn't noticed, but when she got up and went into the living room there was sunshine. She went across the carpet and into the kitchen and looked out the window. There were several police cars and steam coming off the bright black road.

'Good morning, sweetheart.'

'Hi, Leelee.'

'Do you want Rice Bubbles or Corn Flakes or fried egg?'

'Fried egg.'

'I think I want fried egg too.'

Leonie was exhausted. She fetched the big pan and put the stove on, but it took an age for the element to heat up so she leaned against the counter and thought about Peaches and how much Ginny had adored that dog. A knock came at the door. It was probably Dorrie. Leonie glanced out the window and saw no hint of Dorrie in her own window, no flash of blue nightie. She went over and opened the door.

'Hi, Leonie.' Barney was standing on the mat, looking like someone who had emerged from the bush after a week of no food or water.

'Hi, Barney,' she said to this blotchy, anguished version of Barney. He really didn't look good. His eyes were all puffy from crying. Leonie heard the sound of police voices from behind him, from over the fence. Her heart skipped. It must be Ginny. They'd found Ginny!

'My cat died,' said Barney.

'Oh.' Leonie looked down at Barney's bare feet, which were covered in flecks of wet grass. 'I didn't know you had a cat.'

'She lived inside. To protect the birds.'

'How thoughtful.'

'I don't know what to do with her.'

'Barney, do you want to come in?'

'Who's there, Leelee?' This was Joe, yelling from the living room.

Leonie turned and said, 'It's just Barney, sweetie. Give me a sec.'

'I won't. I won't come in,' said Barney. He was kind of muttering and there was a brown stain on his shirt. Leonie just felt so bad for him she could bawl.

'I'm so sorry, Barney. About your cat.'

He blinked a few times, staring at the ground. Leonie saw him take a deep breath and exhale. He looked up and said, 'Can you imagine that it feels gauche to bury her in my yard?'

'Yes, I can.'

'I don't really know why I came here. I'm sorry, Leonie. It's just—I wrapped her in a towel.'

'Barney, why don't we bury your cat in *my* yard? Just keep her in the towel and bring her over this afternoon when I get home from work. We can give her a little send-off.'

Barney cleared his throat and said, 'Yes, okay. Thank you, Leonie.'

She said, 'What are neighbours for?'

38

A slightly tedious morning at Harvey World Travel Clarke Plaza—Wanda and Leonie had client after client until at least eleven thirty. Wanda booked a two-week cruise on the *Fairstar* for a thorny Dutch woman who didn't once smile and who insisted on being called 'Mrs Visser'.

'Certainly, Mrs Visser. Of course, Mrs Visser.'

Wanda was a consummate professional.

Leonie printed itineraries for Clarice, she finalised travel insurance for Clarice, she talked about *all that rain* with Clarice.

'And then as soon as it stops, every mower in Clarke starts up,' said Leonie. 'It's either that or it's people out walking their dogs. On the way to work this morning I heard a hundred mowers and saw a hundred dogs.'

Clarice laughed and said, 'Speaking of dogs, I just got some photos developed. Would you like to see a picture of my new dog, Leonie?'

'I'd love to.'

Clarice reached into her bag and retrieved an envelope with the logo on it from the one-hour photo place next to the RTA. Clarice flipped through and selected a photograph and held it up: a white fluffy dog in a gingham coat.

'Clarice, he is *adorable*. What type of dog is that?'

'He's a Bichon Frisé,' said Clarice. 'His name's Monsieur.'

'Monsieur!' said Leonie. 'You know, I need a pet story with a happy ending today. What a darling.'

'He's like a little cloud,' said Clarice.

'That's just wonderful.' Leonie stapled a pile of papers together and slid them inside a manila folder. Clarice was wearing moleskin trousers and a button-up shirt and looked like she'd bought her whole outfit at Country Road in the city. 'While you're here, Clarice, for your WA trip later in the year, Ansett have this new frequent flyer program, so I'm just going to fill in the form for you and then you can sign it.'

Clarice nodded and put her photos away. She picked up a snow globe (London) and tipped it sideways and then set it down again. She looked up at the poster above Leonie's desk: *A Club Med Vacation Begins Where Civilisation Ends*. Clarice said, 'I always love the music you play in here. What is it?'

'This is Arto Tunçboyaciyan,' said Leonie.

'Oh,' said Clarice. 'How unusual.'

Clarice hummed along awkwardly. And, when they'd finished everything, she signed the form and thanked Leonie profusely, like Leonie had rescued Monsieur from a fire. After Clarice left, and Mrs Visser left, Leonie stared across at the opposite wall, where her and Wanda's AFTA awards hung in silver frames. *Leonie Wallace, Best Travel Consultant—Leisure (1989). Wanda Zhang, Young Agent of the Year (1986).* She wondered what compelled people to dress animals in little clothes.

Wanda swivelled her chair around, her back to the window now. She looked at Leonie and shook her head and said, 'I can't believe Lou Lawson murdered Peaches.'

•

The police had returned to the lemon tree and squelched around the marquee. The grass was not so much grass as mud. Barney made tea in the kitchen. He read some of the paper, an update on Operation Desert Storm. He looked at the date at the top of the page and vibrated with sadness.

Levins and O'Leary were together on the sunny mud-lawn and a new policeman in the full forensics outfit came out of the marquee and called them over and they both disappeared inside.

Barney went down the hall and into his study and crouched next to the cardboard box by his desk. Comfrey was inside, wrapped in a blue towel. Barney put a hand on the material and held it there. It was Deb's birthday today. She was fifty-four. The towel was soft and new and Barney could not believe—could not tolerate—how still it was.

Last year, Deb's sister Irene had taken Deb out for breakfast on her birthday. According to Rita, New Deb had really
enjoyed herself. They'd gone to a cafe along from the Plaza.
Maybe they would be there again now. Barney picked up
the telephone and dialled. His heart raced as he listened
to the ringing tone. Please, he thought. Please. And then,
yes. A wash of relief. The familiar click of the answering
machine. What would he hear? Had she changed it?

Sweet torture, no, she hadn't.

He heard Deb's old voice like a ghost in his ear.

*Hello, you've called Barney, Deborah and Ben. We can't come
to the phone right now but please leave a message after the beep
and one of us will call you back. Bye for now.*

•

'When are you and Joe going to come have dinner with me
and Mickey and the kids?' said Wanda. 'How many times do
I have to invite you?'

'I know,' said Leonie. 'I'm awful.'

'You are awful.'

Wanda and Leonie were on a bench on the Clarke Plaza
terrace in a spot of shade. It was nice to be outdoors after
all the rain, and it wasn't too hot either. Wanda was eating
a wrap with mung bean sprouts in it and Leonie had bought
herself a Hot Bake pie.

'So you were feeling bold at Panda Garden?'

'You would have been proud of me, Lee.'

'And what did Jenny say?'

'Jenny said the police order a lot of Peking-style pork ribs.'

'And?'

'And that the other day one of them thought his soup was cold, so he held up his bowl and yelled at Jenny across the restaurant, "Needs more hot! Needs more hot!"'

'Oh for god's sake,' said Leonie. 'This town.'

'So I asked Jenny what she heard, back in the day. Like, why she thinks Ginny killed herself. And she said that the police go into Panda Garden, and they drink and drink and drink. And then they talk and talk and talk.'

'Ugh.'

'And when Ginny went missing, they were all drunk and so Jenny just asked them straight out.'

'Good on her.'

'Yes,' said Wanda. 'Jenny had read about it in the papers and she was interested and so she asked one of the policemen what was happening with the missing woman, and if they thought they were going to find her. And she said the policeman said, "We don't know if we're going to find her, but we know she topped herself."'

'Bullshit,' said Leonie.

'I know.'

Leonie took a bite of pie. It was inferior to the pie-cart pies, but a fine enough and piping-hot pie. She swallowed and said, 'I can't believe they'd say that.'

'I asked her if she knew the name of the policeman who said it.'

'And did she?'

'No. She said they all look a bit the same.'

Leonie laughed. All she could smell was pie. On the other side of the terrace, the women from the nail salon were sitting together in the sun, and two men in high-vis vests were also eating pies. Even alfresco the smell of the pies was quite oppressive. Leonie felt she should have ordered a salad.

'Jenny said every backroom deal in Clarke is done at Panda Garden.'

'What backroom deals?'

'Like dodgy land deals and all kinds of corruption at council and whatnot.'

'Huh.'

'Apparently your beloved Mayor Simmons was no angel.'

'*No*,' said Leonie. 'Not our Neville.'

Wanda smiled. She said, 'I think they're all just in it up to their necks,' and she set her half-eaten wrap down in her lap and began to peel a boiled egg.

'I can't believe they'd just say, *Oh yes, we know she killed herself.* How could they have *known* Ginny killed herself when they didn't even know where she was? I mean, based on what evidence?'

'Who knows,' said Wanda, who was putting all the pieces of eggshell in a tissue on her lap.

Leonie had burnt her tongue on the pie. She should have ordered a salad. She watched as one of the women from the nail salon took out a packet of Longbeach and offered them around to her co-workers.

Wanda said, 'So you're going to bury the cat?'

'Yes. I've organised to send Joe across to Dorrie's.'

'Poor Barney. Honestly, if I were to lose either of mine I'd be absolutely devastated. They're like my other children, Lee. I adore those cats. Part of me holds on to this feeling that they're immortal.'

'I hate to break it to you,' said Leonie.

'No, I know,' said Wanda, and she bit the top off her boiled egg.

39

When Leonie opened her front door, Barney was standing on her porch with a cardboard box in one arm and a shovel in the other.

'Hi, Barney.'

'Hi, Leonie.'

'Come on in.'

He came on in and set the shovel against the wall, next to Leonie's oak bookshelf. The shovel was so clean it was as if he'd polished it for the occasion. Barney stood in the kitchen, there near the table, holding the box. It was muggy in Leonie's house—she'd sweated up a little storm in her shirt.

'Still a lot of action next door,' she said.

'Apparently it's quite boggy, even with the tarpaulins they had.'

'They haven't found anything more?'

'Not that I've heard. I've taken to hovering in the laundry from time to time so I can listen through the window.'

Leonie went to the counter and switched on the kettle. There was never a question over tea. No matter how hot the weather, it was always tea. She said, 'Tea now, or tea after?'

'Maybe tea after,' said Barney.

'Okay. I just need some water then. Do you want water? It's getting hot all over again. You can put the box on the table if you like.'

'I'll just . . .' Barney held the box as one would hold a flotation device. 'I'll just hold it.'

•

They chose a spot at the far end of Leonie's neat and rather empty yard, as far from Barney's as possible. From where they were, the police activity was largely concealed by the washing on the Hills Hoist. Specifically, Leonie's billowy clothes. The ground was moist. When Barney began to dig, it was not so much dirt but mud that came out, and soon a muddy pile had formed.

Leonie stood by, mostly wordless, an unusual state for her, until she said, 'What was your cat's name?'

'Comfrey.'

'Comfrey?'

'The miracle herb,' said Barney, who was perspiring. And, when Leonie looked baffled, he said, 'My wife was an ardent gardener.'

'Right,' said Leonie. 'Well, as you can see, I'm not. The only thing I grow is chokos and I really don't mean to.'

Barney stopped digging for a moment and wiped his brow with his shirtsleeve, but there was mud on his shirtsleeve which then became mud on his brow.

Leonie said, 'Actually, once I grew a huge tasteless pumpkin.'

Barney had sweat running down the sides of his neck.

'I feel bad because Joe loves gardening,' said Leonie. 'He always wants to do gardening stuff with Clive across the street—he's my friend Dorrie's husband. They have a beautiful garden with fruit trees and vegetables and all sorts of things. Anyway, one of these days I'll have to organise Joe a spot out here so he can plant some seeds of his own.'

'Do you think this is deep enough?' asked Barney, who was very focused on the hole. 'I mean, it's your yard. Do you feel comfortable with this depth?'

Leonie peered at the hole, which looked both deep enough and very unappealing, as far as final resting places go. She could hear several nearby lawnmowers and the sound of the police next door, men's voices. She said, 'I think I'm comfortable.'

'I'll just make it wider.' And Barney dug some more

around the edges, so the hole became a rectangle. 'She was really my wife's cat.'

'But you got her in the divorce?'

'My wife didn't want her anymore.'

'Golly,' said Leonie. 'It sounds like your wife really had a change of heart. On a couple of things.'

Barney appeared to contemplate the hole and deem it finished. He speared the shovel into the turf in a rather manly gesture. His muddy face looked kind of poignant when he said, 'My wife had a traumatic brain injury.'

'Jesus,' said Leonie. 'Barney.'

'Yes, I know,' he said, as they stood there next to the hole and the box.

•

In the kitchen, Leonie stirred a single spoon of sugar into Barney's second cup of tea. She added milk to both mugs. Barney remained seated where he had been for the past half-hour, the cardboard box empty now on the floor beside him.

There was a small pile of books on the table. Barney picked up one of Leonie's several Lonely Planets. It was *South America: includes Chile, Argentina and Easter Island.*

'Are you going on a trip?' he asked.

'Oh, no,' she said. 'I just have some of those for work. Actually, that one was my sister's.'

It just came out—just like that. *It was my sister's.* What was this ease with which she spoke?

'Huh,' said Barney nonchalantly, because how was he to know this was a big deal?

Leonie felt surprisingly comfortable with her new friend. Look at his kind face, with its smudge of dirt. There was something naturally familiar about Barney, and also reassuring. And Leonie really must have felt secure, because she went ahead and said, 'Joe is my sister's too. He's my sister's son.'

'Where's your sister?'

'She died.'

Barney recoiled, like someone had thrown a plate at him. 'Leonie,' he said. 'I'm sorry.'

'So am I,' said Leonie, whose great big heart was racing now. Racing, yet triumphant! *She died. Maurie died.* Leonie had said what she needed to say and she had not shattered into a thousand pieces. She had not collapsed or fainted or perished. Leonie was still Leonie—just the same. Without thinking, she put a hand on her own shoulder and patted herself there. *You're okay, Leonie.*

She picked up her mug of tea, full of relief and pride. 'Anyway. Not to worry.' She raised the mug in the air. 'To Comfrey.'

Barney nodded and raised his mug too. 'To Comfrey.'

They sipped their tea and Leonie said, 'Aren't we a pair?'

40

There was a patch of sun on the front porch. Barney set the empty box in this patch of sun. Comfrey always liked to lie in the sun. Although this was just an empty box now. What would a box care where it was? Barney could hear music playing, the police people had a radio on in the backyard. He opened the screen door and went inside to the sound of 'Dancing Queen' by ABBA.

In the bathroom, Barney took off his dirty clothes. He turned on the shower taps and waited for steam to come. Steam came. He stepped in. He stood under the rush of hot water. Barney was, at this point, desperately sad. He rubbed the soap in his hands and covered himself in a lather. The water ran brown with the mud from Leonie's yard. And Comfrey was just sitting out on the tiles, waiting for him to get out!

No, she wasn't.

Comfrey wasn't there. Deb wasn't there.

Barney closed his eyes.

•

When Deb was still Deb, she had come into the old bedroom one rainy morning, picked up Comfrey from her spot on the bed, and popped her gently on the floor. 'Off you pop,' said Deb.

Barney had been lying under the sheet, fresh from the shower, and Deb had crawled in and leaned towards him in her bed shirt. It was one of his old t-shirts. It looked great on her. His big shirt on her smaller body—although not too small; there was a perfect amount of Deb. It was a green shirt that said *Gather Region Bushwalkers Club: Since 1975* and had the club's emblem: a lyrebird.

Barney had learned from Deb, not *National Geographic*, that lyrebirds displaced an extraordinary amount of soil. A lyrebird spent much of its life shifting soil and leaf litter around the forest floor. Moving soil was their special skill— much like the arctic ground squirrel, or the northern pocket gopher, or Deb with a pitchfork and an ambition to aerate a pile of compost.

Deb had leaned in, in the lyrebird shirt, and Barney had closed his eyes. And when she climbed atop him, in the holey old shirt, the blissful weight of her was like freedom and home.

•

A nurse had led Barney through to the ward. Deb was sleeping. Barney stood beside her bed and he could hear Deb's neighbour—another patient behind the curtain. A man the size of a small cow. The man let out a tremendous groan and a high-pitched fart.

The nurse didn't flinch. She said, 'Deborah was awake for about an hour this morning and she had something to eat.'

Deb looked like a balloon with the air gone out. Everything about her was sunken. And her hair, so grey.

'What did she eat?'

'She had some fruit.'

'Fresh fruit?'

'No, it's peaches in syrup.'

'I'll get her some fresh fruit,' said Barney. 'I'll bring some in tomorrow.'

Never had he felt more helpless. The cow-man behind the curtain made a noise like he was being stabbed. The nurse smelled like antiseptic and had a bruise on the side of her neck.

'Did she say anything?' asked Barney.

'She spoke a little,' said the nurse.

'What did she say?'

'She's still just very confused.'

Barney was so afraid. He got the feeling that the nurse needed to be going on her way to someplace else, but he felt desperate for her to stay.

'Will Dr Prakash be coming around?'

'I'll check,' said the nurse.

Barney read her name tag. He said, 'Thank you, Judy.'

'Not a problem, Mr Clarke.'

•

Barney stood in his new bedroom now, his damp towel strewn on the floor. It was like his mind was separate to his body, the way he had dressed himself and not even noticed. What was he wearing? Just an old shirt, some old shorts. Barney's body was going about its routine. He sat down on the edge of the bed and rested his hand on a patch of cat hair on the blanket.

41

'Hi, sweetie,' yelled Leonie from Dorrie's back deck.

Joe and Clive were in the yard among the fruit trees. Clive had various types of citrus, a fig tree, an olive tree, and something called a feijoa, which produced an oval green fruit that Leonie struggled to enjoy.

'Hi!' said Joe. He was wearing one of Clive's hats. It looked comically large. Clive was crouching before a lime tree, pointing at the leaves, explaining something leaf-related.

'They've been having the best time. I think Joe will go into market gardening,' said Dorrie. 'How was the burial?'

'It was sad,' said Leonie. 'Barney cried.'

'Did he?'

'Just at the end, when he was shovelling the soil back in. He had some tears. And next thing I know, I had some tears too, because I just felt so bad for him. And then I felt like a total imposter, because I never even met the cat.'

'I'm sure Barney appreciated your solidarity.'

'Are you thirsty, Joe? Do you need some water?' Leonie was sort of yelling now. She had her hands on her hips in the glinty afternoon. She stepped back under the deck roof into the shade.

'No!' said Joe.

'We made lemonade earlier,' said Dorrie. 'It's got about a kilo of sugar in it. Do you want some?'

'Sure.'

And the two of them went inside to the kitchen and Leonie sat on a white stool while Dorrie fetched a jug from the fridge.

'I guess today's the last day,' Leonie said.

'The clock's ticking,' said Dorrie.

'I just want to know either way. She's either in there or she isn't. I don't understand why it has to take so long.'

'Because of all the reasons we've discussed about why it's taking this long,' said Dorrie. 'They can't just bring in a bulldozer.'

'No. I know.'

Dorrie set a glass on the benchtop and filled it with lemonade. There were still some ice cubes in the jug and the ice plopped into the glass. 'Guess who I spoke to?'

'Who?'

'Flora McDonald.'

'And?'

'And she had some very interesting information about your old friend Senior Constable Marrel.'

'Ugh.' Leonie felt sick just at the mention of him. She could still see him now—white eyebrows hovering over cold eyes.

'Apparently Senior Constable Mark Marrel has been quietly stood down, hence we haven't seen him. Stood down and living with his parents in Solent Inlet.'

'Why?'

'Because he's been charged with about a hundred counts of assaulting his wife.'

'*No*,' said Leonie.

'Yes,' said Dorrie. She poured herself some lemonade too. There was piano music playing in the living room. Dorrie said, 'He'd been at it for years, apparently, and the wife was terrified of him. They have two boys, and the boys saw all kinds of violent things. Flora said he was only arrested because he dragged the wife down the driveway and smashed her head into the letterbox in broad daylight. And there's the next-door neighbour, pruning her hedges. The neighbour called the police, even though she knew Marrel *was* the police. And the police took Marrel away. But before that, Flora said, the police would tell the wife not to say anything and just to carry on. They'd say, you know, *Cook him a nice dinner. He's really sorry.*'

'Oh, for god's sake,' said Leonie.

289

'But the wife's a solicitor. And she finally decided to press charges. Apparently there's some new police here in Clarke, up the chain, and they're more receptive. So. Marrel's waiting to go to court, and he's in Solent on leave without pay.'

'Where's the wife and kids?'

'I have no idea,' said Dorrie.

Leonie sipped her lemonade, which was cold and sweet and sour. She recalled Senior Constable Marrel at Clarke station, the second time she went up there. Disdain had radiated from his chalky face, like Leonie was just some nuisance woman sent to ruin his day.

'He used to threaten his wife with his police gun, Flora said. Threaten to shoot her and the kids.'

'Jesus.'

Dorrie was leaning forward on the benchtop, next to a cookbook by Marcella Hazan, wearing a navy apron dusty with flour. She said, 'Apparently it's very rare for this to have happened.'

'For a policeman to beat his wife?'

'No, for him to get charged for it.'

'Oh,' said Leonie. 'Right.' She gripped her cold glass. Dorrie's kitchen had begun to smell of pie. The light was on in the oven. It glowed under the benchtop.

Dorrie said, 'No wonder Senior Constable Marrel didn't give two shits about Lou Lawson.'

Leonie shook her head and said, 'He didn't even give one.'

•

On the deck, at the outdoor table, Leonie could see Joe and Clive in front of the shed at the back of the yard. She could see Joe using a little spade, putting soil into a small black pot.

'I've read a bit about that,' said Dorrie. 'People can become different after a head injury.'

'But completely different,' said Leonie. 'Barney said she used to be energetic and thoughtful and warm. That she had this enthusiasm for everything.'

'And then what?'

'Well, that afterwards she became distant and self-absorbed, which she had never been before. And really irritable, like she'd blow up at him over the littlest things. And when she wasn't angry, she was just flat. He said she lost her passion for pretty much everything. Before the accident she was really into gardening, and then she wasn't interested in gardening. She was really outdoorsy, and then she wasn't. They used to go on bushwalks all the time, and then she just didn't want to leave the house anymore.'

'But she wanted Barney to leave the house?'

'Yes, and not come back.'

Dorrie reclined in her chair, her arms folded. 'Poor Barney.'

'I know,' said Leonie. 'Now he doesn't go bushwalking anymore, even though he loved bushwalking. It was this huge part of his life.'

'Well he should go bushwalking again,' said Dorrie. 'Dare I say that he's experienced a loss of coherence in the narrative of his life. He needs to reconnect to those parts of himself. Without her.'

'I love it when you pop out of retirement,' said Leonie. 'And actually that's kind of what I said to him, but less eloquently.'

'And what about the son?'

'We didn't talk about the son. We didn't talk about the son and we didn't talk about how the wife actually got the brain injury. I was that close to asking, but . . .'

'Practising restraint?'

'I hear it's character building.'

Joe was crouching on the grass now in the shade of the shed and Clive was sitting opposite him. They had all these little plastic pots set in rows on a big plastic tray.

Dorrie stared off at the little pots. She said, 'God, that's a sad story.'

'And you know what else Barney said? He said that his wife's hair turned completely grey within four weeks of being in the hospital. Can you believe that? Completely grey.'

'All the colour went out of her,' said Dorrie.

'Exactly,' said Leonie.

●

Barney stood at the kitchen sink and washed Comfrey's bowls. He washed her water bowl and he scrubbed her food bowl, the smears of old dried cat food. He had to scrub it quite hard. It was a white bowl with cat paws printed on it, and relatively expensive, as far as cat bowls go. Barney rinsed it and dried it with a tea towel, and he dried the water dish too. He set them neatly on the bench. Then he went across the tiles and stood on the patio, with the sliding door all the way open.

Detective Sergeant Levins was up near the lemon tree, speaking with one of the forensics officers. The sun was blazing on the yard, and Barney felt he needed to clean the pool. Levins saw him there. He gave a nod and Barney nodded back. Then Levins came down the grass and along the pavers and said, 'We're finishing up.'

'Just like that.'

'It'll take a bit to pack everything down, but we'll be out of your hair in a couple of hours.'

'So you didn't find her.'

'No, we did not.'

Barney stood on the patio. The other policeman, O'Leary, walked across the lawn, past the empty space where the shed used to be, and disappeared down the side path.

'How's your optimism?' asked Barney.

Levins said, 'Ask me that next week and I might have a different answer.'

Barney nodded and tried to look unmoved. What was it to him whether they found Ginny Lawson or not? He had not known her. He was not like Leonie, who had been her friend. And yet the intensity of his disappointment was as surprising as it was overwhelming. They had not found Ginny Lawson and everything was empty and futile. Everything was sad and unfair.

Barney kept nodding, he was like a dashboard figurine. But he didn't want to show his dismay to Detective Sergeant Levins, so he refrained from lying down foetally on the kitchen tiles, which was, oddly, what he felt like doing. Instead, he went over to the bench and retrieved Comfrey's bowls and he handed them over.

'Thanks,' said Detective Sergeant Levins. 'Appreciate it.'

'I don't know what else to do with them,' said Barney.

•

The first thing that Leonie noticed was fewer police cars. There were only two now. Leonie and Joe were coming hand in hand across the street as a policeman was loading white plastic chairs into a van in Barney's driveway. The young one, the police guard, was not in his position. Leonie did not know what to think about this absence of guard.

Joe said, 'There's Barney.'

Leonie looked up and yes, there was Barney, on his front porch in the summer evening light. He was speaking to a policeman, and then the policeman went down the front steps and around the side path towards the backyard. Leonie could see Barney's cardboard cat coffin on the porch, and that Barney had changed his clothes and washed his face.

Joe flapped his tiny hand. 'Hi, Barney!'

Barney smiled and said, 'Hi, Joe,' and then he looked at Leonie and shook his head and Leonie just knew exactly what that meant.

She nodded. And she would have expected to feel something, surely, but she felt nothing at all. *Ginny's not there.* Everything on earth slowed down around Leonie, but she continued walking at normal speed. *Ginny's not there.* Joe swung himself around the pole of the carport. Barney was standing stiff and helpless on his porch.

'Tomatoes are a fruit,' said Joe.

Leonie spoke loudly, across the lawn, and her voice sounded so strange and distant, like she was hearing an echo of herself. She said, 'I'll talk to you tomorrow, Barney.'

42

When tomorrow came, Leonie woke up too early and stared at the ceiling fan. She counted the rotations and lost count. She thought about Ginny, while trying very hard not to think about Ginny. She picked up her shame book and read numbly. Three pages later and she had comprehended nothing at all. The dawn was in the curtains; a little glow was there. And the house was so quiet when Joe was sleeping. She could only hear lorikeets and the bedside clock, which unfortunately said 5.40 am. Leonie wanted to close her eyes and sleep forever. But, no, no. She couldn't do that. She got up and set the book on the bedside table.

Leonie went down the hallway. Everything, so still. It was such a rarity for her to be up before Joe. It seemed like, in the mornings, Joe was always awake. The instant his eyes opened, he was up and talking. There was no slow rousing for Joe.

Leonie opened the back door and went outside where it was almost cool. On one side, Barney's fence. On the other side, a patch of disturbed soil where Barney had buried his cat. What was the cat's name again? Something to do with herbs. She walked barefoot across the trim lawn to the fence and looked over into Barney's yard. Into *Ginny's* yard.

The police equipment was all dismantled and gone. The place where the shed and concrete had been was just an empty space. Leonie looked at the large square of exposed earth. She looked at the area near the washing line, where some dirty turf had been plopped back on top like an afterthought. At the spot next to the lemon tree, where they hadn't even bothered to do that.

Leonie held the palings. What a fool she was. She had been absolutely certain that Ginny was under that concrete. For six years, she'd thought she could sense the nearness of her friend. This had been Leonie's most powerful intuition, even though she didn't really believe in intuition—and she shouldn't have believed in intuition, obviously, because Ginny wasn't there.

•

A knock came early, around eight.

Leonie thought: Dorrie? Barney?

She was standing at the sink, washing the breakfast bowls. Joe was in his room. She took off her rubber gloves, rested them on the counter and went across to the door. At least Barney's cat couldn't have died *again*, was what she thought.

A very tall policeman was standing on the mat next to another, regular-sized policeman. She recognised both these men. They had been next door for days. The tall one was the man in charge. Leonie knew, from Barney, that his name was Levins.

'Oh,' said Leonie.

'Good morning, Ms Wallace.'

'Hello.'

'I'm Detective Sergeant Levins. This is Senior Constable O'Leary. I'm sure you've noticed that we've been doing a bit of a search next door.'

'Have you?' said Leonie.

Levins smiled. There were crinkles around his eyes. He looked older close up, like someone's grandpa, and actually rather dignified. 'Would you mind if we asked you some questions?'

'Now you want to ask me questions?'

'I know you've given a statement in the past. And I am aware that there has been some frustration in the community over the lack of developments in this particular case.'

'Yes,' said Leonie. 'I think you'll find some people took a dim view of it.'

'I understand that, Ms Wallace. But we're reinterviewing several people, yourself included. I want to impress on you that this is a new investigation.'

Joe appeared at Leonie's side. He grabbed hold of the synthetic material of her work trousers. She felt the tug of him. She said, 'To be honest, it takes a lot to impress me these days.'

Levins looked down at Joe and back at Leonie and said, 'If now's not a good time, perhaps you could come down to the station.'

'When would you like me to do that?'

'At your earliest convenience.'

'Well then, I'll come this afternoon.'

'How's four thirty?'

'Four thirty is just fine,' said Leonie.

Detective Sergeant Levins nodded, and the other one just stood there on the porch, looking blankly at the bucket where Leonie kept umbrellas.

Then the policemen left and Leonie closed the door, and she stood stunned on the linoleum. Joe held her trousers. He wrapped his arm around her leg. She barely noticed he was still there until he began to cry.

'Sweetheart.' Leonie crouched down and Joe looked to the floor. She took his face in her hands. She looked steadily at him and saw the tears fall down his cheeks and onto his shirt. 'What's the matter?'

Joe said, 'Are you going to jail?'

'Oh, honey,' said Leonie. 'Oh, sweetheart. No, I'm not going to jail. I'm not going anywhere.'

43

Next door, Barney woke late and spent a long time lying in. He was never one to lie in. There was always something to get up for. He had to feed Comfrey. Or Deb would have needed her morning tablets, and his assistance to do her dreaded physio exercises in the sunroom. When she first came home from Clarke Base, she needed help to dress and to pee.

Before the accident, Deb would have been padding around softly in her batik robe, listening to the ABC, making a stovetop pot of coffee. Barney stared at Deb's old armchair in the corner, and the patch of fabric that looked lighter than the rest of the chair, where he had cleaned off Comfrey's excrement.

He sat up and put his bare feet on the floor. Down the hall, through the kitchen, Barney opened the sliding door and looked at his destroyed lawn. It was strange to leave the back door wide open behind him, but he did, and he wandered out onto the mud and dirt. A dog barked, somewhere nearby. And closer by, he heard noises from Leonie's house, some indistinct movement inside. The earth was cool under his feet. His lawn looked like fifty lyrebirds had been let loose there to displace it. Barney squeezed some mud between his toes. Then he inspected every dig site methodically, taking in every patch of loose turf. And after he was satisfied that there was absolutely nothing of interest to see, he used the long blue-handled scoop to clear the myriad leaves from the pool.

•

On the highway, Barney drove slowly and recited in his head the stages of decomposition: *fresh, bloat, active decay, advanced decay, skeletonisation.* For no particular reason, he went the long way to town, over the bridge, where the river below was brown and flowing faster after the rain. Barney saw a pied cormorant. He saw a pelican. He felt absolutely terrible, like he wanted to submerge himself deep in the water.

Perhaps Ginny Lawson's body was in the river! This thought occurred to him as a revelation. But why would she be in the river any more than she would be in his yard? Barney couldn't think clearly. Perhaps the absence of Ginny's body had become an absence in himself? A new absence, a new emptiness, which sat on top of the hole that Deb had left, and the hole that Ben had left—and now even Comfrey too. Barney tried to focus on something else. He silently conjugated the verb 'to submerge' in French.

Je submerge, tu submerges, il submerge.

Nearing the McDonald's, Barney realised he was driving behind Helen Last. God, Helen had had that Sigma forever. He could see the faded sticker on the bumper: *Royal National Park Centenary, 1879–1979.*

Helen's indicator came on. She was going to the McDonald's. Which meant Barney would certainly not risk going to the McDonald's and being seen by Helen Last. He watched her turn in and glide towards her regular spot. Barney kept driving, pointlessly—where would he go now? He pulled over outside the newsagent. He sat in his car and turned off the engine and almost as soon as the air conditioning stopped the car became unbearably hot. Barney got out and wandered along the pavement. He was thirsty, or hungry. Actually, he hadn't had breakfast. He should buy something substantial for dinner. A few shops along there was a butcher, Noble Meats, which Barney had never set foot in in his life. Deb had been such a committed vegetarian that the only time Barney ate meat was when they went to the Bowlo, or when they were camping with the club and someone brought sausages.

Noble Meats was written on the window in the font of a western saloon. Barney pushed on the glass door, which made a bell ring, announcing his arrival. This bell embarrassed him. And the meat smell confronted him. What an unfamiliar smell raw meat was. A woman was ordering a bag of chicken necks. Who would want to eat the necks of multiple chickens?

'You're Barney, aren't you?'

The butcher was bald and familiar.

'I am.'

'I'm Clive. I live across the street.'

'So you do.'

'What can I get for you?'

Barney said automatically, 'Just a scotch fillet.'

There were pig carcasses hanging beyond a door that led to the rear of the shop. Clive put the steak in a plastic bag, and the plastic bag in a paper bag, which said *Noble Meats* in the saloon font. Barney watched the bag go into the bag. He thought of an *item of clothing*, covered in dirt.

'I'm a good friend of Leonie's,' said Clive.

'Ah,' said Barney. 'Well, it's a bit quieter this week on our side of the street.'

'To our great disappointment,' said Clive, and he winked. What did that wink mean? Barney would never wink. Maybe some people just winked? Clive grinned and turned his head slightly and looked beyond Barney and said, 'What can I get for you?'

The chicken neck woman had left, and another woman was waiting to be served, somewhere over Barney's shoulder. Barney stepped aside, holding his bag. The doorbell rang again.

'Barney?'

Hell, it was Helen Last, holding an enormous drink.

'I thought that was you. What a coincidence.'

Don't say the reason it's a coincidence, thought Barney.

'Because I saw Ben just now at McDonald's,' said Helen Last.

'You did,' said Barney. His face was, just now, very cold.

'I'm ashamed to admit that I've become completely addicted to these strawberry thickshakes. I can't help myself. I try to drive past the McDonald's and I think, *No, Helen, not today.* And the next thing I know, I've swerved in and I'm parking. They must put drugs in these things.' Helen took a thick sip and swallowed. 'I'm so glad to see you, Barney. Phil and I talk about you a lot. We so wish you'd come back to the club.'

'Oh,' said Barney. 'I don't know about that, Helen.'

'Barn,' said Helen, 'I know we've been through this, but I've been thinking maybe you just need a little push.'

'I don't think I do.'

'But after everything you've been though, it'd just be so good for you. Remember the fun we used to have? Rae's leading Sunday week, if you're interested. We're doing Wibung Creek. Why don't you just *come*?'

Barney was holding the paper bag against his thigh. He began to notice the coldness of that too, of the raw meat in there. And his neck, so cold. Barney thought of the stage of decomposition known as 'bloat'.

'We're just putting together the autumn program actually,' said Helen. 'There's going to be an overnight hike in the Royal.'

Barney saw an image of Deb unzipping their old two-man tent and crawling in. They were so real to him, these visions. He even smelled wood smoke, just before he fainted.

44

'So she's just not there,' said Wanda.

'She was never there,' said Varden.

'No,' said Leonie. 'It appears she's not there.'

Pat, who was sitting over at her desk in the front window, looked up and said, 'What an anticlimax.'

'So what do the police have to discuss with you then?' asked Varden. 'That she might be in *your* yard?'

Leonie gave Varden a look and said, 'I really don't know. They just said they want to ask me some more questions. I mean, at least they're asking questions.'

'Can they charge someone with murder without a body?' asked Wanda.

'I don't think they can,' said Varden. 'I think they need a body.'

Varden was playing his favourite album, *Kef Time Fresno*, which he'd dubbed tirelessly from vinyl to cassette. And a fly was hovering above Varden's head. Leonie watched the fly. It was lolling in big uneven circles. Strange, for a fly to be here, in a shop inside the Plaza.

Leonie looked at Varden now and said, 'What about Lindy Chamberlain?'

'Hmm,' said Varden. 'That's true.'

'Not a great advertisement for charging someone with murder without a body, though,' said Wanda.

'That's also true,' said Varden.

'I'm just not instilled with a feeling of trust in our justice system,' said Leonie.

'That reminds me,' said Varden. 'If the Hamiltons come in asking about accom, that new Red Centre Hotel at Ayers Rock is doing a two-night special.'

●

A woman was speaking to Barney as he lay on a stretcher bed in a makeshift camp at Wibung Creek. There was a coolish breeze there by the water. Moss grew on the rocks at the silty bottom. Barney was looking forward to a charred sausage wrapped in soft white bread.

The woman said, 'He's had the most terrible time.'

Barney was coming to. He was nowhere near the creek. He was on a floor of cold grey tiles, looking sideways at someone's shoes.

'His wonderful wife—Deborah—she was in an accident and she had a brain injury that changed her whole personality.'

Barney looked up at Helen Last. He squinted at a long fluorescent light on a beige ceiling.

The butcher/his neighbour, Clive, said, 'Here he is. You okay there, Barney?'

'Barney, can you tell me who the prime minister is?' said Helen.

'Bob Hawke.'

'He's okay,' said Clive.

Barney sat up and looked around.

'Take your time,' said Helen, who smelled syrupy, like fruit left in a hot car.

The woman who had been standing near him—before, at the counter—was now crouching beside him. She was a middle-aged woman who seemed unremarkable, except that her eyes were the colour of grass and she was taking Barney's pulse. A damp cloth that had been applied to his forehead fell into his lap.

This must be the bottom—of the creek, the river, the lake. He thought, I must have reached the bottom.

Helen said, 'Do you want a sip of my thickshake, Barney? It's full of sugar. Maybe drugs too, but definitely sugar.'

45

*H*eadquarters of the Police District of the Gather Region and South Coast. Leonie walked up the brief slope towards the enormous concrete building. The Clarke Police Station seemed built to intimidate—or built to be ugly? Two storeys of concrete and bricks and darkly tinted windows, it looked like several squares plonked together to make one big rectangle.

Joe liked to watch reruns of a space cartoon called *Voltron*, in which robot lions joined together to form one big robot. This building reminded Leonie of the big robot, but in a hostile way. She pushed the glass door open and went warily to the desk, where a policewoman was writing on a thick form with a biro. This woman was so pale, she had not an eyebrow to speak of. She could be Marrel's sister, thought Leonie. The whole building could be crawling with Marrels.

'Can I help you?'

'I'm here to see Detective Levins.'

'Detective *Sergeant* Levins.'

'Whatever his name is,' said Leonie, who was in no mood.

'Your name, please?'

'Leonie Wallace.'

Two other officers were sitting at desks behind the counter, busy-looking with their paperwork. The whitest policewoman on earth disappeared through a mysterious side door that Leonie remembered from last time—it led to mysterious side rooms. A floor fan spun noisily. The place needed air conditioning. Leonie had read about this in the newspaper: the calls for an upgrade for the station, which was described in the article as both too hot and too cold.

The policewoman reappeared and gestured to a row of plastic chairs along a fawn-coloured wall. She spoke in an unpunctuated monotone: 'He's just on a call he won't be long take a seat.'

•

Helen Last found a window table at the Crispy Biscuit and ordered Barney into a chair. He sat down unsteadily. The cafe was right next door to the butcher and Helen had hoisted him in like an injured hiker.

Barney was fatally embarrassed. 'This is not necessary, Helen. I'm fine.'

'Barney, ten minutes ago you were unconscious. What will you have to eat?'

'I don't know if I'm hungry.'

'Hello there,' said Helen to the waitress, who was hugely pregnant. 'Can we get some raisin toast and an orange juice? And I'll just have a black tea with milk. Do you have Earl Grey?'

'We have English breakfast.'

'That'll do,' said Helen.

Barney sat framed in the window signage. *The Crispy Biscuit*, backwards on the glass, curved like a rainbow. The waitress wrote their order with some kind of novelty pen—it was a plastic macaw, but also a pen—and Barney felt an urge to reach out and touch her belly. He remembered when Deb was so pregnant it felt impossible, and yet she kept becoming more and more pregnant, until Ben was finally born. Rivers were often described as 'swollen' after a lot of rain.

The back of Barney's head throbbed. The room smelled of fried bacon. And the bacon smelled absolutely delicious. Barney wondered if he had ever been this hungry.

The waitress went across the room to another table.

'They actually do a nice focaccia,' said Helen.

'Are their biscuits crispy?' asked Barney.

Helen smiled and said, 'You know, I've been here a few times, and they never have any biscuits.'

•

In a side room which was bland and not at all mysterious, Detective Sergeant Levins sat opposite Leonie in a plastic chair. This was not the same side room she'd been in six years ago, with Senior Constable Marrel, but it was that room's twin. She had noticed a number of doors off the brightly-lit corridor. Perhaps all these side rooms were exactly the same.

Here was Leonie and Levins. Here was a dictaphone and a notepad. Leonie couldn't tell if she'd been there for twenty minutes or twenty seconds, such was the way that the stress of it all affected her sense of time. And was it just the stress? No, it was many things. Excitement, grief, strangeness to the point of it all feeling like a dream.

'And do you recall whether the residents of nineteen Calboonya Avenue had any pets?'

'Ginny had a dog.'

'What kind of dog?'

'A dachshund.'

'A sausage dog.'

'Yes, Peaches.'

'And do you remember what happened to Peaches?'

'Yes, I remember that Peaches went missing. Supposedly. This is what Ginny told me at the time. She said that the gate got left open by accident and Peaches ran away. I suggested to her that we put up posters and go doorknocking and that sort of thing, but Ginny didn't want to. She said she'd called both the vets, and that she was just going to wait until someone handed Peaches in. Which they did not do.'

'I see,' said Levins, who was writing left-handedly on a pad. His right hand was resting on the table, next to Leonie's original statement, a typed document from 1985.

'You found Peaches, didn't you?'

Levins looked up and said, 'We found the remains of a dog.'

'Did the dog you found have its skull bashed in?'

Levins gazed across the table impassively. 'The dog we found had sustained injuries.'

'I knew it,' said Leonie.

•

When Barney's raisin toast arrived, it was already buttered and had, for a garnish, a sprig of parsley and a Mintie.

'Rita said you had a nice night at the Bowlo.'

'Yes, we did,' said Barney. 'It was nice.' He sipped orange juice through a straw, his hand around the plastic bottle. This orange juice, at this moment, was the best thing Barney had ever tasted. He could feel it reviving him from within. He could feel himself coming up from the bottom of the murky river, of the silty lake.

'It's good for you to get out,' said Helen. 'You need to see people.'

Barney ate a piece of the thick buttered toast in three bites. He was ravenous. When had he last eaten? Last night? Barney swallowed. He said boldly, 'Helen, how is she?'

'Rita? She's fine.'

'I don't mean Rita.'

Helen looked at Barney like he was behind glass in a zoo. An animal—perhaps a macaw—trapped and alone and away from its natural habitat. She said, 'Oh, Barney.'

'Tell me. I can handle it.'

Helen sighed and said, 'She's okay. She's how she is now. She's very different. Seeing her can be hard, and I know Rita finds it hard. But I see her and we have a chat and she's actually very funny. It's so weird because Deb has always been funny, and now she's funny again, but in a totally different way. She cracks up Irene. You should see Irene laughing at Deb's jokes. And Irene's there and I think she's doing a good job. But Deb's not like she used to be, as you know. She doesn't care about the same things. I mean, obviously.' She put her hand out, gesturing at Barney. 'Case in point.'

'I was so distracted,' said Barney. 'I keep thinking about how distracted I was back then. I mean, before the accident. I don't know what I thought was so important.'

'Ah, yes,' said Helen. 'Are you having a good time beating yourself up?'

'Not really.'

'Do you want me to slap you? Because you sound like you might need it.' Helen lifted her teabag out of the cup and set it on a saucer and it leaked a pool around it the colour of the lake.

Barney sucked on the straw till the bottle was empty. He said, 'Where's Ben living?'

'In one of those crappy fibro places near the uni. He loves it. Deb says it has no insulation and they'll freeze in winter and boil in summer, but I think it's definitely better for him to be out of the house. Deborah agrees. She's still able to be a decent mother, I think, in some ways. She certainly wants what's best for him.'

'He's with the girl from his work?'

'Yes, Tara. Tiny little thing. She makes a good strawberry thickshake.' Helen laughed.

'Okay,' said Barney. 'Okay.' He wanted the waitress to bring him more toast and juice. He unwrapped the Mintie and put it in his mouth and found it impossibly chewy.

'It's better this way,' said Helen. 'You not seeing her. Especially the way it was in the end, with all that anger she has. I mean, Deb of all people. Who could've expected that anger?'

Barney looked down at the sprig of parsley on his crumby plate.

Helen said, 'I feel terrible for you, Barney, but I say this as your friend, as well as being her friend: You have to try to move on. You have to get back to having a life. A new life.

See your friends again, come walk with us again. You have to start living again.'

Barney nodded and sucked on the Mintie, holding it against the inside of his cheek.

'What else are you going to do?' said Helen Last. 'Sit around forever, wishing things were different? There's no point in that. That gorgeous light Deb had inside her? That light's gone out, Barn. You have to let her go.'

•

Detective Sergeant Levins reached down and retrieved something from the floor. It had been sitting down there, next to the leg of his chair: a large paper bag. He took something out of the bag and set it on the table in front of Leonie, and Leonie felt like someone had knocked the breath out of her.

'Do you recognise this?'

In a clear plastic bag there was an orange cardigan with flowers embroidered on it, all covered in dirt. The dirt was of several different shades. Black dirt, pale clay dirt, red dirt; was that blood? Leonie had a flash of memory, of Ginny sitting at Leonie's kitchen table. Ginny was drinking hot tea and laughing—and she had laughed so much, and the tea was so hot, Ginny had to take off her cardigan.

Leonie looked at the plastic bag and her eyes covered over with tears. She said, 'Yes.'

'From where?'

Leonie blinked. Tears fell out and hit the table. She wiped her eyes with the back of her hand. 'It was Ginny's.'

'You're sure?'

'I'm positive.'

46

At the end of the bushy cul-de-sac, at the base of the inland mountain, Barney stood in front of the big sign that displayed information about the walking tracks. The Birrung Track, the Mountain Walk, the Waterfall Ring Track, the various fire trails that were marked only by numbers. Barney looked at the large map and the illustrations of notable flora and fauna. He scanned the list of 'viewing opportunities'. He had viewed at all of these opportunities. He had walked all these walks. Under the subheading SAFETY, he read: *Darkness descends quickly. Ensure you allow adequate time to complete your walk in good light.*

Barney was headachy and tired. He would drive home in a minute. He'd just felt this compulsion to come and look at the leafy dirt track that disappeared off into the bush. He had not returned here since the day of the accident. This was the place he had been. The earthy damp smell was so familiar it overwhelmed him. Barney closed his eyes and remembered how Deb had pulled the old Subaru into this spot in the early morning. He remembered how he had packed enough food and water for eight hours—to get the most out of the day.

•

'Do you need another minute?' asked Detective Sergeant Levins.

'No, I'm fine,' said Leonie.

'Would you like some more water?'

Leonie sighed. He was very courteous, this Detective Sergeant Levins. Leonie was fighting the urge to respect him. 'No,' she said. 'I'm fine.' She looked at the plastic cups on the metal table. They held a small amount of water. Levins had disappeared for a moment and then reappeared with this scant offering of hydration.

'Before we finish up, I just want to know if you can remember anything else about the days before Mrs Lawson went missing.'

'Before?'

'Yes.'

Leonie's eyes darted upwards and around. The ceiling was textured and grey. She saw a small wall-mounted camera. She noticed she was tapping her foot on the floor and wondered how long she'd been doing that for.

'Well, it was rainy around that time.'

Levins wrote this down. 'Okay. What about the day before? May the seventh?'

'Oh god, I don't remember the day before.'

'You've said the last time you saw Mrs Lawson was on May the fifth, which was three days before Mr Lawson reported her missing. Is it unusual that you wouldn't have seen her for three days, given she was your friend and she lived next door?'

'No. Ginny kept to herself a lot—or Lou kept her to *himself*. I work full time. Sometimes we just wouldn't see each other. Also, it'd been raining, so she and Tobias wouldn't have been out in the yard. I would often chat to her over the fence when they were in the yard, when Lou was at work or when he was off fishing or hunting. Or Ginny and Tobias might come over for a cup of tea at those times, when Lou was fishing or hunting.'

'Is it your opinion that Mr Lawson spent a lot of time at Grant's Lake?'

'Yes. He spent a lot of time fishing and a lot of time hunting.'

'You said in your original statement that you didn't believe Ginny would have gone off for a day shopping at the Plaza.'

'No, because she always had Tobias with her. Always. They went walking or to the playground or on the bus to the library—stuff like that. But shopping was not a thing Ginny could do, because Lou was so controlling about money.

He was like that about everything. She didn't have her own car. She wasn't to drive Lou's Land Rover. It might have looked like Ginny was taken care of, because Lou bought her those show-offy things, like her jewellery and dresses, but he wouldn't let her have her own money.'

Levins appeared completely unmoved, like he'd heard it all before, which he had, because he had Leonie's old statement there on the table. He wrote down one sentence, which Leonie could not make out. She could see the tiny tape in the dictaphone, though. The reels were rolling slowly around.

'I guess I'm just wondering, given your proximity, if you might have seen or heard anything else out of the ordinary. Or something that might seem unusual in retrospect. Night-time, daytime, anything unusual.'

'It was unusual that your colleagues didn't do a proper search of the property. They might have had a look around inside the house, but I never saw them in the yard. Gerry over the back fence, he never saw them in the yard. They never searched the yard.'

'I have in your original statement your information about the addition of the concreted area and the disturbance of the landscape near the fence line.'

'My neighbour Clive made a statement about that too. Clive Little. I know he came up here.'

'Yes, he did,' said Levins. 'I think the reasoning at the time was that the landscaping was due to the sale of the property.'

'Which is what Lou said. But now you've found Peaches and a cardigan.'

Levins picked up his white plastic cup, which looked tiny in his hand, like a child's cup. It held just a mouthful of water and Levins drank this mouthful. He looked at Leonie with no expression, but Leonie could sense his expectation that she should produce some new memory out of nowhere. Or was it her expectation? She couldn't tell.

She said, 'I don't remember anything else. I don't know what you're asking for, specifically, but I feel like I said it all back in 1985.'

'Okay,' said Levins. He closed his notebook. He backed his chair out so it made a most unpleasant scraping sound on the concrete floor. 'I think that's everything then.'

Leonie wanted to snuggle up next to her mother. She wanted to be under a blanket on Eunice's old settee, watching *Columbo*.

'Just one more thing,' she said. 'I know you've been talking to Earl Banovic again. Word gets around pretty fast. I know your colleague, Senior Constable Marrel, thought Earl was a great suspect for a hot minute, back in the day. But the more time you waste on Earl Banovic, the more time Lou Lawson spends walking around on bail for assault instead of in jail for murder.'

Levins stood up. A giraffe of a man. He said, 'I wouldn't worry about that, Ms Wallace. Mr Banovic is not a suspect. He's a witness.'

47

On the old settee at Eunice's, Leonie had liked the crochet blanket that Aunty Iris had knitted. She always chose Aunty Iris's blanket. Eunice preferred the cheap throw from Fosseys and never had a kind word to say about Aunty Iris. Come to think of it, Eunice didn't have a kind word to say about many people. Come to think of it, Eunice seemed almost thrilled to deliver the news that Verna Swan had a herniated disc and wouldn't be joining them.

Eunice had had too many sherries, which meant two. She said, regarding the episode of *Columbo* they were watching on the wood-panelled television, 'They're all wearing such terrible wide ties. Men's neck ties used to be wider, didn't they?'

'I don't think I notice men's ties,' said Leonie.

'Why is this creepy guy helping the other guy?'

Leonie said, 'We've seen this one before. He's the police commissioner and he's helping his friend who's strangled his wife. He's making it look like a burglary, because then the police commissioner kills his own wife, for the inheritance, and makes it look like the same burglar. So he's really helping himself.'

'It's coming back to me,' said Eunice. She was in her recliner, the one that ended up at Sunset Gardens. The hall light was on behind her, silhouetting her poetically. She said, 'That's too obvious. Who turns the sheets down in preparation before they go to bed? It looks totally staged.'

'Don't think Columbo's not going to notice that.'

Ad break. Leonie stared at the television and wanted a packet of Ruffles.

'You know, Joanne's son Rod just got a job at the disposal store in the Plaza.'

'So?' said Leonie.

'So, you know.'

'No, I do not know.'

'He's a nice man,' said Eunice. 'Joanne said he's lost a lot of weight.'

'I'm not interested in Rod, Mum.'

'Joanne just thinks you two might hit it off. Rod's put all that stuff behind him, you know. He's making a fresh start. And he really didn't mean to start that fire. He just flicked his cigarette into the bush and didn't realise.'

'Mum.'

Eunice set her silly crystal sherry glass on the coffee table. It was part of a silly set of two. Eunice had spent over one hundred dollars on two small glasses. *Never in her life* had Eunice seen such beautiful craftsmanship. Leonie couldn't care less if a glass said 'Waterford'.

The ads finished and *Columbo* came back on. The original wife-killer was speaking to the future wife-killer on a telephone at a bar. Staring at the television, Leonie assumed a look of deep concentration in an attempt to ward off Eunice's inevitable next move.

'Lee, I just don't get it. You can't just have one failed relationship and then give up for the rest of your life. Come on. There are thirteen thousand people in Clarke. Surely you can find one man.'

Leonie didn't look away from the screen. She hoisted up dear old Aunty Iris's blanket so it covered her chest. She said, 'I'm not looking for one.'

'It's my fault, isn't it?' said Eunice. 'It has to be.'

'What do you mean?'

'I mean I thought at least Maureen would have found someone by now. She's thirty-seven! I think we all know I can forget about grandchildren.' Eunice looked down at her lap, at the cheap pink throw. 'I'm sorry, Lee. Sometimes I think I've been such a dud.'

'Oh, Mum,' said Leonie wearily. Her guilt was like an arrow. 'You're not a dud.'

•

As Leonie drove back from the police station, towards the Plaza, she felt as though she'd just emerged from a cave. The day was too bright. The sky too blue and cloudless. It wasn't often that Leonie drove alone and, when she caught sight of Joe's empty car seat in the rear-view mirror, she was struck by a sick feeling in the pit of her belly. She had forgotten Joe! She had left him somewhere unattended!

But, no. Joe was *fine*. She would be at the preschool in ten minutes and she would pick him up.

Leonie was approaching Clarke Stockfeeds. She glanced left at pallets and hay bales. Stacks of timber posts. What was she supposed to remember, *before* Ginny went missing? It had been raining, she remembered that. It had been a very rainy week. And actually the last time Leonie had gone to Ginny's house was just a couple of weeks before she vanished. Lou was in Queensland with the hunting club, and Leonie had offered to sit with Tobias so Ginny could have a nap.

That Ginny accepted had astonished Leonie. Ginny was such an uncomplaining person. But Ginny accepted, and Leonie had walked up that neat lawn where Ginny had her rose bushes. Up the steps and onto the porch. She had knocked and heard the *thud thud thud* of sweet Tobias running up the hall.

And then Ginny had opened the door, all tired smiles and loose hairdo. Tobias at her ankles. She said, 'Leonie, you're a lifesaver.'

Leonie turned now, onto Colonial Road. The big statue in Clarke Park was gleaming in the sun, and, as always, covered in the shit of a hundred birds. Leonie had the strangest thoughts sometimes. For instance, right now, this is what she wanted to do: she wanted to pick up Joe from preschool and go over to her old family home where Eunice would be waiting, and then all three of them would get under blankets together and watch television and everything would be just *fine*.

48

Later that afternoon, under a flawless sky, Leonie stood on Ginny's old porch again. It really was a bizarre feeling. Standing there, in the place where Ginny used to come and go. Leonie peered around to see what was the same and what was different. And really, she could barely remember. She'd only been over to Ginny and Lou's a handful of times. But the front door was definitely the same, the screen door was the same, the paint was the same blue. Leonie knocked, and then she stood back on the wooden boards, between Joe and Dorrie.

The three of them stood in a row and waited. The sound of footsteps emanated from within. And then Barney appeared in a pair of shorts and an old green shirt with a lyrebird on it.

'Oh,' said Barney. 'Hello, everyone.'

'Hi, Barney,' said Leonie.

'Hi, Barney, we've met once before. I'm Dorothy. I live with Clive across the street.'

'Of course. Hello.'

'I brought your steak,' said Dorrie, who was clutching a paper bag from Noble Meats. 'You left it at the shop.'

'Right,' said Barney.

Leonie had expected Barney to look awful, but he didn't look awful at all. He looked partly embarrassed and partly amused. Also, freshly showered and ten years younger.

'Hi, Barney,' said Joe.

'How are you, Joe?'

Joe said, 'Dorrie made you eleven biscuits.'

●

Inside Barney's plain kitchen, Leonie sat at the dining table and Joe sat on her lap and Dorrie insisted on making tea.

'No, you sit down, Barney,' said Dorrie. 'You just relax.'

'I really am fine. I think I just hadn't eaten.'

'Well, have a biscuit,' said Leonie.

Barney took a chocolate-chip biscuit from Dorrie's metal biscuit tin, which sat in the centre of his table. Leonie let Joe take a biscuit, and then Leonie took a biscuit. The kitchen was entirely different to how Ginny had it. Ginny had it exceptionally neat, but homey. It was always homey. This kitchen was like a display kitchen in an appliance shop.

'This kitchen is very intuitively organised,' said Dorrie, pouring boiling water into a mug. She set the kettle down and put the red Twinings box back in a cupboard, and she opened the bare white fridge, which had no magnets on it at all.

Where were they? That's right: 'So anyway, yes, Lou's out on bail,' said Leonie. 'And Tobias is with Janice's family. Did I tell you that, Dor?'

'You did.'

'Which I was relieved about, obviously,' said Leonie.

'And what about the children Lou and Janice had together?' asked Barney.

'Levins said they're all with Janice's family, which is to say somewhere in Queensland.'

'Right.'

'Levins is the tallest man I've ever met,' said Leonie.

'And he's very interested in exotic cats,' said Barney.

Joe did not appear to be listening to any of this. He was kicking one foot up and down and looking around the room, holding a portion of biscuit.

'Where are your things?' asked Joe.

'Joe . . .' said Leonie. She put her chin on his head, her arms wrapped around his middle.

Barney looked at Joe and said, 'What things?'

'Your stuff,' said Joe.

'Well. Most of my stuff is still in boxes. I should probably start unpacking all my boxes at some point, do you think?'

'I think so,' said Joe.

•

Outside, Joe walked up the slight slope of lawn and held on to the pool fence, peering in.

'Jesus, they really did a number on this yard,' said Dorrie.

Leonie stood next to her friend, under the awning. She said, 'What about up along the back fence, behind the pool?'

'Yes, and that whole section in front of where the shed was,' said Dorrie, pointing. 'It doesn't look like they even touched that section.'

'They didn't,' said Barney. 'I mean, it's not hard to see the bits they touched.'

'I wish now that they didn't pay so much attention to what Clive and I said about the concrete and the lemon tree. I wish they'd just dug up the entire thing so we could be sure that she's not just, I don't know—*there*.' Leonie was pointing to a patch of undisturbed grass.

'They dragged the radar over the whole yard, though,' said Barney.

'Maybe the radar can give a false negative,' said Leonie. 'Or a false positive, as it were. Or they might never have dug at all.'

'Yes, I wonder what the radar actually showed,' said Dorrie.

'You know where the radar didn't go?' said Barney.

'Where's that?' said Leonie.

'Under the house. There's a good amount of clearance under the house. They sent some guys under there, but not with the radar. I thought about it just earlier. I was thinking, Well, how can they tell if something's buried under the house just by looking at the topsoil?'

'They can't,' said Dorrie, shaking her head. 'Surely they can't.'

Joe was making his way slowly around the perimeter of the pool, holding on to the fence bars one by one, letting one go and grabbing another.

'Shall we?' said Leonie.

'Sure,' said Barney.

And so Leonie called to Joe: 'Joe, we're going around the side here to have a look under the house.'

Joe nodded. He had reached the shade of the big eucalyptus tree that hung over the pool. Barney had scooped so many leaves out of that pool and yet now there were more leaves, there in the pool.

Barney led the way around the back of the house to the side path, and Leonie and Dorrie followed.

Leonie said, 'I've never even seen this side of the house.'

Then the three of them crouched down on the path, peering into the dark, where there was enough space to crawl all the way to the other side, where the light came in. Barney could just see the base of Leonie's paling fence.

And what was there to see under the house? Barney saw things he had not really noticed before. Soft sandy soil. A sheet of corrugated iron. A dog's ancient chew toy, a pile of white stones.

'Huh,' said Leonie.

'Hmm,' went Dorrie.

'Yes,' said Barney, and he thought of how when Ben was a crawling baby, maybe ten months old, he would crawl around the house and lift up all the rugs. Baby Ben would lift every corner of every rug to see what was underneath.

Leonie, still crouching, said, 'Maybe the concrete was a misdirection. Maybe what I'm supposed to have seen or heard—the day before, or the day after, or whatever Levins is thinking now—was Lou digging a grave under here.'

Barney nodded.

Dorrie said, 'I guess it would have been sheltered from the rain.'

49

When they got home, Joe and Leonie had somewhat of an argument about the use of permanent markers. Joe cried because Leonie wouldn't let him blow bubbles in the house. Joe slammed the door of his bedroom, which was a first, because Leonie said it was too late in the day to organise a play date with Milo. And then, when a knock sounded at the front door Leonie thought: There are so many knocks these days.

She set the knife down on the board and stared at a pile of diced onion. Her eyes had watered; they stung. She went over to the front door and decided not to speculate. It could be anyone, she thought. Surprise me.

'Hi, Leonie.'

Holy crap, this *was* a surprise.

'Hello, Eileen.'

Her surprise must have been evident, because Eileen said, 'Sorry for the surprise visit. I was just coming back from work and the girls are with Nathan. And I wanted to drop these off. So here I am.'

Eileen was beautiful and holding a large yellow envelope. She was in her work uniform—a shirt and slacks—with a name tag that said EILEEN in capital letters. Leonie had changed into her house clothes and was therefore untagged, unidentified. She had on her floppy house pants and no shoes and a t-shirt that said, *Don't Worry Be Happy*.

'What have you got there?' said Leonie.

'Have you been crying, Lee?'

'Oh, no.' Leonie laughed. 'I was just chopping onions. Do you want to come in?'

•

In the living room, on the carpet, Eileen Swan looked slightly more beautiful, if this were even possible. Leonie thought Eileen would look beautiful in any setting. She imagined, briefly, being in a hospital bed and Eileen swanning through the door offering nursely comforts. Eileen would no doubt be exceptional at her job. And it was true that Leonie had had a recurring fantasy of being in hospital, where she was unable to do anything but await food and sedation. She saw that Eileen had a flush of colour on her neck.

'Where are Annie and Patty?' asked Joe.

'They're with their dad,' said Eileen.

'I don't know my dad but he lives in South Africa,' said Joe.

'South America,' said Leonie.

'South A-mer-ica,' said Joe.

'That sounds like a nice place to live,' said Eileen, who was sitting cross-legged in her slacks and had her hands in her lap. 'Did you go to preschool today, Joe?'

'Yes.'

'Which preschool do you go to?'

'Joeys.'

'I think I know Joeys. Does it have a kangaroo on the sign?'

'Yes,' said Joe. 'It has a kangaroo.' He was rolling a blue Hot Wheels along a row of flat blocks that went across the length of the living room. He lifted the car up, making it fly, and then landed it again. 'This is my road. Leelee won't let me get a train set.'

Leonie was perched on the edge of the couch. She felt Eileen's eyes on her and sensed the sympathy in them. Eileen radiated warmth and something close to affection. Leonie felt unworthy just being near her. Being near Eileen—what a heady feeling. It was unworthiness mixed with some kind of longing. A longing to be more like Eileen? That must be it. Who wouldn't want to be more like Eileen?

Eileen said to Joe, 'I can understand that. It looks like you're making do pretty well without a train set though. You've made such a big long road.'

Leonie said, 'Joe, why don't you have some special treat TV while Eileen and I have a cup of tea.'

•

'Lee, that must've been awful,' said Eileen from her seat at the kitchen table.

Leonie sat opposite. The kitchen smelled of raw onions and Leonie felt a little self-conscious about the smell. She should have bought some air freshener with the scent of lily-white flowers. She said, 'It was. It made me feel sick seeing it all covered in dirt like that. Ginny used to wear that cardigan all the time.'

'I wonder why it would be buried just on its own?'

'I don't know,' said Leonie. 'Dorrie and I were just talking about that before, at Barney's. Why bury a cardigan? The only explanation we have is that it's evidence. We thought maybe under all that dirt there's blood.'

'There probably is.'

'I just couldn't believe it, when the policeman showed it to me. First, I felt sick. Then I felt devastated. Then I felt angry, like I could kill someone myself—specifically Lou Lawson. But then I also started looking at it furiously, at every dirt stain, thinking, *Is that blood?*'

Eileen was sitting back in her chair, as comfortable as anything. She'd been like that for the past hour. It was like you could just pop Eileen anywhere and she'd look like she'd been there her whole life.

'Well, you're very invested in this. Of course you want to know.'

'It felt a bit macabre.'

'It is macabre,' said Eileen. She took a sip of water and set her glass down. Eileen had said no to tea. Who says no to tea? Eileen Swan—because she was in charge of her own destiny.

'I know,' said Leonie. There was a kilo of mincemeat in a paper bag on the kitchen counter that said *Noble Meats* in big black letters. It was so hot—she should put the mince back in the fridge. Eileen had a way of making her distracted. The theme from *Inspector Gadget* was drifting over from the television. Leonie glanced at the stack of books on the table and hoped Eileen wouldn't see Maurie's Lonely Planet guide to South America.

But Eileen didn't seem to notice the book. She ran her hand through her hair and gestured to the yellow envelope. 'Lee, I don't want to upset you with these. I just thought you and Joe might like to have a look at them.'

Leonie had that feeling in her belly, like being on a swing that was swinging too high. Maurie used to push her so high at Clarke Park that Leonie felt a part of the sky. 'Thank you,' she said.

But Leonie must have sounded wary, because Eileen gave her a most disarming look. She said, 'You're very good company, Leonie. And I have a feeling you're much stronger than you think.'

50

The next morning, Barney lay in his warm dim room and tried not to think of that day. He tried not to think of the back of the old Subaru as it drove away and left him at the start of the walking tracks at the base of the mountain. That was the last time he had seen Deb as Deb. The last thing she had said to him, as her original self, was: 'Be careful.'

Be careful.

He had been careful. And even if he had said it back to her, like he wished that he had, it wouldn't have made any difference.

Barney realised he was lying on his side, cuddling a pillow. He let the pillow go. He missed Comfrey. He missed his beautiful old cat. He rolled onto his back and looked at the manhole in the ceiling. He thought of Leonie, on all fours on the side path, peering into the dark space under his house, looking for a grave. Barney let out a laugh. What a funny woman she was. And soft, like a Rubens painting in a travel agent's uniform. Barney felt better then, thinking about his comforting neighbour and knowing she was close by.

•

Sitting on the edge of her bed, Leonie stared at the yellow envelope that sat on the bedside table, next to her stack of books, her glass of water, her alarm clock, her vanilla candle. She picked up the envelope and held the thickness of it in her hand, and she remembered how Maurie had sat on the edge of this bed too. How, one time, Maurie had been chatting away while Leonie was lounging around, propped up on some pillows, a book on her lap.

'He adores you, you know,' Maurie had said.

'Well, he has excellent taste,' said Leonie. 'And luckily the feeling's mutual.'

Maurie had smiled. She said, 'I better get his snack ready. He's going to wake up any minute.'

Leonie had picked up her book and was going to keep on reading, but instead she said an unusually earnest thing to Maurie. She said, 'I'd do anything for him, Maur.'

Maurie had said, 'I know you would.'

It was true—Maurie had known that Leonie would do absolutely anything for Joe.

Leonie set the envelope down now, unopened. She could not open it last night and she could not open it this morning. She could not look inside. It would ruin her, melt her, she'd be a puddle. She stood up and tried not to think about that day when Maurie went to get the peanut butter and the milk and whatever else they had found strewn about.

'Can I watch *Pinocchio?*'

Here he was—her beautiful Joe. He'd appeared in the doorway and Leonie was just standing there in the middle of her bedroom.

'*Pinocchio*, hey?'

'Yes,' said Joe. He came into the room and hopped up on Leonie's bed and sat down, his feet dangling off the sides.

'I don't think I've ever seen *Pinocchio*,' said Leonie. 'But some of those old Disney movies can be very upsetting.'

'Milo said in *Pinocchio* the boy turns into a donkey.'

'I heard that. It sounds a bit scary.'

Joe kicked his heels against the bed. 'Leelee?'

'Yes, Joe?'

'Would you still love me if I was a donkey?'

Leonie said, 'Sweetheart, I'd love you no matter what you were. If you turned into a donkey, I'd just find us a house with a big barn and a beautiful paddock.'

•

Sitting on an outside chair, Barney put his old walking boots on. He tied the laces so they fitted tight around his ankles. Laces so old they looked set to disintegrate. He rubbed sunscreen on his legs and forearms and sprayed Aerogard on his shins. He went inside and, in his backpack, he put an apple, a bottle of water, *The Field Guide to the Birds of Australia*, Burnum Burnum's *WILDthings* and two of Dorothy's chocolate-chip cookies wrapped in foil.

In the study, Barney knew exactly what box to look in. He opened the cardboard flaps and retrieved his Akubra hat. His *hat*. Deb had loved him in his hat. Barney's father had given him this hat in about 1973. He'd told Barney that it took the fur of thirteen rabbits to make one Akubra hat.

Barney put his hat on, there in the study, next to the cardboard boxes. He felt almost silly, like he was dressing up as himself. But he wasn't dressing up. He was Barney Clarke, and this was his hat.

•

Joe spent ten minutes doing forward rolls on the carpet while Leonie ironed her trousers and her work blouse. She got dressed and went outside and pegged up the washing in the hot sun. Then she came back in and tidied up the kitchen table, and tidied up the toys from the living room carpet.

Joe was in his viewing spot at the window, holding the bottom of the aluminium sill. He said, 'Leelee, can I have bread and butter?'

'You can have toast and butter.'

'I don't want toast. Why can't it be bread and butter?'

'Because the bread's too stale. It needs to be toasted.'

'Leelee, that man is at Dorrie's.'

'What man?'

Leonie went over and looked out the window too.

There was Detective Sergeant Levins and the other one—O'Leary?—standing on Dorrie's front step. The two policemen were in their blue uniforms and Dorrie was in the doorway, arrayed in her pretty nightie with the pattern of blue flowers.

Leonie said, 'Come on, sweetie—I'll make you some toast and you can eat it in the car.'

•

'So when they say Earl's a witness,' said Varden, 'what did he witness?'

'Your guess is as good as mine,' said Leonie.

Wanda looked preoccupied. She said, 'I should go back and help Pat with the window display.'

The three of them were sitting at a table in the food court. Varden was holding a plastic container at chest height, reclining in his chair. He said, 'Maybe he saw the actual murder. But he's a criminal himself, so he can't tell the police that he saw it. Oh! I know! Because he was doing his illegal things when he saw the murder.'

'Sure,' said Leonie. 'He was dealing marijuana from a stolen car when he witnessed the murder.'

Wanda smiled. She set down a paper cup with some frothy-looking coffee in it and pushed her chair out to depart.

'It's actually possible,' said Varden, forking around in a container of caesar salad.

Leonie said, 'Dorrie and I think Earl must have seen Lou do something suspicious before the murder, or before he reported Ginny missing—because of how Levins kept asking me if I'd seen something before.'

'And if Levins was talking to Dorothy this morning, he was probably asking her the same question,' said Wanda, standing now, coffee in hand, handbag on shoulder.

'Exactly,' said Leonie. 'I'm dying to talk to Dorrie.' Their table was right in front of Hot Bake and Leonie was considering a croissant. A frothy coffee and a croissant. She said to Wanda, 'Do you want me to bring you back a croissant?'

'Ooh,' said Wanda.

And Varden. So earnest, with that smear of mayonnaise on his beard. He looked at Leonie and said, 'So Earl is a witness, but we don't know what he witnessed, or when he witnessed it, or if he told the police at the time that he witnessed it.'

'Correct,' said Leonie.

'So,' said Varden, 'why don't you just go over to Earl's and ask him?'

Leonie frowned a moment, confused, and then broke out in an enormous smile. 'My god, Vard,' she said, shaking her head. 'That's so funny. I honestly hadn't thought of that.'

51

At the big sign at the start of the walking tracks, Barney stood with his backpack on, his Akubra on, his binoculars around his neck. This had been like a uniform for him in his past life. Walking boots, dusty jeans, faithful old hat. Barney loved the accoutrement of walking. He loved the preparation of walk snacks and the smell of Aerogard. At the bottom of his pack he kept a film canister of salt in case of leeches, and a pair of fine-nosed tweezers in case of ticks.

Darkness descends quickly, said the sign. But it was bright and early. Barney set off, his binoculars bumping against his chest. The bush was scrubby and dense. He heard a whipbird call, as if to welcome him. The male whipbird, and then the female doing the follow-on notes. How bizarre it was to be here, and how familiar. How difficult it was, and how easy. It was wonderful, dreadful. Barney felt like he was existing in the past and the present at the same time. How could he be here? But how could he not be here? He approached the old Scout camp, off to the left. There was rustling in the undergrowth and he saw a yellow-throated scrubwren.

The path divided where it always had. Which way to turn?

Deb had loved the waterfall—and Barney realised he was crying. Tears dropped off his chin. They splashed on his chest as he felt that Deb was with him, striding ahead just slightly. She was speaking softly, her head wrapped up in one of her brightly coloured scarves.

Barney went up the pine steps that had been built into the side of the mountain. It was muddy still from the rain. He needed new boots. His boots were like relics. The higher he went, the further Deb receded. She seemed to seep away slowly. Barney saw a brown cuckoo-dove. The terrain became ferny for a section and then opened out for a stretch of flattish rocks. He saw so many leaves. Leaves that were grey green, pea green, fern green, moss green.

When there was a space in the canopy, Barney tilted his face up to the sun. When there were steps again, he found himself springing up them. His legs would be sore in the morning. He ascended, panting, sweating a waterfall of his own inside his shirt. Barney felt a strange sense of embodiment. He was becoming himself again. He had forgotten—and now it was all rushing back in, along with other things he had forgotten, like how many shades of green there were.

As he reached the bench that he and Deb had so often sat on, perched halfway up the mountain, he gulped water from his bottle. Something began to ebb like a tide inside him. He went on. His body flowed forward. Amid the blackbutts, he realised he had stopped crying. He realised he was even smiling.

•

Back at her desk, Leonie thanked Belinda at Hertz rentals and hung up the phone. She leafed through a brochure for Pinetrees Lodge and considered suggesting Lord Howe Island to Clarice. She watched Pat and Wanda fuss about their arrangement of the Gold Coast package deal posters in the window. And then the door opened and in walked Di Hickey. She'd just been talking about Di the other day, with Barney! Di was giving Wanda a wave. Sometimes Clarke felt like such a small town.

'Speak of the devil,' said Leonie. 'I was just talking about you the other day.'

'Singing my praises, I hope,' said Di, as she sat down in Leonie's customer chair. 'I spied you through the window and thought I'd pop in. God, Leonie. I've been thinking about you all week.'

'Did you see it in the paper?'

'I did, and I thought: they've got him. I mean, please tell me they've got him.' Di was clutching a bookstore bag and a punnet of strawberries.

'I don't think they've got him,' said Leonie. 'They didn't find her, Di. They don't have a body. And I don't know if they're going to get him without a body.'

'*No,*' said Di. 'I've been waiting to see pictures of him in handcuffs!'

'We live in hope,' said Leonie. 'I was just telling my new neighbour, Barney—who has the misfortune of living in Ginny's old house—how you'd told me about Lou's wandering eyes on those hunting club trips. How he was on the prowl up in Queensland and met Janice and all that.'

Di had picked up a snow globe from Leonie's desk. New York. She shook it and set it down again and, as the snow fell, she said, 'The good old Clarke Hunting Club. Or, as I used to call it, the Lou Lawson Appreciation Society.'

'Really?'

'Did I get you this one?' said Di, pointing at the miniature Statue of Liberty and the tiny plastic buildings in the glass dome.

'No, you got me Chicago.'

'That's right,' said Di. 'Leonie, honestly, the men in that club all just worshipped the ground Lou walked on. Robert and I still fight about it. I've barely spoken to him this week because it's been in the papers and so it brings it all up again. He thinks Lou's innocent. He's all like, *He might be a cheater, but he's not a murderer.* Bullshit, bullshit. Pardon my French.'

'I will never understand the cult of Lou Lawson,' said Leonie.

'It's as old as the hills. It's just the cult of the alpha male,' said Di. 'He's a peacock. And everyone in the club was just falling all over themselves to impress him, and to impress each other in front of him. I used to say to Robert that it sounded like one of those nature documentaries about lions or gorillas. But this was supposed to be a group of grown men.'

'Grown men with rifles,' said Leonie.

'And the odd Smith and Wesson revolver,' said Di.

'Oh,' said Leonie, who didn't know a thing about guns.

'There were a couple of police officers back in the day who used to show off with their police guns, shooting at kangaroos and things of that nature,' said Di. 'Just being very aggressive. Trying to impress Lou Lawson, no doubt. Thankfully those men didn't last very long. I am just glad the club is back now to what it started out as, which is legal licensed hunting. Keeping down feral animal populations. Conservation. That's what it should be about and, according to Robert, that's what it is again now.'

Leonie leaned forward on her desk, in front of her Club Med poster. She said, 'Do you remember the policemen's names?'

'No,' said Di. 'This was years ago, Leonie. This was probably 1983. I do remember one of them was very short, though. I used to say that he must have had a Napoleon complex.' Di hooted out a laugh.

'A short blond man?'

'I used to say to Robert, *That little aggro one should put his gun down and join a support group.*'

'Was the short policeman called Marrel?'

Di stopped smiling and, a beat later, she said, 'Marrel. Yes, it was. It was Mark Marrel.'

•

Barney pulled into the McDonald's car park, did a quick scan for Helen Last's old Sigma, and backed into his spot under the tree. He turned off the engine and rolled down the window. He was still damp with sweat from his walk, moist under the arms.

Hello, Ben.

Barney smiled across the car park at his son. He watched Ben walk along the back of the counter and disappear into the kitchen area. Barney waited, peering at Ben's co-workers, and at the back of a woman standing at the counter. God, he felt fantastic. He felt like he was glowing.

Ben hadn't come back from the kitchen yet and Barney tapped his fingers on the steering wheel with a new kind of energy inside him. He reached over to his backpack and retrieved the last of Dorothy's chocolate-chip biscuits. Delicious. What a nice woman she was. A real salt-of-the-earth kind of person. She reminded him almost of an older version of Deb.

Still no Ben. Barney chewed some biscuit. He opened his hardcover first edition of Graham Pizzey's *A Field Guide to the Birds of Australia* and flipped through the pages, and he smiled at the green ticks he and Deb had made next to the hundred or so birds they had seen. Rufous fantail: tick; sooty oystercatcher: tick; nankeen kestrel: tick; superb lyrebird: tick. Barney looked at the illustrations and skimmed the descriptions.

The male lyrebird will construct several circular mounds of bare dirt on the forest floor, for the purpose of conducting courtship displays.

A quick glance up at the counter and, good, Ben was back. Barney set the book down on his lap and watched his wonderful son. It was hot in the car, but he didn't mind. Ben turned to the silver shelf where the burgers stayed warm, tucked in their paper wrappings. Barney would stay a while today. He felt happy just to sit here. He switched on the radio and the ABC were doing a story on Lithuania's newfound independence.

Barney watched Ben make a soft serve. He watched Ben scoop French fries into a small paper bag. He listened to the radio and learned that approximately two million people had joined hands to form the Baltic Way in August 1989. Two million! He hadn't known it was that many. The human chain stretched for six hundred and seventy-five kilometres across Estonia, Latvia and Lithuania. Barney imagined all those people, holding hands on roads and in fields, and he felt that he could wait for his son forever.

52

Dandelions, clover, tall grassy tufts. This was Earl's lawn. Leonie and Dorrie stood ankle-deep in weeds, looking at the grimy steps that went up to Earl's porch. There was a bumper bar leaning up against a wall, and two old hub caps on a patch of bare dirt.

'His car's not there,' said Leonie.

'That's a relief,' said Dorrie.

'I thought you agreed that we should ask him.'

'I didn't say I *wanted* to ask him.'

The two women peered up at the porch from the relative safety of ground level. Leonie saw an esky that said EARL, an ashtray of cigarette butts, a car radio, a pair of discarded shorts.

'Why would he take his shorts off on the porch?'

Dorrie, who looked fetching in a patterned linen dress and sneakers, said, 'I think it's best not to think about the particulars.'

'I guess we come back later?'

'Or we send Clive?'

'I think Earl's more likely to talk to us,' said Leonie. 'You know how men get threatened by other men?'

'Like how men get threatened by women?'

Leonie laughed. She read the three metal signs hanging next to Earl's front door. One said, *Wishin' I was Fishin'*. One said, *Fart Zone*. One said, *Beware of the Dog* with a picture of a German shepherd. 'He doesn't have a dog, does he?'

'I've never seen a dog.'

The sun was burning Leonie's freckly forearms. The street was so quiet she could hear bees on the weeds. 'Let's go,' she said. 'We must look like lunatics. Imagine if he comes home in his muscle car and finds us on his lawn.'

They turned and trundled glumly down the slope.

'Maybe he's off looking for a golliwog to go with his lawn statues,' said Dorrie.

'They actually sell golliwogs at the chemist in Mulamang,' said Leonie.

'You're kidding.'

'I'm not. They have them in the window.'

'For god's sake,' said Dorrie, shaking her head.

'I know,' said Leonie. 'This town.'

●

On Dorrie's back deck, Leonie said, 'So Levins and the other one went to every house?'

'It seems that way. I saw them go to Ruth and Dave's, and they went to Teela's, and Doug and Sandra's, and the one on the other side of your house. What's that guy's name?'

'Oh, Warren,' said Leonie. 'But he won't know anything. He moved in after Ginny went missing. Warren has said about five words to me since 1986. I wonder if they went to see Gerry over the back fence.'

'Probably,' said Dorrie. 'I had a physio appointment at eleven thirty, so I had to cease my surveillance.'

Leonie sat in one of Dorrie's director's chairs and watched Clive demonstrate to Joe the planting of seeds in garden beds, as opposed to little plastic pots. Clive sprinkled tiny seeds in a neat row along the centre of a raised bed. Then he gave Joe some seeds and let Joe sprinkle them in. 'What are you planting?' yelled Leonie.

Joe conferred with Clive and then yelled back, 'Radishes!'

'The impatient gardener's favourite vegetable!' yelled Clive.

Leonie smiled. Then she turned back to Dorrie and said, in her deepest voice, 'So, Mrs Little, do you remember anything unusual about the days leading up to the eighth of May, 1985?'

Dorrie said, 'I wish I did.' She sipped some iced water and set the glass back on the deck slats. 'I thought about it the whole time I was doing my very slow-motion exercises at physio.'

'And?' said Leonie.

'And I agree that it makes sense that Lou must have waited a day or even two after he killed her before he reported her missing.'

'To give him time to bury her.'

'Which he would have done at night-time.'

'Definitely at night-time. He would have needed Tobias to be asleep.'

'Or our former theory: that Lou would have taken his own suggestion and sedated Tobias.'

'But regardless of Tobias, night-time, so no one else would see.'

'But someone saw.'

'Which was Earl,' said Leonie.

'While Earl was breaking every law known to man,' said Dorrie.

Leonie had been feeling numb and practical, but now she laughed. Then she quickly became sad, as she was prone to do quite abruptly. At the reality of Tobias, who had been as innocent as Joe. At the reality of Ginny, who was as alive to Leonie as if she were still here. Leonie said, 'If Ginny is under the house, they'll need another search warrant if they want to come back and dig there. That's what Barney said.'

'Poor fainty Barney,' said Dorrie. 'I think he's very emotionally repressed.'

'I'd assumed low blood pressure.'

'So a coincidence that he'd just bumped into his wife's old friend?'

Leonie looked away from Dorrie. She turned to the garden, where Joe was watering the line of seeds with a watering can and Clive was crouching on the thick healthy grass.

'Lee,' said Dorrie.

Leonie thought of Eileen Swan, with her yellow envelope. She turned back to face Dorrie and had that feeling she often got, which was that Dorrie wanted to say a whole lot more, but that Dorrie held it all in because Leonie was made of glass. Because Leonie was not strong after all; Leonie was emotionally repressed. Because—what if Leonie fainted?

Dorrie just said, 'I'm going to put dinner on. Do you and Joe want to stay?'

•

That night, after Joe was asleep, Leonie sat on the edge of her bed, on the soft quilt. Aunty Iris had made that quilt. Aunty Iris had never married and lived her whole tiny life in the Mulamang house that she and Eunice were born in. Aunty Iris died at the age of forty-five of ovarian cancer. Leonie had adored Aunty Iris.

Don't be stagnant, thought Leonie. *You're stronger than you think.*

She picked up the yellow envelope, on which *Leonie xx* was written in Eileen's messy wild scrawl. What spirited penmanship! Leonie's writing was conventional and small. Leonie closed her eyes a moment. She steeled herself. And then she pulled a photo out, as simple as that. It was a photo of Maurie and Eileen when they were teenagers. Maurie was grinning in denim overalls and rollerskates.

Leonie looked at the picture and—oh, *Maurie*. Her easy beauty. It just about flattened Leonie to see her sister again. There was a boy at Clarke High called Matthew Davies who said to Leonie, when she was thirteen: 'Maurie's the pretty one, you're the funny one.' Leonie hadn't thought of Matthew Davies in almost thirty years. She hated him as freshly now as she did then.

Leonie's hands were shaking when she pulled out another photo: a polaroid of Maurie and Eileen on their last day at Clarke High, in the old uniform. Eileen had a cast on her arm, covered in signatures. Skinny Maurie looked like she was the smartest girl in school, which she was. Smartest and saddest—but they only gave out an award for one.

Leonie sat quivering on the quilt. She had resolved to look at everything in the envelope. It was hard. It was very hard for her, but she had made this resolution and she knew now that she would do it. Her pulse was racing, but she put her hand inside the envelope again and retrieved a postcard addressed to Eileen.

Maurie's handwriting! It was like a whiplash to her heart. *Dear E, greetings from Pucón. I can see a volcano from where I am sitting.* Leonie felt the tears come. She blinked and they fell on her gaudy nightie, and she wiped her eyes to read on. *You'd be proud of me—I've eaten my weight in empanadas.* Leonie sat up straight and pulled her shoulders back. She took a breath, trembling and weeping. *I don't miss work, or Sydney. I do miss Lee, though—I call her every Sunday. She's my home base.*

Leonie sobbed a bathtub of tears. She sobbed until she felt herself dissolve.

53

It was just after dawn. A warmish morning. A burst of cockatoos flew squawking over Calboonya Avenue. And, for the first time in two years, Barney opened the glove box in his car. He wanted the small torch that was in there. Unfortunately the torch was under the pamphlet he'd been given at Clarke Base Hospital: *Helping Young People After Loss*. In order for Barney to get the torch, he needed to touch the pamphlet. And, how ridiculous, he hesitated even to touch it! Like it might bite him and infect him with—what? More sorrow? More regret?

Barney was sitting sideways in the passenger seat of his car with the door open and his feet on the concrete driveway. He picked up the pamphlet. Lo and behold, it did not bite him. He could have scrunched it into a ball or merely set it aside, but instead he scanned the front page. A subheading said, *Let young people grieve in their own way.* A photo of an adult comforting a child. *Barney* had been like a child. This pamphlet had been so terrifying to him it had rendered him a frightened infant, covering his eyes.

'Normal' grief for young people doesn't just mean feeling sad. It often involves anger (that their whole world has been turned upside down).

Barney considered this and sighed. He wanted so much to see his son and to talk with him. He wanted to put a hand on Ben's broad shoulder. What a useless father Barney had been on so many occasions. That fact was not going to change. So, what to do? Gather information! He sat in his car and read the pamphlet from start to finish. Then he turned back to the front and read the whole thing again, which was what Barney sometimes did when he wanted to commit something to memory.

Back in the house, he set the pamphlet on his desk, next to a manuscript titled, *Theories of Social Reality and Their Importance for Schooling as a Social Project.* He looked around the bare study and decided that it was terrible like this. It was like working in a coffin. He needed to unpack some boxes. He needed to remember the things that were important and alive to him.

But first, carrying his red torch, Barney went out through the kitchen, out the sliding door, and down the side path. On all fours, he shone the torch into the darkness. The concrete hurt his knees. His thighs ached, his calves ached. It was so satisfying to be achy from walking. His body felt stronger already.

The soil under the house was soft and silty and grey. Barney saw a broken terracotta pot. He crawled over to the rusted sheet of corrugated iron. He couldn't see anything of interest, but he didn't know what he expected to see. He went further and put the torch down and rummaged around in the earth with his bare hand. He should get his gloves. This was absurd.

He pushed his hand around, making wide circles in the soil. What was that? Something hard was buried there. Barney unearthed it and set it on the soft ground and aimed the torch.

A bone.

Barney had found a bone. The shape of it was so familiar. It transported him back to weekday dinners as a child. His parents had been such quiet, restrained people. He was never sure what his mother thought or felt about anything—except God, who, she said, had 'perfect timing'.

As a child, Barney never knew what that meant. But right now he thought of Ginnny's little dog, Peaches. He'd read once that dachshunds had a strong prey drive and would bury their food to protect it. He nudged the bone with the torch. It was just an old dirty bone from a lamb chop, and Barney's knees and hands were filthy as he crawled backwards into the daylight.

•

Next door, Leonie woke to Joe's voice.

'Leelee, are you asleep?'

Leonie had been very asleep. She rolled over on the bed, yanked out of a gentle dream. Maurie was in a fishing boat on a lake. Leonie had a sense of Eileen being there, but Eileen wasn't there. She opened her eyes. In real life, Joe was standing by her bed in his space pyjamas.

'What's this?' said Joe, his hand on the yellow envelope.

Leonie sat up and squinted. She said, 'Eileen gave that to me.'

'What is it?'

'They're photos of your mum and some postcards and stuff like that. Things that Eileen had.'

'Can I see it?'

'Of course you can,' said Leonie, who felt suddenly awake. She reached for the glass on the bedside table and drank all of the water in it.

'You're thirsty,' said Joe.

'I was.'

Leonie had forgotten to close the curtains and the bright sun was coming through the windows. The room looked so alive with the morning. Perhaps she should never close the curtains again. The quilt and the carpet and the lining board walls were shining. There had been a swan in her dream. It was a big black swan, gliding on the water. Leonie felt lighter somehow. She had a feeling of relief for no apparent reason. She patted the quilt and said, 'Hop up here and we can look at them together.'

●

In the hallway, Barney picked up the receiver and pressed the buttons and waited.

'Hello?'

'Helen, it's Barney.'

'Barney! How're you feeling? How's your head?'

'I'm terrific, thank you, I really am.'

'I was worried about you.'

Barney had washed his hands and wiped his knees with a damp cloth. He looked down and noticed how dusty his shorts were, how filthy his shirt. He said, 'Don't be. I feel much better. It might have been a blessing in disguise.'

'Fainting?'

'Just a reset.'

Helen was quiet a moment on the other end of the phone. Then she said, 'Okay, well I'm all for silver linings. Did you want to talk to Phil? I think he's still in the shower.'

'No, I don't need to talk to Phil. I just wanted to let you know that I've been thinking about what you said about coming back to the club. I went for my first walk in a very long time yesterday.'

'You did?'

'I did.'

'Where'd you go?'

'Just the waterfall.'

'Gosh, I bet that felt good. It just gives you a lift, being out there. I never know how else to describe it, but it just gives you a lift.'

'That's right,' said Barney, who was in such an expansive mood. 'That's exactly right. Although I'm a bit rusty. My legs were shaking all the way back down.'

'That'll happen the first few times,' said Helen.

'Did you say it's Wibung Creek next weekend?'

'Yes, Sunday week. We're meeting at the sign at eight. And Rae's leading, so we'll have to fight for morning tea. There's always a grumbling in the ranks by ten thirty when Rae leads.'

'I remember.'

'I thought I'd make banana bread just to annoy her,' said Helen, and Barney laughed.

He thought of how the dawn light made the mountain turn pink and orange. He wished they were meeting this Sunday, at dawn. Helen said, 'Phil and I will be thrilled to have you back, Barn. Everyone will. We've missed your commentary.'

'You never know when an irrelevant fact might come in handy,' said Barney.

•

In the kitchen, after a cup of strong tea, Leonie stood at the window watching the street. She watched as Earl's old orange car pulled into his driveway. The car was shiny and the engine growled loudly. Leonie couldn't understand why anyone would want such a loud car.

A knock sounded and Leonie knew it would be Barney. Joe set his toast down and rushed over to the door.

'Hi, Barney!'

'Good morning, Joe.'

'Come in,' said Leonie, and Barney came in. He stood hovering in the kitchen with a warm expression and a surprisingly filthy outfit. Leonie had the radio on and the house was filled with the saxophone solo from 'Careless Whisper'.

'Earl's home,' said Barney.

'Very audibly,' said Leonie.

'Are you going to try again?'

'Yes, I think Dorrie and I will brave it when I get home from work.' She went over to the table where she had a manila folder full of newspaper clippings. 'This is everything. I kept it all.' She opened the folder and the most recent article sat on the top of the pile, with the picture of Ginny and Lou on their wedding day.

'Thanks,' said Barney. 'Saves me going to the library.'

'Have you been rolling around in the dirt, Barney?'

Barney looked down at his shirt and shorts. 'I went under the house.'

'And?'

'And I found a disappointing bone. A remnant of Peaches, I suspect. By which I mean something she must have buried.'

'Lamb chop?'

'Yes, lamb chop.'

Leonie smiled. Barney searching under his house for a grave—how adorable! She said, 'I do appreciate your enthusiasm.'

'What are neighbours for?'

Leonie was still smiling when she picked up the article on the top of the pile. Ginny looked so gorgeous. She was wearing her thick gold bracelet and a veil like Princess Diana's. Leonie said, 'I guess you've got this one from the other day?'

'I have that one, yes.'

'I might read it again,' she said, and she lay the sheet of newspaper on the table.

Joe was back on his chair now, kicking his legs, eating Vegemite toast.

'I'll bring this back when I'm done,' said Barney, picking up the folder.

'No rush,' said Leonie.

'It's so sad when bread gets stale,' said Joe.

Barney held the manila folder to his chest and said, 'Yes. That is sad.'

•

After Barney left, Joe went out to the backyard with his toy digger and Leonie brushed her teeth in the bathroom. She noticed for the first time that the dental floss had a use-by date and spent a minute wondering why. She attached her name tag to her work shirt and read it backwards in the bathroom mirror. ƎINOƎ⅃.

To her own reflection, she said: 'Leonie, you're much stronger than you think.'

Then she went to the kitchen and studied the number she'd written down on the notepad in blue biro.

Since when did a telephone number give off such a feeling of terror and excitement? Since when did a telephone number on a piece of paper make a person feel light-headed?

Leonie braced herself and dialled.

'Hello?'

'Hi, Eileen—it's Leonie.'

'Hi Lee,' said Eileen. 'How are you?'

'I'm very well,' said Leonie. 'I just wanted to say thank you for the photos and postcards and et cetera.'

'You're welcome,' said Eileen. 'I wasn't sure about bringing them around, but I hoped that they might be of some benefit.'

'Yes,' said Leonie.

She was in the kitchen by the window and she watched as Clive walked out his front door and put two fishing rods into the back of the ute and went around to the driver's side and got in. A flash of Dorrie went past Dorrie's front window.

Leonie said, 'Joe was very interested. We looked at the photographs together.'

'I'm glad,' said Eileen, and Leonie could hear Annie and Patty in the background. Eileen said, 'Patty, can you not bring the potion into the house? Just take the jar out the back and leave it in the yard. Sorry, Lee.'

'That's fine.'

'I don't think I should have given them the bicarb soda.'

Leonie let out a shrill laugh. She was terribly, embarrassingly nervous. She pushed her hot cheek against the phone and said, 'Eileen, maybe we could get together again sometime.'

'Patty!' said Eileen.

Leonie waited there in her kitchen, pink-faced and fidgeting with the springy white cord. She stared down at the crusts she had cut off Joe's toast.

'Sorry, here I am,' said Eileen. 'What did you say, Lee?'

This was like hell. One part of Leonie wanted to hang up the phone immediately. Yet another part took over and ploughed on. She said, 'I was just thinking that maybe we could get together again sometime.'

'I'd love that,' said Eileen easily.

'Oh. Well, okay. Good.' And Leonie couldn't believe that she said the next part out loud, but she did, dry-eyed and not wobbly. The words came out quite well, despite her nerves. She said, 'I was thinking it would be good if we got together and maybe talked about Maurie.'

A brief silence came from Eileen, and there was the sound of either Annie or Patty's high-pitched screaming in the back-ground. Golly. Whoever it was, one of those girls was really letting it all out. It was like one child was about to kill the other, or potentially kill Eileen. But probably this was just what happened every other day, because Eileen said, warmly and completely focused, 'Lee. Yes. Let's do that.'

54

They ran that many tests on Maurie, Leonie couldn't keep up. Maurie was taken to specialists at Clarke Hospital— this was before there was Clarke Base Hospital. The old Clarke Hospital was in a weatherboard building near the park, and had since been damaged by fire.

Leonie remembered, as a teenager, accompanying Eunice and Maurie to one of Maurie's appointments there. It was depressing as hell. All those sad, ruined people, waiting in chairs. Walking the corridors with stoic Maurie and nervy Eunice. Looking back on it now, the whole experience for Leonie was like being damaged by fire.

Eunice had entrusted the health of the family to a GP called Brian, who seemed, firstly, too young to be a doctor; and secondly, one of the dullest people Leonie had ever encountered. Brian's waiting room was all brown. The walls and the counter and the carpet were brown, brown, brown. Perhaps Maurie had migraines. For a while it was thought she had focal epilepsy, but then apparently she didn't. She might have had a concussion that went forever. Or was she prone to high fevers? Or perhaps it was epilepsy after all; Brian was not the finest diagnostician. Whatever it was, Maurie was certainly too thin, according to everyone, which thrilled Eunice.

'She takes after her mother,' said Eunice, who was, disappointingly for Eunice, not thin in a way that caused concern.

•

On Joe's first birthday, Eunice was let out for the day. Maurie picked her up from Sunset Gardens and brought her to Leonie's for lunch. Eunice lumbered into the living room on purple blotchy legs.

Joe loved to be read to. He picked up a book and shuffled across the carpet to Leonie on his knees: 'Da. Da.'

'You want to read this one again? Okay, up you get.'

Joe crawled onto Leonie's lap and Eunice was shipwrecked on the big couch, lost in her own thoughts. Leonie began reading to Joe.

Then Eunice spoke right over Leonie: 'This brings back memories. Seeing you read to him like that, Lee.'

'Of you reading to me?' asked Leonie.

'Oh,' said Eunice. 'No, of my mother reading to *me*.'

'Oh.'

Joe said, 'Da da.' He pointed at the book: 'Ah-da.'

Eunice said, 'I guess I read to you. And Maurie. I must have. I don't remember.'

Maurie glided in across the carpet, holding a large bowl. One thing about Maurie, along with all the other things, was that she had terrific posture. This was on account of the ballet classes Eunice had dragged her to as a child. Leonie, instead, was tutored in Italian by a woman from Eunice's book club. Eunice said Leonie was 'the wrong shape for ballet'.

'So how was work this week, Maur?' said Eunice.

Maurie lay a salad nicoise on the coffee table. She said, 'It was fine.'

'So descriptive,' said Leonie. 'I feel like I was there.'

Maurie said, 'Well, I want to move more into collection care. I had a meeting this week, actually, about doing training with the preventative conservation team.'

'For books,' said Eunice.

'The library has more than just books,' said Maurie.

'Huh,' said Eunice, who'd lost interest already.

Then Joe looked up from the book and crawled straight over to Maurie, as if he hadn't seen her for a month. He pulled himself up and yanked at her jeans. Maurie bent over and picked him up and, oh, how Joe smiled! How Maurie smiled! Joe put his cheek on Maurie's chest. The two of them together was like some kind of natural magic. It was like Maurie had been born to birth that child and to hold him close.

'Look at that,' said Eunice. 'He loves his mum.'

'He sure does,' said Leonie.

'You're wonderful with him, Maur,' said Eunice. 'He's very lucky to have you.'

•

Now, on the way to the Plaza, Leonie and Joe had all the windows down in the car. The radio was on and the Bee Gees were singing 'More Than a Woman'. They went past Maurie's old ballet school, which was now a hairdresser called Combing Attractions. Poor Maurie: god, she hated ballet.

But Leonie didn't really dwell on Maurie, or not as much as usual. Actually, Leonie was tapping the steering wheel and, whenever she remembered a lyric, she would sing along. It was like she had created a feeling in herself by calling Eileen Swan. It was pride—and perhaps elation? That was strange, but Leonie didn't dwell on that either. She just felt that the morning had a real shine to it. The intensity of the sunlight—the way it lit up the sign on the Shell station.

Joe said from the back seat of the car, 'My mum was beautiful.'

Leonie glanced at him in the rear-view mirror. Sometimes he looked so much like Maurie it was enough to make her cry. Leonie said, 'She sure was.'

Leonie watched the road. She thought: You're okay, Leonie. It's okay. She liked the way the breeze felt coming through the car window.

'Leelee?'

'Yes, Joe?'

'You're beautiful.'

'Oh, sweetheart,' said Leonie, gliding along the highway. 'So are you.'

55

As always, Barney checked the letterbox. He'd checked it first thing that morning, and he checked it again just now, as he got home from Camping & Beyond. There was no letter from Ben. But he did find a magnet advertising a local plumber and a takeaway menu for a new pizza store on the highway, which was called I Love You To Pizza's. Barney was so tired of misused apostrophes. But look, the pizza shop had a two-for-one special on Wednesday nights. Barney had an unexpected thought: he wondered if Leonie and Joe liked pizza.

Barney brought the magnet and flyer in and set them on the hall table, and he put his shopping bag on the floor. It contained a new pair of walking boots, which were brown and offered ankle support, arch support and a new technology in waterproofing.

Earlier that morning, Barney had read half of the articles in Leonie's collection. Now, he would read the rest. He took his old boots off and sat down. He learned that witness reports of Ginny walking down a residential street in Lismore, New South Wales, constituted an 'unconfirmed sighting', which was one of 'a number of alleged sightings of Mrs Lawson since her disappearance'. He learned that Ginny's maiden name was Cayley, and that her mother—Carol Cayley—had told the media that her daughter had been the light of her life. Carol was living an 'emotional nightmare'. When asked if she'd been able to find any closure, Carol had said, 'Closure is for doors.' Plucky, thought Barney.

He also learned that Janice's Pomeranian had won a silver medal at a dog show in Emerald, Queensland. And that, on the five-year anniversary of Ginny's disappearance, police dressed up a mannequin in a wig and 'similar clothing' and plonked it on the road outside Clarke Plaza with a sign that said: *Did you see this woman?*

Barney pushed his chair out and stood up. He walked over to the boxes lining the back wall of the study.

He opened one and retrieved an ancient framed photo of his mother and father, and he set it on his desk. He lined up his collection of banksia pods. He unpacked what Deb called his 'decorative binoculars', which she had bought him from the big antique store in Cedar Valley. He blu-tacked his pictorial poster—*Birds of the Gather Region and South Coast*—on the wall next to the door. He affixed, above his desk, his favourite historical image: a photocopied drawing of the Aboriginal tracker John Watkins ('Sir Watkin Wynne'), during the arrest of the Clarke Brothers at Jinden Creek in 1867.

Barney returned to the boxes. Oh, his notepads. A thousand notes-to-self. He would need more shelves for his books, magazines, journals, manuals, guides.

He found his favourite framed photograph of Deb, standing on a bush track in a pair of shorts and one of Barney's button-up shirts. He considered it a moment, and then put it in the bottom drawer of his desk.

Then he went out to the kitchen and, with his new magnet, he stuck a year twelve school photo of Ben in the centre of his shiny white fridge.

•

Wanda said, 'So what do you think happened to Barney's wife?'

'I don't know,' said Leonie. 'When someone says "accident", I think car accident. But maybe that's just me.'

'I don't think it's just you,' said Wanda, smiling gently from her desk chair.

Pat was sitting in the window, talking on the phone, staring at a banana. This banana had been on Pat's desk all day, next to Pat's Filofax and Pat's tea mug.

'But a person can have all kinds of accidents,' said Leonie.

'That's true,' said Wanda. 'You know, I just read the other day about this terrible thing that happened a few years ago in

Buenos Aires. An older lady was walking along the footpath and she was killed by a falling poodle.'

'She was not.'

'She was. The poodle fell thirteen floors.'

Leonie began to laugh.

Wanda said, 'And then another woman—who saw the first woman get hit by the poodle—rushed across the street to help. And in the process of crossing the street the second woman got hit by a bus and she also died.'

'She didn't.'

'She did. And then a man who witnessed both deaths was so shocked that he had a full-scale heart attack. And he died too.'

Leonie was properly laughing now. She wobbled with laughter. She said, 'What about the poodle?'

'The poodle sadly passed.'

At this, Leonie really lost it. She had to wipe away tears. Golly, it was good to laugh.

Wanda grinned widely and said, 'These are real people, Lee. It's not funny.'

Pint-sized Pat, at her desk in the window, held the phone to her ear and turned to face the glass. The banana just sat there as if it might never be eaten. Leonie looked out and saw the bright glow of the Plaza, and that flathead fillets were on special. Her cheeks were wet with tears and she felt warm in her belly from laughing.

Wanda said, 'So what time's good tomorrow?'

'Six?'

'Six it is. I'll make a reservation. The boys are really looking forward to seeing Joe.'

'I can't wait to be terrified of Jenny.'

'Oh, you will be.'

'Will we get pineapple pork?'

'Of course we will,' said Wanda. 'Best pineapple pork on the South Coast.'

•

Joe and Clive set about picking every leaf off two uprooted basil plants. Joe was very focused on the task. He gently picked the leaves and put them in an enamel colander there on Dorrie's back deck.

Leonie said, 'Dorrie and I are going up to Earl's now.'

'Okay,' said Joe.

Clive nodded at Leonie, and Leonie nodded at Clive. This was the knowing look of two people who felt certain they were about to solve a crime.

Then Leonie and Dorrie went through the house and out the front door and along the thick grass verge past number twenty and then there they were at Earl's, because it was just one house up. Leonie felt a sense of profundity as they climbed the grimy steps.

'Hello ladies,' said Earl, who was opening the screen door. He seemed to be coming outside anyway. He looked at Leonie with eyebrows raised and then at Dorrie the same way. Leonie could hear Lynyrd Skynyrd from inside the house and there was a smell, too, like yoghurt past its expiry date.

'Hello,' she said. 'I don't think we've formally met. I'm Leonie from number twenty-one. This is Dorothy.'

'I think you know my husband's cousin,' said Dorrie hopefully. 'From the Wreckers.'

'I know who you are,' said Earl, like they were both daft, which perhaps they were, being there on the porch like this, looking for new answers to an old question. Earl sat down on a folding chair and took out a Winfield Blue and proceeded to light it. 'Is this about Lou Lawson?'

Leonie said, 'It's about Ginny.'

56

In Dorrie's kitchen, perched on a barstool, Leonie said, 'So even then, even in 1985, Earl was never a suspect.'

'So why did we think he was?' said Clive.

'Because we saw the police over there questioning him,' said Leonie.

'And because Lou said he was,' said Dorrie. 'Lou was telling everyone that Earl was a suspect.'

'The same way Lou said Ginny might have run off with a cult,' said Leonie.

'Or with some other man,' said Dorrie.

'Or killed herself,' said Leonie.

'Or moved to Lismore,' said Dorrie.

'Did Lou say that one?' asked Leonie.

'I was just getting into the spirit of things,' said Dorrie.

The three of them were huddled around Dorrie's kitchen

counter and Joe was sitting cross-legged over in front of the television, watching *Care Bears.*

Clive leaned back and folded his arms and said, 'Marrel's a very pathetic character in all of this.'

'I can't believe the things that men will do to impress other men,' said Dorrie.

'You both smell like cigarettes,' said Clive.

Dorrie sniffed her own shoulder. 'I felt like I could smell a rancid dairy product.'

'We should invite Barney over and tell him what Earl saw,' said Leonie.

•

An hour later, mosquitoes aplenty, Barney sat at Dorrie's outdoor table, clean-shaven (no cuts) in a light beige shirt. Leonie thought he looked quite nice. Dear, avuncular Barney. She noted some colour in his cheeks. Barney said, 'So this is the night before Lou reported Ginny missing.'

'Yes,' said Leonie. 'And Earl's just sitting on his porch at two am because that's what Earl does.'

'I guess you get a different perspective on things at two am,' said Barney.

'Earl certainly did,' said Dorrie.

'So it's pitch dark and rainy and et cetera,' said Leonie. 'And he was just sitting there in the dark, smoking, when he saw Lou back his Land Rover out of the carport onto the road and then go forward a bit, and then back it up the drive again, so the boot was facing the house. At two in the morning.'

'Ah,' said Barney. He took a sip of the Heineken that Clive had bestowed upon him. The two men had already had a spirited chat about home brewing after Barney arrived. Clive was very interested, it was something he'd always wanted to try, and Barney had offered a tour of his systems, perhaps on the weekend.

Leonie said, 'And then Earl saw Lou get out of the car, go up the side of the house, and come back with something heavy, which he proceeded to put in the boot of his car.'

'All of this illuminated by that conveniently located street-light,' said Barney.

'Exactly,' said Leonie. 'Earl said he didn't see what Lou was carrying, but he could tell by the way Lou was moving that it was something big and heavy. And then Lou drove away, at two in the morning, and Earl thought that it was all a bit weird, to say the least. So Earl waited. And then Lou came back about forty minutes later and drove the car up frontways like he usually did and went inside. And that was it.'

'Except the next evening, Lou says, "Oh heck, my wife's missing",' said Clive.

Barney said, 'So he moved her. He moved her and dumped her somewhere.'

'Yes,' said Leonie.

'Where?' said Barney.

'I'd put money on the lake,' said Clive. 'Lou fished the lake all the time. It's twenty minutes away and it falls away deep at the boat wharves. If he weighted her down well enough, then it's a quick solution.'

'And he would have been in a rush on account of Tobias being at home asleep,' said Leonie.

'And then he buried the cardigan for what reason?' said Barney.

'It must have been evidence,' said Clive.

'Maybe it got left behind by accident on the night of the murder,' said Dorrie. 'And he couldn't just put it in his bin.'

'And he couldn't burn it in the yard, because it was pissing down with rain and windy as anything,' said Leonie.

'So Earl told all this to the police in 1985 and they just sat on it?' said Barney.

'No,' said Leonie. 'Worse. Earl told Senior Constable Marrel. And Senior Constable Marrel told Earl that, if he wanted to stay out of prison for the numerous charges he had against him at the time—drugs and cars and what have you—then he should keep his mouth shut.'

Clive let out a laugh, shaking his bald head. As if it was all just so bleakly amusing. He re-sprayed an elbow with Aerogard. And beyond Clive was Joe, on the rug in Dorrie's colourful lounge room. The television was off now and Joe was busy with Lego.

'So why is Earl reporting all this now?' said Barney.

'Because our new best friend, Detective Sergeant Levins, told Earl that if he wanted to stay out of prison for all the numerous historical charges he has against him—drugs and cars and what have you—then he should make a statement immediately,' said Leonie. 'And because, as Earl told us, he's always thought Lou Lawson was an up-himself prick who had it coming.'

'There's one thing we and Earl can agree on,' said Clive.

'If nothing else,' said Barney.

'Earl's my second-least favourite person of anyone I've ever met,' said Leonie.

Dorrie took a sip of beer. Her grey hair was up in a tremendous bun, and she was wearing a pair of blue jeans and a white cotton singlet. She looked like she'd just elegantly milked a cow. She said, 'Before we all die of hunger, I'm going to whiz up that pesto. Barney, why don't you stay for dinner?'

•

After what turned out to be an extremely convivial evening, Leonie, Joe and Barney went across the street in the almost-dusk.

Joe rushed up the slope to the carport and swung himself around the metal pole.

'Well,' said Leonie, 'I guess we won't be expecting any more search warrants.'

'And I can stop crawling under the house with a torch,' said Barney.

God, Leonie felt sad; but she laughed anyway. The moon was a sliver in the pink sky.

Barney said, 'Clive's right. They might never find her body.'

'I know.'

'And I gather that without a body, there's very little chance the police will be able to charge him.'

Leonie nodded. 'I just thought we'd find her eventually.'

'Maybe Janice will still produce the smoking gun.'

'I don't know,' said Leonie. 'It just feels like it's over.'

And then she and Barney stood together wearily and watched as Joe stopped swinging and stood dizzily on the concrete. He stared at his own bare feet and swayed. Then he hopped up on the low brick wall between the properties and began to walk along it, muttering to himself.

Barney smiled. 'He's a delight.'

'He sure is.'

'My son's name is Ben. I think he blames me for what happened to his mother. He certainly blames me for leaving, and for not staying at home and sticking things out.'

Golly, Barney had really blurted that out. If ever someone needed to get a few things off their chest. Leonie nodded carefully. She said, 'But didn't your wife'—how to put it delicately?—'didn't your wife make that decision?'

'She certainly did.'

'Right,' said Leonie, who had been desperate to ask what happened to Barney's wife. Absolutely desperate. And she almost did, there in the driveway, but instead she said, 'Well, as far as I know, the definition of an accident is that it's no one's fault.'

Barney smiled. 'You're absolutely right. By definition an accident is unintentional.'

'Chancy.'

'Yes it is.'

'You'd spend a lot of time thinking about definitions in your line of work.'

'Yes I do.'

'Well, take some comfort in them,' said Leonie, who felt like she had done a very good job at being both restrained and perhaps even wise. Her mind went to Maurie, popping off to buy peanut butter and milk. Joe was going along the brick wall on his knees. It seemed he was pretending to be an animal of some kind. He crawled towards the carport.

Barney looked at Joe and said, 'You're lucky to have him.'

'*Yes*,' said Leonie. 'I am.'

57

That night, after Joe was asleep, Leonie finished *Healing the Shame that Binds You*. Afterwards, she put the book down on the bed and thought about it for twenty minutes. She got up and went to her bedroom window and peeked around the edge of the curtain. She could see Earl's disembodied cigarette tip glowing red in the dark on his porch, moving around with his smoking. Then she closed the curtain and went back to her bed, where she had set a photo of Maurie on the quilt.

Maurie with baby Joe. Leonie could tell the photo was taken in Eileen's kitchen, now that she had been to Eileen's kitchen. Maurie's cheeks were rosy and Joe was on her lap. Maurie had both arms around Joe's precious middle.

Leonie closed her eyes and thought of the day Maurie had left to get peanut butter and milk—and the other simple groceries that she bought at Con's Convenience & Deli, the little store next to the South Coast Philippines Association.

•

Barney worked late on account of having a sense of needing to fix something unnameable and not knowing what else to do. He finished the Duncan article. He sat at his desk, staring at the folder full of newspaper clippings about Ginny Lawson. He should take them back to Leonie's. He felt there was no point in them now. He leaned over and opened the bottom drawer of his filing cabinet and put his hand on the tab that said *DEBORAH* and he pulled out the whole file folder.

When he opened it, the first thing he saw was the article. He had saved the whole of page three of the *Gather Region Advocate* from Friday, 17 March 1989. Barney stared at the grainy photo of the level crossing and at the mangled back end of their old Subaru.

•

Leonie placed the photo of Maurie and Joe on her bedside table ceremonially. Then she went out to the kitchen and got the newspaper article about Ginny and she folded it down the middle, so Lou's face was folded under and she didn't have to look at that up-himself prick a minute longer.

Back in the bedroom, she placed Ginny next to Maurie on the bedside table, and then she lit the vanilla-scented candle to complete this simple shrine.

•

Barney read the article about the accident from start to finish, and then he read it again and he couldn't believe the language used to describe this crash, which had ended Barney's life as he knew it. ONE DEAD, ONE INJURED IN RAILWAY CRASH. This was the headline. Deb was the injured, and Barney had felt like the dead. But of course he was still here living. He was here in his study holding a piece of newspaper, which described in plain unadorned English how a Nissan Pulsar had ploughed at speed into the back of a Subaru wagon, which was stopped and waiting at the level crossing on Albion Street. That was Deb, who had been on her way to pick up Barney from his day-long walk. Deb had finished work and was waiting for the train to pass. There'd been no gate at the Albion Street level crossing in 1989. Deb had sustained such injuries that she was put in an induced coma. The other person's car had been dragged for over a hundred metres by the train and ended up on its back. Some of this other woman's possessions, Barney read now, were 'strewn along the railway line'.

•

Leonie sat and watched the candle burn and she thought of the afternoon when Maurie went off to the shops. Leonie had gone over it so many times as to drive herself insane. If only Leonie had already bought groceries. If only she drank less milk. If only Maurie had chosen to go to the Woolworths at the Plaza instead, and then the timeline would have been all different, because the Plaza was further away, and she could have crossed the tracks at Horsham Street. And if she'd chosen Albion Street anyway, then she would have crossed there at a different time, and there might have been no train, and she might not have ploughed towards the railway line, where another car was parked waiting. Maurie was going so fast that she pushed the other car clear over the tracks, which left Maurie there, in her car, in the path of the train.

The other woman had blessedly lived. Leonie didn't even know her name.

All she knew was that Maurie was so clearly dead that the paramedics who attended saw no need to check her vital signs. Leonie was told that Maurie had sustained injuries that were 'incompatible with life'.

•

Barney had heard at some point—at the hospital, perhaps— that the other woman had suffered a medical episode.

A seizure? He recalled now the horrible fog of Clarke Base, where information came at him like knives and made cuts all over his skin. He had floated down hallways which smelled of disinfectant. He had purchased Smith's crisps mindlessly from a vending machine. He had glazed over when Dr Prakash uttered sentences like, *Initially there might be problems with word finding or comprehension.* Barney had been outside of his own self. He had not cared about the woman who had died, whose name he could not recall. Did he ever even know her name?

All he cared about was that Deb would wake up. And she did! She was awake! Oh, *Deb*!

But she was no longer Deb. She had gone outside of herself and never went back in.

•

Leonie sat on the edge of the bed and wept for Maurie and for Ginny.

She was a wet mess by the time she blew out the candle. She wiped her face with the back of her arm and felt somehow lighter. She lay back on her pillow, got under her sheet, and kicked the quilt down.

Then she fell asleep under the spinning fan and stayed there until Joe called in the wee hours and she stumbled sleepily into his room.

'I need you,' he said.

'I'm here,' said Leonie, as she crawled into his squishy bed.

He threw his arm over her and snuggled in and she lay on her back and stared at the glow-in-the-dark stars. Sometimes she felt that Maurie was looking over them, as an angel might, which was silly, since Leonie did not believe in angels.

'I love you, Leelee.'

'I love you too, sweetie.'

58

On Sunday the following week, Leonie and Joe and Clive began early in the morning, planting out a garden bed on the north side of Leonie's backyard.

'Barney did a good job of this bed,' said Clive.

'I helped,' said Joe.

'I bet you did,' said Clive.

'It was so thoughtful of Barney,' said Leonie.

'And then we swam in Barney's pool,' said Joe.

'That sounds nice,' said Clive, as he planted a tiny lettuce.

'Lee!' Dorrie was at the back door. 'I've got mangoes.'

So Leonie went inside, and Dorrie went about unpacking mangoes and half a watermelon onto the red formica table.

'How was last night?' said Dorrie. 'Did you go to the Bowlo?'

'We did,' said Leonie. 'Eileen and I had a nice meal. They do very good hot chips.'

'They do,' said Dorrie. 'And how did Joe go with Verna and the girls?'

'He had a great time. Verna got them a Viennetta.'

'How posh,' said Dorrie, smiling. She was slicing off the mango cheeks, doing the crisscross pattern with the knife and then opening them out like flowers. She said, 'Did you talk about Maurie?'

'We did.'

'And how many times did you cry?'

'Four times.'

Dorrie looked at Leonie so warmly, but Leonie did not blush. Dorrie said, 'And was that tolerable?'

'I think it was,' said Leonie, who sipped iced water and felt a deep pride. She drank the rest of the water so there were just ice cubes left in the glass. Leonie was thirsty from her first foray into gardening. She was in a wonderful, wonderful mood. She said, 'Eileen does so much stuff. She does dance classes. She takes the girls snorkelling and camping, all by herself. She's very *Life. Be in it.*'

'Good for her.'

'She wants me and Joe to go up north with them on a holiday,' said Leonie. 'She's taking the girls to Yamba for five days.'

'And?'

'And I don't know. I mean, I don't know if I can get the time off work.'

Dorrie had laid the mango pieces on a big blue plate and was now cutting watermelon into thick slices. Dorrie had a wry smile on her face as she arranged the watermelon, and Leonie thought it was a very good presentation. It looked like one of the photos she showed clients at work of a tropical resort buffet.

'Lee?'

'Yes, Dorrie?'

'Go to Yamba.'

•

Barney was last on the trail, which was a position he preferred because he liked to look around as much as possible.

It was single file from the signs along the loop track, four kilometres that circled all the way around the old Scout camp. There was an ancient wooden sign, covered in lichen. Barney, in his new boots, reeked of Aerogard. His binoculars beat gently against his chest. He could see the back of Helen Last's green shirt. *Gather Region Bushwalkers Club: Since 1975* and the emblem of a lyrebird. It was so moist as they neared the creek. Barney saw, on the track, a native blue flatworm.

From up ahead, Rae said, 'Bush wee.'

'Bush wee,' said Helen Last.

The group stopped. It was just a small group today: Barney, Helen and Phil, Rae, and also Norma King. Barney hadn't seen Norma for two years, yet she looked like she'd aged ten.

Had Barney aged ten? He probably had. He waited with Phil and Norma while Rae and Helen bush-bashed off to urinate on the peaty leaves.

'New boots?' asked Norma.

'Yes,' said Barney. 'The old ones were—you know.'

'Old,' said Norma.

'I felt like starting fresh,' said Barney.

Phil Last said, 'I was just thinking about being up here when I was in the Scouts. I loved the orienteering. It's the only reason I can use a compass and a map. You just learnt every inch of this bush so well.'

Then Helen's voice yelled from the bush, 'Phil!'

'Helen?' said Phil.

'You all should see this!' yelled Helen. 'There's a bunch of lyrebird mounds! They're so beautiful!'

•

Joe and Clive and Dorrie ate mango and watermelon at the kitchen table, and Joe was gloriously covered in dirt. He had dirt all over his face, and his fingernails were caked with dirt, and there was dirt smeared on his thin brown arms.

'Do you want tea too, Clive?' asked Leonie. She was at the sink filling the kettle, and she looked out the window to see a green car outside Barney's house and a young man standing on Barney's front lawn.

'Sure, I'll have tea,' said Clive.

'There's a shadow shining on the table,' said Joe.

'Just a sec,' said Leonie, and she put the kettle down. She went through the kitchen and out the front door and walked down the driveway.

•

Barney waited on the track with Norma King, who didn't want to push her way through the bush for twenty metres to see lyrebird mounds because she had seen that many lyrebird mounds in her life, and it was Gather Region Bushwalkers Club policy never to leave a walker alone.

'I count ten of them!' yelled Phil.

Barney could not see Phil anymore, he could only hear him. There was no obvious path to Phil. But there was a faint suggestion of path. There was space around the trees enough to push through. And right in front of Barney was the most beautiful *Banksia ericifolia*. He stared at the burnt orange flowers, the grey-green leaves. He felt that one flower in particular was looking back at him, and he smiled to himself at this thought.

'You can see the circular clearings—they're very distinct,' said Helen. 'Phil, take a picture. We should put this in the newsletter.'

The breeze stopped and Barney could hear his fellow walkers like they were right next to him now, the bush being so quiet and still. He heard a snap of a branch, and an acknowledgement of the snap by Helen.

'I've stepped on something,' said Helen. 'What's this?'

•

The young man was on Barney's front porch now, knocking on the door. He was just a teenager, in a McDonald's uniform.

'Barney's not home,' called Leonie, from her driveway.

'Okay.'

The lanky young man began to come back down the steps—and Leonie was so glad. She'd been feeling unusually happy for herself. And now she felt unusually happy for her friend Barney.

'Shall I tell him you've dropped by?'

'I'm his son.'

Leonie smiled and said, 'Yes, I can see that.'

•

Oh, did Helen Last scream when she saw what she'd stumbled on next to one of the mounds. Barney would see, only moments later, that the body was almost entirely covered in scrolls of bark, leaf litter, small branches, scratched earth. He learned, much later, that a gold bracelet had been found, still intact, around the bones of Ginny's wrist.

But when Helen screamed, and Barney was still on the path with Norma, he went cold all over and something in him just knew.

He heard Phil say, 'It's bones. Helen, come forward towards me. Those are a lot of bones.'

Barney ignored all protocol. He left Norma on her own. He pushed his way through the bush, breaking small branches and scratching up his Aerogarded arms so much that blood came in several places. He rushed forth, full of a terrified, exhilarated knowing.

After twenty metres, he saw his friends. Helen looked pale and Phil looked confused and Rae looked like Rae, and ten beautiful lyrebird mounds lay before them—large circles of cleared earth.

'Those are bones,' said Phil, pointing behind Helen, who had frozen in shock, and Barney fell to his knees when he arrived at where Phil was pointing.

Here she is, he thought. We've found her. We've got him.

Barney felt as if a train was running through his body. It dragged him a hundred metres. It scattered his belongings. Tears sprung to his eyes.

Wait till Leonie hears about this! he thought. I need to tell Leonie!

Acknowledgements

I live and work on unceded Dharawal country and I pay my respects to Elders past and present.

Thank you to Annette Barlow, Courtney Lick, Ali Hampton and the team at Allen & Unwin.

Thank you to Ali Lavau for expert advice.

This story was partly inspired by the search for Lynette Dawson, and I am thankful to *The Teacher's Pet* podcast, which brought the case to my attention. Although this book is entirely a work of fiction, my sympathies are with Lynette Dawson, her family and friends.

For information on police procedure, I am indebted to former NSW Detective Sergeant Bob Wells.

I am grateful to Dr Daniel Siegel: a real-life scenario described in his book *Mindsight* provided inspiration for the character of Deb.

Thank you to my mum and to my friends for ongoing support.

Endless thanks to my partner Zoë and to our children Alvy and June.

And thank you to my friend and mentor Richard Walsh for seeing this book through with me from start to finish.